Also *by* Michael Coolwood

The Unexpected Death Of A Soldier
(published by Verse Publishing)

Michael Coolwood

Confessions *of a* Gentleman Arachnid

MONTAG

First Montag Press E-Book and Paperback Original Edition November 2015

Montag Press
ISBN: 978-1-940233-28-4
Cover art © 2015 Stuart F Taylor of chainbear.com
Cover, layout, & e-book © 2015 Blush Book Design

Montag Press Team:
Project Editor – Mara Hodges
Managing Director – Charlie Franco

A Montag Press Book
www.montagpress.com
Montag Press
1066 47th Ave. Unit #9
Oakland CA 94601 USA

Montag Press, the burning book with the hatchet cover, the skewed word mark and the portrayal of the long-suffering fireman mascot are trademarks of Montag Press.

Printed & Digitally Originated in the United States of America
10 9 8 7 6 5 4 3 2 1

For Jen

Michael Coolwood

Confessions *of a* Gentleman Arachnid

1

MY LATEST ADVENTURE STARTED AS SO MANY OF MY DAYS had at that time in my life: with toasted globbits in bed, accompanied by a hot cup of chitterlings and that morning's newsfeed.

The third war in the Creatic was really hotting up, according to page one. This was rather jarring to my peace of mind, as I'd spent most of my second tour whizzing about the place during the last war. My chums and I had just got the place into a decent state by the time my tour had ended, and I wasn't altogether happy with the idea of the place getting messed up again.

Page two led with an article about the endangered species act, and whether humans should have been removed from its protection last year. The mammals, the author pointed out, were still barely able to rub two sticks together without causing some sort of cataclysm. This was true, albeit rather patronising. Humanity had managed to reach the stars, after all. Not any particularly impressive stars, mind you. Without the benefaction of their various neighbours it is unlikely they'd have ever made it out of their home solar system… but there is something about those chaps that just keeps them plugging away.

Page three was devoted to the latest actions of the growing conscientious objector movement. Several chaps had attacked the parliamentary network with bags of flour. The article was careful not to let on whether the author was in favour of these actions or not.

Page four was mostly advertisements for exotic goods and tweed.

Page five contained the letters to the editor. I skipped page five. I have nothing against the scribblings of my fellow arachnid per se, it's just that such writings were regularly devoted to wars, and how we as a species weren't involved with anywhere near enough of them. This was where my opinion deviated from that of the arachnid about town.

It was the summer of 2568. I had just completed my third tour of duty with the 92nd Grand Battlefleet and I was feeling a little down in the dumps. This was partly because adjusting to civilian life was proving dashed difficult. I had forgotten just how focussed chaps were on the wearing of ties. There are only so many conversations a chap can endure, concerning whether a Childermass would be just that little bit less presumptuous than a Full Norrell. It was also because the second anniversary of my dear Emily's death had come and gone, leaving my mental state in five or six oddly shaped pieces.

I'd met up with one or two old school chums last night. They were the sort of chaps and lasses whom I'd considered close at the time. We had been at basic training together, before parting ways when picking our specialties. This reunion, whilst having all the makings of a capital idea, had turned out to be anything but. The chums in question, it transpired, had not had the fight knocked out of them to quite the same extent I had. They gaily chatted about their fourth tours of duty, all of which had already been signed up for. One was returning to his breaching squad after being made a chosen man on his previous tour. Another had been made an officer, to my surprise. Another was in intelligence, which caused several hearty laughs from the group. I had joined in the laughter and hoped like the blazes that it didn't sound as hollow to them as it had to me.

I cast my newsfeed to the winds, wrenched myself out of bed, and threw open the curtains. The modern metropolis of Eggart greeted me, much as it did every morning, with a cheery wink that was quite difficult to make out through the rain. The tallest buildings, such as the Science and Arachnid History Museum, wore a crown of cloud. Their shorter brethren, such as the twelve-metre-tall statue of Lord Archibald the Bloodthirsty and Bitterly Sarcastic, had to settle for being drenched.

Last night had been boat race night. Skelbet College had rowed to victory over Wizbloot and the wrecks of various craft from both sides were littered on the riverbank, in nearby fields, in the public parks, up trees, and I was sure I could see one or two embedded in the walls of the police station. One or two fires speckled the horizon and, as I wondered if anything had to be done about them, I heard the whoop-whoop of a siren as a fire engine blazed past my window and on through the sky towards the fires.

I nodded to myself and decided it was probably time to leave my sanctuary. Forsythe was waiting for me in the sitting room. His vast hulking form eclipsed the view from my windows thanks to his storage tanks, utility tendrils, and caterpillar tracks.

He bore a tray, upon which was an envelope. Such things might have looked foolish in the grip of someone similarly massive, but without the fundamental dignity of a valet or personal attendant. Dignity is one of those things Forsythe has in spades. He just can't get enough of the stuff. He is a person who can make the simple act of proffering an envelope towards his employer seem an act with centuries of tradition and nobility behind it.

The envelope had a Newbury postmark on it, betraying the author of the letter contained therein. I unsealed the envelope using my security hashsign and found a small smile playing across my mouth for the first time in what felt like two years.

I had hit upon the idea to write to my cousin Gertrude, asking after her health, after reasoning that writing pleasantries to a relative would be a considerably better use of my time than staring at the empty legchair in my flat for the third day in a row. Her reply, which I now held in my claw, contained an invitation to stay at her family seat in Newbury Towers.

At first my instinct was to reply saying I couldn't possibly drag myself away from the city. I mentioned this to Forsythe, intending him to draft a reply to the young lass. Forsythe rumbled slightly at the suggestion. This demanded that I tilt a quizzical eyebrow at the fellow, so tilt I did. In response, Forsythe replied that he merely wished to point out the merits of Gertrude's suggestion. He pointed out the impact Emily's empty chair was having on me. He also drew my attention to the unhealthy company I had been keeping, viz. the aforementioned unhelpful chums.

Put like that, the prospect of spending time with Gertrude was far more pleasant. She and I have known each other since we were in short trousers, which meant she was well accustomed to my shortcomings. More importantly, though, was the fact that Gertrude had spent her last two tours of duty with the special operations network – a unit whose purpose is to deal with the areas of war that require subtlety, skill, and a great deal of properly directed violence.

Such work takes a definite toll on a person. If you were to encounter one who has served in that illustrious network, you would no doubt find them less enthusiastic about conflict than most other fellows you may happen to bump into.

Gertrude, I felt, would offer supportive words when needed. She might also provide cheery distractions when I was found to be dwelling on the fact that my life was, at present, rather lacking in Emilies. I would have accepted her invitation with as much gusto as I could summon, were it not for one final stumbling block: Angus Wermacht.

Angus Wermacht, or Sir Angus Possingthrut Woebuston Wermacht IV, to be slightly more exact about things, is

Gertrude's father and my uncle by marriage. He, along with his sister Ophelia Slavarington, has never enjoyed my company. As a result, the atmosphere of any home containing myself as well as Sir Angus can become dashed chilly. Some might even describe our interplay as glacial.

I replied to Gertrude, saying that I would be delighted to accept her invitation, were it not for the matter previously mentioned. A letter received the next day put my fears to one side. Sir Angus was attending to a family matter several light years away and wouldn't be back for some weeks. My spending a week with Gertrude would allow me plenty of time to slip from the place unobserved.

Considering myself thoroughly braced and completely out of excuses, I decided to give my old two-seater a bit of an airing. I selected a hat, checked that my tie was just so, and settled myself behind the wheel of my beloved motorcar. I instructed Forsythe to follow with the heavy luggage and pressed the engine activation stud with my claw. The car's chlorine triflouride powered engine thrummed to life and, in very little time at all, I was shooting through the sky of Eggart and on my way to the express lanes.

There was some sort of rumpus happening in low orbit. As I drew closer, it appeared to be between a few postgraduates from Skelbet College and the police. If I had to guess, I'd say it was probably because the latter were upset that one of the boats belonging to the former had been inserted into their police station.

The conflict appeared to be in its later stages. Battle lines had been drawn and the two sides were exchanging good-natured fire. From the looks of things, both sides were using non-lethal rounds, but even so such things would risk damaging my two-seater's paintwork. Going around the rumpus would have cost me not an insignificant amount of time, so I reasoned it was best to bring my trusty two-seater to a halt and wait for the conflict to peter out.

To my chagrin, one of the police officers must have had his suspicions raised by the way I slid my car to the side of the conflict. I'd used a trick my old wing commander had taught me involving an inverse half dangler and I hadn't considered it overly complex. The police officer must have, though, because it raised a claw and bellowed: "There's another one!"

Before I could say Thursday (I always get stuck on the 's'), several officers had abandoned their task and had taken great jet-assisted leaps from behind their squad cars to the open area of sky directly in front of my trusty transport. Several weapons were raised in several legs. Claws moved to triggers.

I re-evaluated my decision to park my two-seater and floored the accelerator. Two of my claws gripped the steering apparatus whilst another felt for the switch that would activate the Azidoazide Azide boosters. At around the same moment the switch was being flicked, two other claws were searching in the glove box for the flash bangs that I kept there.

It took a little more time than I might have liked to locate them because I had to search through what appeared to be a mountain of gloves in order to locate the things. I got my claws on the things just as my Azidoazide Azide boosters activated and my car leapt forward like a racehorse that had just remembered it had left the oven on.

I tossed the flash bangs out of my window as I passed the police officers and only neglected to activate one of the six. A tremendous bang confirmed that five of them had activated just as I'd hoped they would. A flash in my rear view mirror confirmed that I had managed to grab flash bangs and not high explosives, unlike the last three times I've been compelled to perform a similar manoeuvre.

The police thus distracted, all I needed to do was perform a quick dovetail over and in-between the ranks of the postgraduates, most of whom were still too intoxicated from the night before to even get a shot off. One or two did manage to wave a weapon in the vague direction of my two-seater, but their shots went pitifully wide, and in two shakes I was out of orbit and heading into the pleasantly traffic-free express lanes.

The village of Newbury is a quick seven-hour drive from Eggart. If I remember my history correctly, the place used to be a planet. There were oceans, biodomes, and various species of flora and fauna. Unfortunately for the planet, it was first discovered by humans. The humans had been expanding into space at the time and were settling on planets as if there was going to be a sudden shortage any day now. They then set about treating the poor thing the way humans usually treat their planets. They extracted all the valuable resources, massacred the fauna, and devastated the flora.

Once they'd got this out of the way, they decided to start a war with the planet next door. I say a war, but what humans do isn't really warfare. When I was young enough to still have my baby fangs, there was a game some of my school chums used to play. They'd ring the doorbell of a house nearby and then run away. I never really saw the appeal myself, but it serves as a wonderful analogy for how humans usually approach war.

The humans attacked their neighbour, destroyed a few cities, that sort of thing. They then declared victory and started planting flags all over the place. Then the counter attack happened. Before you could say "whoops", the humans had been driven from the planet they'd invaded, and a planet cracking team had reduced the planet of Newbury to a small cluster of asteroids.

Still, some humans survived. They do that. Individually they may be more fragile than the china ornaments your mother-in-law insists on scattering about her home, so that she can leap out at you with a triumphant stare the second you bump into one... but as a group, as a *species*, they cling to life as if merely existing is something that needs to be held onto at all costs.

The remaining humans cobbled together a village on the asteroids that were all that remained of their planet and, rather than have the whole sorry cycle repeat itself, one of Sir Angus' ancestors was granted a title and a couple of plots of land overlooking the village. If you were to visit Newbury, simply cast your eyes to the northern end of the village. There you will see a pleasant green biodome linked to a stately home and garden by one of those tri-filament rotational lift things. That is Newbury Towers, Sir Angus' estate. The home orbits around the land, and the land orbits around the home, whilst everyone on both does their best to not get dizzy.

From a distance, the estate, and the village it overlooks, is really rather easy on the eyes, and it just becomes more pleasant the more you approach. Under the watchful eye of Newbury Towers, the humans in Newbury have managed to avoid wiping themselves out or getting into any more ill-advised wars. Picturesque might be the word I'm searching for. There's a lovely sort of statue thing in their village square, their town hall is pleasant to gaze upon, and the place is largely disease-free, so there aren't corpses clogging up all the gutters.

The entire place looks like one of those villages I read about during my humanthropology studies in secondary school. It was thanks to these studies that I won the prestigious prize for Human Culture Knowledge during that year's prize giving, but I mustn't go on about that.

I pulled into orbit around Newbury Towers and plotted my approach. As I landed, I saw a solid-looking figure poking a sharp implement at a rosebush. It wore a gingham dress, boots that had a decidedly military tone to them, and the sort of mask one wears if one is about to attend a dinner on one of those planets where acid volcanoes are considered pretty much the normal thing. This, I surmised, was my cousin Gertrude. I pulled up alongside the rosebush she was poking at and bunged a greeting her way.

She reacted in a rather unusual fashion. She flung herself to the floor, rolled about under the rosebush for a bit, and then bounced upright holding a sort of shotgun thing, which she unloaded into the broad side of my two-seater.

I didn't quite know what to make of this. I wiggled a claw in the old external auditory meatus to try and shift the dashed ringing that had started immediately after the shot. By the time I'd formulated a suitably pithy riposte to four rounds of shot ruining the paintwork of my car, Gertrude had reloaded and levelled the gun at my head.

I was considering that line from Rosencrantz and Guildenstern Are Dead, about being allowed to sleep and perhaps dream or however it went, when I realised that Gertrude had not pulled the trigger. Instead, she was frowning.

"Milli?" she asked, removing her breathing mask and lowering the weapon a touch. "What the devil do you think you're playing at?"

I was less than a ninetieth of my way into what would probably have been a rather well-put soliloquy about my motivations for greeting her, when she held up an authoritative claw. "Hold on a tick," she intoned.

I held on as per instructions. The relative proceeded to flip open her skull and fiddle about a bit. This took rather longer than a tick, but the Clodthorpes are always willing to stretch a point for an old chum.

As the second stretched on, I decided to inspect the damage the relative had caused to my two-seater, so I stepped out. I'd barely made a preliminary inspection, though, when a solid implement inserted itself between my shoulder blades and bowled me forwards.

"Milligan!" roared Gertrude, "you nearly gave me a heart attack!" I turned and we greeted each other in the traditional manner, although I made sure to keep one claw on my pocket watch.

I started to speak and then hesitated, unsure as to whether whatever malady she had been suffering from when I arrived still afflicted her. She laughed, heartily.

"Oh that. Don't worry, light of my life, you can talk again without causing me uncontrollable agony. You know I lost my ears in my last tour? Well, I haven't managed to sort out all the settings on the mechanical replacements they fixed me up with, as of yet. Your voice was merely registering on the same harmonic frequency as gunfire, what larks, eh? I say, I'm sorry about your two-seater, but into every car's life some rain must fall, what?"

I was beginning to regret my decision to trouble Newbury Towers with my presence. Gertrude's method of communication is both boisterous and difficult to follow. I may have mentioned the speech she gave at my wedding, where she went on at such great length on such a variety of subjects that most of us quite forgot what we were there for.

A morsel of my chagrin must have shown on my face, though, because the relative checked herself and threw four of her legs into the air.

"I am being thoughtless!" she cried, and then checked herself again. She returned her legs to the ground. "My apologies," she said in a more reserved tone. "My excitement at seeing you safe carried me away a little."

"Come," she said, linking a leg through one of mine that wasn't really doing anything useful and leading me up to the house, "let me fill you in on the changes that have occurred since your last visit. Daddy has repainted all of the bedrooms upon the advice of some artist or other. I believe our people have set you up in what has become known as the Ghastly Green Bedroom, so I hope you enjoy being driven to the point of madness by tasteless décor." She cackled, then resumed. "I'm only kidding, Milli, that hardly ever happens.

We dress for Brunch now but only in prime colours and, of course, there are the traps."

"The traps?"

"Yes, don't worry about the traps. They're not for you. Ah, here we are."

We were walking up the steps at the house. There was a rather splendid architrave or epistyle over the entrance, which put me in mind of one of those old temples people used to wander in and out of all the time. Just below that was a portico, and just below that was a butler, who was in the middle of a shallow bow.

"Mr Clodthorpe," he intoned, his voice booming like the something or other of Thor. "Welcome back to Newbury Towers."

I thanked him a few times and commented on how lovely the architrave or epistyle was. He agreed that it was, indeed, and the mouldings displayed on it were particularly fine as well. I asked him what he meant, and he made a sort of growling noise which prompted Gertrude to lead me past him and into the house. She muttered some quick instructions with regards to how I might find the Ghastly Green Bedroom and then scuttled off to talk to one of the domestic staff about my car.

I stood rooted to the spot for a solid moment. You can learn a lot from a stately home by its entrance hall: the choice in wallpaper, the security systems, the decorations on the wall. Newbury Towers was pleasingly old-fashioned. Wood from two or three of the better sort of trees had been requisitioned to panel the walls. The floor was lined with a pale grey stone, of a sort that would soften or harden depending on the tread of those who walked on it. Light was provided by a lighting array of the sort my grandfather had in his home.

Sir Angus hadn't brushed Newbury Towers' origins under the carpet, though. Partly because there wasn't a carpet and partly because, as George Satriani said, those who ignore their past are sure to wind up just repeating the same sort of stuff over and over again. Weapons were still on their racks at the base of the great staircase leading to the first floor. There were also telltale control panels at various points throughout the hall that would activate intrusion countermeasures or would cause pieces of hard cover to leap out of the floor.

This was all because the Wermacht family had been charged with preventing the humans in Newbury from wiping their village from all but the most out-of-date of maps. This would occasionally require protecting the humans from external aggressors. It would also necessitate preventing the humans from taking action that would cause their village to self-destruct, whether by starting wars they were ill-equipped to fight or by experimenting with power generation methods they had heard about but hadn't fully understood.

Well, given that Gertrude would likely need some little time to see about getting my two-seater repaired, it would be best to establish quite how ghastly the green in my room was. I climbed the stairs to the first floor and paused on the landing, trying to recall whether Gertrude had said I was in the second bedroom in the west corridor or the third bedroom in the east corridor.

The mystery proved a thorny one, and I was just getting my fangs into it, teasing apart the precise details involved in the case, when I heard a noise from down in the entrance hall.

I scuttled over to a balustrade so I could get an unrestricted view of the hall. The door that separated the hall from the elements blasted open, and my heart leapt into my mouth at the sight of Sir Angus Wermacht thundering in.

2

I COULDN'T TELL YOU IF I'D EVER SEEN SIR ANGUS WERMACHT truly angry before that moment. Sir Angus always considered me completely unworthy of the love his niece, dear Emily, held for me. This, coupled with his dislike for clumsiness and those who lacked his intellectual calibre, led him to view my company as something to be enjoyed from afar — several hundred light years, preferably. Sir Angus is a gentleman, though. He considers his guests' comfort to be the highest priority. He often grew so concerned about his hostly duties towards me, and whether he might be neglecting them by allowing his feelings towards me to become known, that he often overcompensated. To put it another way, he usually treated me, and others he disliked, with more thought and care than he treated those whose company he enjoyed.

Because of this, I was more used to Sir Angus smiling at me, although usually showing a great deal more fang than might otherwise be necessary. As he strode into the entrance hall of his home, though, he looked rather like one of those thunder gods that used to be all over the place.

"The irresponsibility!" he was roaring. "The recklessness!"

I threw myself to the floor in a desperate attempt to remain unobserved. I then remembered I had a personal cloaking field that would have performed much the same function, but, given that I was already out of sight, I didn't feel the need to drain my auxiliary energy reserve. I scuttled around for a few moments, trying to reach the closest corridor whilst remaining out of sight. My plan was simple: Hide, and if I heard Sir Angus' clawsteps on the stairway, I'd bolt down the corridor and conceal myself in one of the rooms.

"It was far from irresponsible!" A voice retorted. I had managed to reach the doorway to my escape corridor, so I squeezed behind the frame and began to listen in earnest. The voice that had replied to Sir Angus was not one I recognised. It was a slightly uncanny voice. It chittered in much the same way you'd expect, but there was something slightly mammalian about it that unsettled me. "I simply wished to continue my duties!"

"We will speak about this further over dinner," replied Sir Angus. This was the moment when he was most likely to discover me. Thankfully, I heard retreating clawsteps and then the gentlemanly slamming of a door. Not one arachnid claw had ascended the stairs. I exhaled.

"I say, hello," said a different, yet also familiar, voice in my ear, "I didn't know you were here. How's tricks?"

I whirled around. I staggered slightly. Behind me was a regrettably familiar object. It was a coffin, albeit a mobile one. Eight legs protruded from it at the points where you'd expect them on a more typical body. A thin tendril with a voice projector at one end was pointed at me. On the tastefully decorated silver plaquette, affixed just below the voice projector, were engraved the words "Sarah Slavarington". Pigstick had died, and her consciousness had been stored in a coffin until she could be downloaded into a new body.

"Pigstick!" I hissed at the youngest in the Slavarington line. "How did you get behind me?"

"Well I saw you hiding here and thought you must be up to something, so I used my cloaking field to slip past you and wait to see what it was you were doing, but after uncle Angus buzzed off to his study, you didn't seem to be doing much of any one thing or another, so I thought I'd draw your attention my way."

I looked around to see if we were unobserved, but Pigstick grasped one of my legs with one of her mechanical ones. She drew me into one of the rooms off the corridor and closed the door.

"That's better," she said, "Milli, look, you *can't* be here."

"But I am here-" I pointed out, not entirely clear on what the young pineapple was getting at.

"I mean you *shouldn't* be here." Pigstick corrected herself. "Uncle Angus is in a frightful mood, and encountering the last of the Clodthorpes might send him over the edge."

She referred, rather insensitively I reflected, to my status as the last to bear my name — my father's brother, Reginald

Clodthorpe, having been lost at sea during a tragic cottaging incident.

"I was invited to stay by your cousin Gertrude…" I pointed out, in an effort to get the facts straight.

"I hate to say it, Milli, but I think it won't matter on this occasion." Pigstick replied. Her voice was grim. The grips on her coffin had a distinct foreboding edge to them.

"You aren't saying…" I trailed off. I was going to say, *that your uncle would neglect his duties as a host,* but certain things are so terrible they're best left unsaid.

"I'm afraid I am, Milli. You'd best leg it."

This was sound advice. Life at Newbury Towers now that Sir Angus had returned would surely be about as far from a quiet week in the country as it was possible to get. I nodded, thanked Pigstick for the sound council, and had my claw on the door grip when I spun around. "But dash it, I can't!" I exclaimed. "Gertrude has introduced several rounds of her finest shot into the delicate areas of my car. Until the poor thing is fixed, something that will take until tomorrow morning at least, if I'm any judge, I can't use that method to escape. How did you get here, Pigstick?"

"Uncle Angus drove me."

"I can't very well borrow Sir Angus' car to make good my escape. Are there any others on the premises?"

"None that I know of."

"Blast." I said, musing. "Might there be some way of my remaining here until my transportation has been repaired? What has caused Sir Angus to be in such a shocking bad temper anyway? Is it because of what happened to you?"

"What, this old thing?" Pigstick asked, waving a mechanical leg at her coffin. "Oh no. I was shot down over one of those lava planets and my organic body was fried to a crisp. Very unfortunate and all that, but my backups were up-to-date, so they downloaded me into this coffin, and that was more or less that for my second tour of duty. My grizzly end isn't the problem. The problem, old spice, is Bainbridge."

"Bainbridge?" I gasped.

Bainbridge was a family friend to the Wermachts — if friend is the term I'm after. Come to think of it, it isn't. Scourge. That's more like it. Bainbridge was the scourge of the Wermachts. Sir Angus and Sir Arthur Lusitania were at school together. Unfortunately, Sir Arthur was injured rather badly during his first tour of duty, and since that day he's spent large chunks of time in and out of various medical facilities. This left his only son Bainbridge as something of a Devastator-class warship without a rudder.

Sir Angus has done his level best to keep Bainbridge on the uncomplicated path towards becoming a gentleman of worth and value. While it is true that I am loath to speak ill of anyone, my refusal to blame Sir Angus for Bainbridge's rotten character is far from mere politeness. As far as I can tell, Sir Angus treated the young Bainbridge as one of his own. Sadly, Sir Angus' efforts were evidently not met with complete success.

Bainbridge is best described as a young carbuncle. He barely scraped his way through his first tour of duty. He then delayed his second for so long that Gertrude and I were making bets as to whether he'd do a runner or not. To both of our surprise, and the satisfaction of Gertrude's wallet, he did not flee the scene when the recruiting officer dropped by. Skip forward two years, and here we are today. Marmalade only knows what tomfoolery he got up to during his tour to get it cut short by this much, assuming he hadn't died as Pigstick had.

"What," I asked, "has Bainbridge done?"

Pigstick leaned in, the better to lower her voice to a conspiratorial volume. "Well, this is all from what I've gathered from one or two parties that were privy to the event, as well as uncle Angus' chats with Bainbridge in the car on the way here... but he died on his last tour."

She paused and wiggled her voice projector subtly. I could only guess at her meaning, but I suspected she was hoping I'd invite her to continue.

"Please carry on, young Pigstick." I urged, "I am hanging on every word."

"He didn't die in combat, though." Pigstick continued, "Apparently his tour had taken him to a relief base where he'd be involved with distributing supplies to local conflicts. Apparently the poor sap didn't pay attention when they showed him how to operate that lifter thing they have there and wound up crushing himself with a crate of plargs."

"What are plargs?"

"Some local animal rich in protein — but I haven't got to the good part yet, Milli, kindly stop interrupting. His backups were up-to-date, as you'd expect, so they were in the process of finding a coffin to stick him in when he panicked. He flipped the emergency download switch."

I was so shocked I couldn't even gasp.

The emergency download switch is one of those things… well, it's like that star eater we developed a few years ago, or that Ju-on virus that human Takashi Shimizu created. They're objects that get developed in the hope that they'll never actually be used.

At the start of every tour of duty, everyone is fitted with an emergency download switch. The idea is that if you die in the line of duty, but there's something so incredibly urgent to deal with that you can't wait to download into a coffin, you can flick the switch and download into the nearest body with a built-in receptor. The bodies with receptors are usually support staff who work on our bases – almost universally non-arachnids. A large number of humans have them because we're one of the only species out there that will employ the little scamps. The process, unfortunately, wipes the host mind of the original consciousness in preparation for the download.

To someone who hasn't started their tours as of this moment, this may sound a little barbaric, but there is a good reason for it. Every once in a while, one of the newer space-faring civilisations gets it into their heads that war is one of those things that can be won. From this bit of ideological insanity, it's only a matter of time before doomsday weapons get involved. If one of these is discovered by a chap and the chap is then killed, it's imperative that the chap stop the weapon before it can be activated and destroy the entire planet.

The creatures that allow receptors to be built into them trust that we will only use the emergency download switch in the direst of circumstances. The idea that Bainbridge used it because he didn't like the idea of being dead is unpalatable.

Pigstick was eyeing me, conspiratorially.

"Quite," she said, after the fiftieth uninterrupted second of shocked silence. "You can imagine how Uncle Angus feels about this…. And this is *why*, Milli, we need to get you out of here with all speed. Uncle Angus is beside himself; he is grief-stricken. He may very well react in an ungentlemanly manner when he discovers his mansion is infested with Clodthorpes."

"I don't think you can count it as an infestation if there's only one of me," I pointed out.

"Now is not the time for flippancy, Milli," Pigstick hissed. "Let me think. We can't very well send you down to Newbury to hide. Your presence would cause considerable comment, and Uncle Angus would be bound to hear about it. Blast!"

Pigstick began pacing about the room, muttering to herself.

"I have it!" she cried after only a few moments.

"Ah!" I cried, "What do you have?"

"We'll bury you!" she exclaimed. "We'll take you out to the garden and bury you. That will stop Uncle Angus finding you!"

Maybe I was being unkind, but this seemed like an idea born out of desperation rather than practicality. "Pigstick…" I said, placatingly, "There must be some other way. Perhaps if you and Gertrude explained matters to your uncle…"

Pigstick rounded on me. "Explain? EXPLAIN?" Her voice projector trembled at me for a few seconds before she was calm enough to continue. "Well, I suppose that might be a solution of sorts. It's probably more practical than my idea, given I have no idea where the gardener keeps her shovels."

Pigstick raised Gertrude on her vox-o-matic, and the two spent a few moments in quiet discussion.

"We have a plan!" Pigstick exclaimed, after terminating the signal. This was probably good news, although I hoped it was a more thought-out plan than the last one Pigstick had suggested. "Gertrude will locate her father and attempt to reason with him. She says that, as a daughter, she can twist her father's mood around her tiniest claw when needed."

"How does she do that?"

"I believe she regales her father with stories of her first tour, when she was compelled to crush the head of an enemy combatant with her fangs, but that's by the by. She says it would be best if you and I take a stroll in the grounds, in case Uncle Angus is prowling about the house. He may come across us before she is able to find him, in which case I am to distract him with grumbles about my coffin."

It was a formidable plan and, what's more, a formidable plan that had several layers of contingency built into it. I agreed to the scheme with enthusiasm, and in the space of only two and five minutes, we had slipped out of a set of human windows that separated the sitting room from the garden.

The human windows were an interesting feature for a stately home to have. I had noted their presence on my previous visit, but had never had the opportunity to enquire as to their origins. Pigstick informed me that the original architect, knowing that the house was to serve as a bastion from which the local humans would be protected and governed, had included several touches of human architecture into the design. Hence the human windows, the human blinds, and the occasional serving of human toast during breakfast.

I couldn't tell you quite why but, as Pigstick and I wandered the grounds of Newbury Towers, I found myself reflecting on the circumstances that had followed my signing up for my first tour of duty. I very nearly hadn't. I very nearly marked myself down as a conscientious objector. How glad I am now that I hadn't followed my conscience at the time, mostly because I would have failed to fall in love with dear Emily during a chance encounter on the frigate she was stationed on. Significantly, though, I feel that I owe much of my current outlook on life to my first tour.

I am one of those people who believe that, deep down, there's good in everybody. There may not be much, but it's important to focus on it. I may well have always believed this, but it was my first tour that really cemented the idea in my... well, you could call it a brain if you were being charitable. Yes, my brain. Some people may find it strange that it took going to war to realise this. Allow me to elaborate.

My species has been engaged in near-constant war for the past few thousand years. During that time we have fought against the Antipodeans, the Trusts, the Ungong, the Rampant Bantams, the Woolly Horsemen, the Yarrrrrrrrrrl, the Crumpet Whisperers, the Humans, the Stiig and... look, we've been at war with a lot of people. If you truly want a list of them, I suggest you visit a library. Occasionally, when newly discovered species learn about us, the above list causes them to think that we are a particularly aggressive species.

This is not an unreasonable conclusion, but it fails to understand the reasons behind war. My species recognised early on that plenty of people have aggression issues. Sometimes these issues manifest in violence towards individuals, sometimes against society itself. A quick solution to the problem was found: encouraging everyone to get involved in at least one major conflict wherever possible. This got the untapped aggression out of the systems of many people. Those who found one or two good wars insufficient to stem their aggression signed up for more. There was little reason to not take part in these wars, given that the death problem had been solved millennia ago. There were enough resources in the galaxy for everyone several billion times over. There was, as the fellow said, no reason to not go to war other than on purely ethical grounds.

Some species, it is important to note, did not have access to the consciousness-swapping technology that effectively defeated death. They were the species we warred with the least. Although it is worth saying that these species were often the most aggressive and, as such, the ones that would necessitate self-defensive conflict the most.

In my youth, I had seen these conflicts as supremely wasteful. I had believed them to be an archaic system perpetuated out of an unwillingness to, as The Kinks put it, give peace a try. That was before my first tour, though. When I was going through basic training, I met a whole slew of people who made me reasonably sure that I'd been wrong about there being good in everybody. There were plenty of good chaps from the word go, of course, but there seemed to be a disproportionate number of people whose negative traits started at the A's with Arrogance and just got more disagreeable the further down the alphabet you went.

Several of these chaps, who I couldn't in all honesty say I got on with, selected the air group alongside me. I gritted my fangs and prepared myself for five years of belligerence, bullying and boorishness. Then, during our third mission, several of our squadron were blown into terribly small pieces by the enemy anti-fighter defences.

Not one member of the squad got through that mission without losing a friend. The fact that the friends would be up on their claws after a matter of weeks was little comfort. It was a jolt. It shook everyone, including me. After the mission, though, something remarkable happened. My squadron mates began to soften, even the worst of them. The tight cliques that had formed during our first few weeks dissipated. There were fewer casual insults, more heartfelt enquiries after people's emotional wellbeing.

For some, this change didn't stick, but the more missions we flew, the kinder everyone was. There is, it seems, something about hurtling through space at several thousand metres per second in a trilinium box with huge weapons and even bigger engines whilst someone else tries to paint a plasma trail on your cockpit that really mellows people out.

These changes I observed are what cemented the idea in my head that there is good in everybody: one just needs to find the appropriate way to tap it. I was smiling at this thought when I was brought sharply back to the present by the sound of Sir Angus' voice.

"Clodthorpe!" he bellowed from some way behind me. I turned to see the knight of the realm standing on the terrace that bordered his house. Gertrude was approaching him at a sprint, waving several legs in the air. I did not focus on Gertrude, though. My attention was drawn to the large rifle that Sir Angus was carrying. He levelled it at me and I threw myself to the floor, hearing a roar and crunch as the shot flew wide and impacted with a rather pleasant stone statue that someone had placed several metres to my right.

3

FOUR SHOTS FOLLOWED THE FIRST ONE. PIGSTICK HAD apparently frozen, so I yanked on one of her legs and she came crashing down next to me. She was shaking.

"Milli-" she gasped, when there was a gap between shots. "I'm having 'nham flashbacks."

She and I had fought in the battle of Cheltenham. We didn't talk about it much. I motioned to my upper lip and silently invited her to drink in how stiff it was. She resumed her normal calm demeanour within a few moments, and I dare say there was a great deal of unspoken camaraderie passing between us. I was never able to confirm this, however, because I heard the tread of approaching clawsteps and surmised that Sir Angus had reloaded and was approaching my position.

I grabbed Pigstick by the leg and made a break for it. I heard a curse from behind me and an unhealthy-sounding click. My fortune was such that Sir Angus' rifle had jammed. Pigstick pulled herself together after the first few metres and was keeping up with me after a few metres more.

We ran together. We kept low, the better to give Sir Angus less to shoot at. There was a hedge maze to the south and we made for it, not because it would be easy to conceal ourselves in, but because Sir Angus would think twice about blowing holes in the elegantly sculpted taxus trees.

A bullet thrummed over my head as we reached the maze, and we jinked around, trying to get the bulk of green leaves between us and the armed aristocrat. I could hear a terrible whining from the servos in Pigstick's legs, though. Her coffin wasn't designed for prolonged movement at above a walking pace.

On the other side of the maze, there was a glade with seven statues depicting the seven favours the first Wermacht at Newbury Towers had granted to the village of Newbury. Pigstick took cover behind *electricity*, whilst I found myself behind *regular meals*. There was a moment when we thought Sir Angus might pass our hiding spot, but the sound of approaching clawsteps disabused us of that notion. Pigstick made a distressed electronic buzzing noise and we both ran once more. A shot careened past me and buried itself into the *electronic tagging* statue.

We jumped a stream on the other side of the glade, and I was in the process of dodging around a small cottage that might have belonged to the gardener when I realised Pigstick wasn't with me. I looked back and saw that two of her servos had jammed, leaving her down to six functioning legs. This wouldn't be an issue for someone at home in their body, but Pigstick had only occupied her coffin for a matter of days and was, as such, unable to stand, let alone evade angry Wermachts.

I returned to her side and helped her to her claws. She thanked me, her voice pained. We turned as Sir Angus stalked into the middle of the glade and levelled his rifle at us.

I stared at the gun, saw Sir Angus' claw move to the trigger, and tried to think of something poignant to be my last thought. Of course, in hindsight I realise I should have thought of myself and Emily skipping through a field or something. Instead, I was struck by an image of dear Emily staring at me, goggle eyed, shouting, *Is this really how you're going to die, Milli? What in blazes have you been doing with yourself since I left?* and then throwing her claws up in frustration.

Sir Angus didn't fire. He stared through the sight at me for some considerable time. Gertrude arrived after a few seconds and stood behind him. I could see her calculating whether she could disarm her father before he squeezed his index claw. I never got to see what conclusion she came to because Sir Angus lowered the rifle. Gertrude gently took it from his grip.

I saw Sir Angus slump. I've seen similar motions before. Sometimes consciousness uploads or downloads don't work. Sometimes someone finds that a friend who died in battle is just gone. Some people, like my dear Emily, believe that the transience of life is what makes it special and, as a result, don't upload or download their consciousness. The news that such an individual has died often results in a slump of the sort I saw Sir Angus exhibit.

Gertrude slipped a leg through one of her father's and began to walk him back to the house. The bowed set of Sir Angus' retreating back was melancholy personified. I wanted to cry out with some encouraging comment, but refrained. My presence had helped the onset of this sudden malaise. Uninvited shouts would only deepen it.

I turned back to Pigstick instead and spent some little time helping her back to the house. There, I encountered Forsythe, who was giving a couple of porters clipped, precise instructions on where to set most of my luggage. A plain van loomed off in the distance, indicating the method of his arrival.

I drew Forsythe's attention and he rallied round. He replaced the broken servos in Pigstick's leg there on the driveway, but remarked that he would be grateful if Ms Slavarington could spare a few moments, so that he could ensure the rest of her moving parts weren't about to suffer a similar fate. Pigstick agreed, and the two strolled off to the house infirmary. I made to follow them, but was stopped in my tracks by a vox-o-matic signal from Gertrude. I enquired as to the health of her father, which caused something of a sigh to come from the young lass.

"I've never seen him like this..." Gertrude half whispered, evidently having only just left her father. "He's in his study just staring into space. I think it's all been a bit much for him."

"Is there anything I can do?" I asked, feeling rather futile.

"I think there might be, actually. If Father's mood persists throughout dinner, he might look more kindly on you – and consider life just the teensiest bit less wretched as a result – if you were to stick up for him."

"Stick up for him?" I echoed. The idea seemed absurd.

"You know," said Gertrude, clearly thinking I'd misunderstood her, which wasn't unreasonable given my track record with misunderstandings in general. "Defend him if one of our number were to be beastly to him."

"I don't think any of our number would be that heartless," I pointed out.

"I think you may be wrong there," said Gertrude. "I've just been having a little chat with Bainbridge, and if his current temperament is anything to go by, you should have ample opportunity. Still, in case Bainbridge disappoints, I shall have a quiet word with Pigstick. She can start being beastly at the drop of a hat, so she'll have a crack at it once the port's out of the way if Bainbridge hasn't stepped up to the matter."

The idea that Sir Angus' current mood was anything other than transient was not a pleasant one. That said, if his mood could be bolstered, and his opinion raised of me as the result of one simple action, it had to be worth a try.

I thanked Gertrude and retired to my room to muse. I mused with my eyes shut, for the most part, because the décor was somewhat unsettling. I'd never seen green in such a variety of shades before. Somehow the colour contrived to clash with itself at various points in the room. In spite of this, after a mere hour or two, I thought I had a couple of juicy phrases that would melt Sir Angus' heart, all whilst bolstering his defences against even the most beastly of attackers.

The dress gong rang as I was noting one or two of these phrases down, which caused Forsythe to shimmer in and assist with my preparations for dinner.

With a gentleman's personal gentleman in tow, it only takes about five and twenty minutes to slip from the rags of the morning into something that would be more appropriate when seen at the dining table of a country house. I dare say it would be possible without Forsythe at my elbow, but I wouldn't swear to it. The Clodthorpe brain being what it is, I expect that by the time I'd made a proper decision about whether, when you got right down to it, a blue suit was more appropriate than a classic dark green, search parties would have been dispatched to locate my body.

My own shortfalls notwithstanding, Forsythe facilitated my dressing to such a degree that I was second to arrive at the dinner table. I say second to arrive because there was somebody already seated at the table when I strolled in. That someone was Sir Angus Wermacht. I contemplated beating a hasty retreat and coming back when Pigstick or Gertrude were present so that the poor fellow didn't have to stomach having only a Clodthorpe for company. Unfortunately, the knight's eyes snapped up as soon as I entered the room, rendering me unable to slip out unobserved.

No part of Sir Angus moved, other than his eyes, but he appeared to glare from me to a chair, so I sat in it, trying to be as inoffensive as possible. One of Sir Angus' claws shot forward and tapped a decanter. I thanked him and waited as the butler appeared and poured me a glass with ice and a shred of lemon peel. The beverage was heavenly. I enquired from the butler as to its origins, not wanting to suffer Sir Angus through a conversation with me. I didn't fully understand the explanation the butler offered, but the words "matured for fifteen years" stood out. I thanked him and returned to the restorative.

Thankfully, Sir Angus wasn't forced to sit quietly watching me work my way through his spirits for long. I had just finished off the third glass of the truly first class beverage when Gertrude entered. She was followed shortly by Bainbridge and, scuttling along behind, Pigstick in her coffin. Sir Angus turned to them, and his face drank them in as if he was a desert feeling the first of the rains on his face, although truth be told his actual expression changed very little.

Dinner was a somewhat muted affair. Sir Angus maintained a stolid silence throughout. Thanks to the refreshment I had enjoyed prior to dinner, I was in high spirits but it looked dreadfully like I was the only one who was. Gertrude was clearly anxious over her father's mood, and Pigstick was sat next to Bainbridge and, as a result, was having to listen to him for extended periods.

Young Bainbridge seemed to have developed a keen dislike of his new human body. I only mention this because, apart from the odd interjection about passing salt or something similar, he never spoke on another topic throughout the evening. He spoke with such venom on the subjects of humanity in general, and the unit he'd been downloaded into in particular, that the rest of us had barely finished digesting his most recent pearl of wisdom before he'd started on the next one.

Throughout the meal, most of the participants had been somewhat downcast by the frequency with which Bainbridge was bending our respective ears with reference to this topic. Gertrude kept attempting to change the subject but never succeeded thanks to Bainbridge's remorseless single mindedness. Pigstick had started to shift about the place after the first hour, which was always a sign of trouble. Sir Angus, though, had been half listening the whole time, with the expression of a man who had thought that life couldn't possibly get any worse, yet every passing second was proving him wrong.

There seemed to be an endless list of complaints young Bainbridge had with his body. The shortage of limbs, the shortage of eyes, the lack of proper fur (what little he had, apparently, didn't count), and the lack of any venomous characteristics in the dental region, were all subjects touched on over the soup. During the subsequent courses, we were treated to speeches on the problems with fingers, why breasts were in completely the wrong place indeed, and a musing on which idiot had decided to lay out the central nervous system in such an unintuitive manner. By the time the port and walnuts rolled round, Bainbridge was really beginning to hit his stride and was just beginning to explain to us all what menstruation was and how, whilst it sounded fantastic, it was in fact the most vile proceeding one could endure, when Sir Angus drew the line. I believe it was at the mention of the human uterus that he stirred, like a leviathan who'd finally become fed up with shipping vessels dropping anchors on him all the time.

"Bainbridge," he began, off to a strong start. He then launched into an erudite speech about how the young ingrate should use this opportunity to better himself. Words like "layabout" were inserted with abandon. Phrases like "complete failure to take responsibility" thundered from his lips. Bainbridge is not one to be easily cowed, though, and I could just see him winding up to lay into the aged relative by marriage when I saw my opportunity.

I could have attempted to tick Bainbridge off at various points throughout the meal, but without an interjection from Sir Angus and a subsequent attempt at a riposte from Bainbridge, it would have had significantly less impact. I could feel Gertrude and Pigstick willing me on. Just as Bainbridge opened his mouth to reply, I interjected.

"I say, Bainbridge," was how I began. This is how I like to begin a light rebuke, as it lures a fellow into what I like to call a false sense of security. You see, the fellow will hear my cheery phrase and feel encouraged. He will then be totally unprepared when I hit him with the good stuff. "I think you've got this all wrong, young rectangle. If I were you, I'd be glad to see life as a human. I mean, to look through another's eyes, well that's something of a rare privilege, what? It seems to me, Bainbridge, and forgive me for going on about this, that whilst you can speak eloquently about the problems you have with this new vessel, you have not truly taken the time to appreciate what it can do for you, if you see what I mean. I think you've been entirely beastly throughout this wonderful meal in subjecting us to your complaints, and the moment Sir Angus points this out to you, in dashed polite terms I might add, given the circumstances, you round on him like a tiger.

Pause, young Bainbridge. Consider the impact your actions have on those around you. Consider Sir Angus, who has been most upset by your actions. Consider the poor human whose mind you wiped in order to occupy its body."

Well, I must say that I rarely see a fellow wilt after my speeches. The best I can hope for is for my opinion to be dismissed out of claw, but on this occasion, young Bainbridge actually paused. He seemed to weigh my words in the balance. Sir Angus seemed as surprised by this development as I was. I actually saw his expression flicker. It wasn't quite the dramatic mood shift I had been hoping for, but it was something to be proud of none the less. I took the opportunity to steer the conversation towards an interesting piece I'd seen in The Weekly Wipe that morning.

Gertrude ran with the new theme enthusiastically, saying that yes, she'd seen that piece and wasn't it wonderful, the sorts of things one could do with goats these days if you had the will and the circular saw blades at claw. Pigstick chimed in occasionally with the sort of pithy comment about goats that made her such a popular raconteur at the club.

I, for my part, had been so encouraged by my effective rescuing of the evening's conversation that I felt it would be an appropriate time to savour a glass of port. I became so caught up in the bouquet and the exquisite nuances of the beverage that I had managed to sink a full six measures before I realised that someone had been trying to attract my attention for a spell.

"I say," I started, "have I missed something?"

Sir Angus rumbled like a dormant volcano that had become bored with retirement and was considering a return to its previous glory. I looked around and found it was just the two of us left at the table, the others presumably leaving for greener pastures. The old uncle by marriage, as politeness demanded, couldn't leave until all his guests had done so, and I realised gradually that the poor chap wanted to give his mattress and pillows a good seeing to. I apologised profusely, he muttered something about it being quite all right, all the time glaring at me as if nothing would give him greater pleasure than to have me fall down some sort of well.

Considering the idea of laying into the pillows a capital plan upon reflection, I staggered in that direction myself. I found my bedroom after making only two or three wrong turns along the way. There, I discovered Forsythe was waiting for me, and together we found some suitable attire for my upcoming night's rest.

Forsythe really is a marvel. I've had some valets in my time that would have been content to whisk me from my garments, fling a nightshirt at me, and then retire to their realm below stairs to chase parlour maids, or play Pai Gow, or whatever it is these chaps do with their spare time. Not Forsythe, though. He takes his time. He considers the effect of the nightshirt with this or that nightcap. He considers the consequences of whether it was the sort of night which required any adornments of the claws.

Forsythe adjusted my wardrobe until my appearance met both of our exacting standards. I think we settled on something figure-hugging in blue silk finally. I thanked him and he murmured something along the lines of, "Not at all, sir," before leaving to see to his own recharging arrangements.

Now, I'm sure I don't have to relate to you how sleep works. I mean, I possibly should in case you're one of those people who never sleep thanks to some sort of brain enhancement. I understand that in those circs, sleep can become something of a distant memory, much like collective self-worth has become for the humans. To clarify, when I sleep, I tend to go unconscious for a while, hallucinate vividly on and off for another while, occasionally wake up screaming at the memory of dear Emily's death, then return to uninterrupted unconsciousness, until finally waking up in the morning.

This night was slightly different, in that the restoratives my uncle by marriage Angus had been supplying me with, not to mention the port, had rendered my sleep somewhat more deep and dreamless than it had been for some time.

I woke up feeling fresh and much like one of those ancient workers by claw and brain must have done. I wanted very much to bound from my bed and get right down to the business of the day. Things were dashed comfortable, though, so I paused for a spell, drinking in the day. The sun shone through the window, and some sort of space-faring parasite was knocking a snail against the window sill, making an agreeable tap-tapping sort of a noise. Generally, all was as well as it could possibly be. Even the horrifying greens my chamber had been decorated in seemed less ghastly than they had the day before.

Forsythe chose to brighten my day still further by swooping in with the breakfast tray. If I didn't know better, I'd suspect that he'd introduced a monitoring device into my pillow that could detect my brain waves and identify the precise moment I awoke, allowing him to time his entrance with the morning gastronomic delights perfectly. In fact, I asked one of those medical chaps one encounters in hospitals from time to time whether this was possible. He pondered the question for a while and then sent me to get the old cranium examined by one of his fellow sawbones.

This chap ran me through several machines, and then spent some time staring at bits of paper. He subsequently fixed me with a stare and informed me that, whilst it would be entirely possible for my gentleman's personal gentleman to implant a device that monitored brainwaves into my pillow, it would make little difference in the practicalities of everyday life, because it transpired that my levels of brain activity were identical whether I was asleep or whether I was awake and fully alert. As you can imagine, this came as something of a relief. One doesn't like to think that one's valet is spying on one.

I don't know if it was the fog of sleep clinging to the old brain, but Forsythe looked particularly imposing on this particular morning. It was possible he'd upgraded himself. Occasionally, when he finds himself in dens such as Newbury Towers, the fellow will find himself chatting to the mechanic who services the estate's vehicles. Soon after, he will have added a few storage pods to his frame or, perhaps, a hydroponic facility for the portable production of tea. I assumed upgrades of this sort were the reason for his appearing considerably larger than I remembered him looking less than twelve hours ago.

My eye was drawn to the tray in Forsythe's claws, as it so often is. The fellow had really outdone himself this morning. No doubt assuming I would be somewhat the worse for wear after dinner last night, he had acquired vast quantities of tea in a cup that was more akin to a bucket than a mere cup. I looked up to thank the valet for treating me with such consideration.

Forsythe, as I may have mentioned before, never looks surprised at anything. If there was a pan-galactic championship for being completely unsurprised in the face of devastating news… that would be incredibly bizarre. Nevertheless, if something of the sort did exist, Forsythe would doubtless place in the top twenty, if not the top ten. On this occasion, I wasn't aware that there was anything for him to be surprised at, if you see what I mean, so I took his complete lack of surprise very much in my stride.

"Good morning, Forsythe," I said. "What ho!"

My voice was a good deal more bovine than I remembered it being. I didn't want to make too much of a fuss about this, though. Beverages of the sort I was drinking last night have been known to have peculiar side effects on the morning after consumption. I remember on one occasion, when dear Emily was still alive, we both consumed more than our fair share of something remarkably pleasant, and the next morning we woke up with a penguin in the bed. No ready explanation presented itself, and even Forsythe considered himself at a loss as to how the animal ended up there. I was all for eating the animal in question, but dear Emily, always one to bring out the best in me, suggested donating it to a Zoo which, on reflection, was a far better idea.

What I mean to say is that, whilst I wouldn't go so far as to admit I was intoxicated last night, it is possible that I might have overdone things slightly, so a little fraying of the vocal chords wouldn't be entirely out of the question. Forsythe's next remark, however, chilled me.

"Ah, sir," he remarked, "I see you have changed."

I, of course, wondered what he meant. I surely hadn't roused myself in the night and dressed myself in dear Emily's clothes so I could be surrounded by her scent again, had I? I looked down. I was not wearing dear Emily's clothing.

"Forsythe!" I choked, "what's happened?"

"Do I divine from your tone, sir, that this development was not entirely the result of action taken by you?"

The question amazed me so that, rather than answering, I found myself only to emit a series of exasperated coughing noises.

"I see, sir," said Forsythe, "would you like me to see if Mr Lusitania is in his chamber?"

"Yes, Forsythe, if you could," was about all I could manage at that moment.

Forsythe drifted out and I was able to assess the full horror of the situation. I was prodding and probing myself when the fellow returned, followed by me. Well, I mean to say, my body.

"Mr Lusitania, sir." Forsythe intoned.

"Bainbridge!" I thundered. "What is the meaning of this?"

Bainbridge shrugged, irritatingly. "What do you mean, Milli old chap?"

"I mean," I growled, like the Sphinx watching Oedipus' retreating back, "what are you doing in my body and what, when you get right down to it, am I doing in your human body?"

4

I'VE NOT CONSIDERED MYSELF YOUNG FOR SOME YEARS NOW. My fur is thinning around the cephalothorax, and there are definite wrinkles around my eyes. Seeing Bainbridge in my body, though, was something of a revelation. Not being weighed down by the years to quite the same extent I was, he wore my body with more vitality than it had seen in some time. I'd never considered the scar that bisects one of my eyes to look rakish; it had always been something I'd tried to hide. He had shot his cuffs on entering the room, a gesture my body had not performed for two summers at least. The body I saw before me was young and carefree. This would not stand.

"What am I doing in your human body?" I repeated.

"Oh that," said Bainbridge, airily, as if I'd just asked him for the name of his tailor, "well, Milli, you were talking at some length last night about how wonderful it must be to be in a human body, so I, quite naturally, assumed that you wanted to swap with me. You knew I found the whole process beastly after all, old salt."

Had I the mandibles, I would have sputtered. "Bainbridge, this is intolerable!" I managed after a spell. "Kindly return me to myself at once!"

Bainbridge chuckled in a way I found perfectly infuriating. "Can't be done I'm afraid, Milli. The chap I borrowed the body-swapping apparatus from wanted it back. He'll have no doubt moved on by now."

I hyperventilated a little.

"Well, I say, there's no need to be like that, old sauce," he said, prodding me where I assumed my ribs were, "I would have thought you would approve of this move of mine."

I glared. Wretched as this new body might have been, I found it exceptional for glaring. It had far fewer eyes than I was used to, but I managed to revolve them in a way that established my objections wonderfully. Bainbridge didn't wither in the face of my glare in quite the way I'd hoped, however.

"Well, mustn't stand around chatting all day, old breadcrumb, I need to be dressing for breakfast. I'll get Forsythe to raid my wardrobe for human clothing. Pip pip, keep your chin up!"

He drifted out like a spectre of some form or other.

Breakfast was a miserable affair. Preparations for the meal had set the tone when I had needed to dress in clothes that were entirely unsuitable for a modern gentleman. They were altogether too small (although they fitted this new body

I was in well enough), and they were distressingly lacking in space for pockets, or any stylish touches such as lapels or buttonholes. I had struggled to get downstairs to the breakfast room, and had then needed to half-climb into the high chair that had previously been occupied by Bainbridge.

Gertrude had tut-tutted at Bainbridge when the sequence of events last night had been relayed, which I took comfort in. Pigstick in her part offered one or two words of sympathy, and even Uncle Angus glared at me in a way which was not even a tenth as hostile as I was used to.

It was this last display of kindness that touched me the most. I realised how much effort it must have taken the relative by marriage to glare at me with dislike instead of cold, hard, eye-bursting fury, given the events of the previous day.

I was ruminating on this matter after breakfast, whilst getting used to my new ambulatory apparatus in the gardens. If you picture the scene, there was a biggish sort of lawn spread out ahead of me, with trees lining the lawn to the left, and a sheer drop into the all-consuming void of space on the right. There are one or two flower beds tastefully arranged hither and thither, as well as one or two pylons, and things that kept the breathable atmosphere just so.

I had just managed to sort out walking to my satisfaction, and was trying to work out how a relaxed stroll might be achieved with only two legs, when I heard a cheerful, "Ho there, Clodthorpe!" from behind me. I spun around, which was a mistake. The sixth and seventh legs which I use for balance when conducting such a manoeuvre turned out to be absent without leave, and so I toppled over.

It took some time for me to work out the necessary movements to bring me back to my claws, and, during this time, the creature who had hailed me approached. It turned out to be Pigstick. A lesser individual would have guffawed at seeing a pal of hers collapse like a society run entirely by economists, but not Pigstick; I could tell that my plight weighed heavily on her mind. She didn't actually say this, and her coffin was inexpressive as ever, but we Clodthorpes are astute.

"I say, Milli," she said, laying a comforting mechanical leg on my back, "what's it like in there?"

I didn't quite know what she meant. I asked for a clarification of sorts. She replied that she was curious as to "the human condition". She'd asked Bainbridge during their drive to Newbury Towers, but Bainbridge being Bainbridge had told her to get knotted.

Now, I don't know how you would deal with such a question, but I found myself more than a little bit flummoxed. I mean, turning the old ocular sensors inwards and gazing deeply into what resides inside your suit of flesh and bone can yield results that are dashed difficult to describe. I suppose a more eloquent scribe than me might have taken the time to talk about the nature of consciousness, and how, when you got right down to it, we are all just minds inhabiting bodies, and the bodies themselves are immaterial. You know how it is, though. In the moment, such pithy remarks rarely occur to you. Instead, I chatted to young Pigstick for a few moments on the obvious differences between my new body and the one that had been hijacked.

If I recall correctly, I touched on some of the subjects that Bainbridge was soliloquising about last night, although in less harsh terms. I don't like to speak ill of a body whilst I'm inside it: I worry that it will take offence. Nevertheless, I was unable to inform Pigstick that everything was lipstick and rainbows.

"Mmm," Pigstick said, gazing at my body and inserting a claw into some of the softer bits. "Well, let me know if you come to any interesting conclusions."

I said I would, and she thanked me.

I spent a few moments gazing at where the herbaceous borders would be if this estate had such things. This done, I found that my memory was jogged. This was such an unusual occurrence that I spent a few moments further enjoying the sensation. Once this was out of the way, I rounded on Pigstick. The sensors on her coffin were pointing every which way, but many of them were pointing in my general direction for reasons I decided not to attempt to fathom just yet. Instead, my memory and my wits working in conjunction, I focussed on the young shaver:

"Did you want something, Pigstick?" I asked.

"I don't know," she replied, "did I?"

The poor cabbage was distracted. I reminded her that it was she, of all people, who had hailed me earlier, resulting in my inspecting the lawn rather more closely than I would normally have liked.

"Ah!" she exclaimed, "yes, yes I did, didn't I? Now, I don't mean to shock you, Milli, but I also can't stand you living under misapprehensions all over the place. I need you to brace yourself. I don't think our plan to soften Uncle Angus last night went particularly well."

I opened my mouth to retort with something along the lines of "I know that, Pigstick, you perennial half-wit," but she didn't give me the chance.

"I know this is hard to hear, Milli, old chap. You may not have picked up on all the signs that I have. We Slavaringtons are a perceptive lot. Now, last night's efforts were not entirely fruitless, but I'm sure you'll agree they didn't produce quite the results we were after. This morning however, old wizbit, the wonder that is that new body of yours has caused him to feel sympathetic to you. I wouldn't go so far as to say he'll offer you a shoulder to cry on, should you be reminded of my dear departed sister by an old portrait or tactless comment, but I would go so far as to say he would empty the contents of a vase or two over you if you spontaneously conflagrated."

I wondered if there was any way I could speed her along the way to her point. Talking at odds to the matter at issue has often been a peculiarity of Pigstick's. It's hard to blame the young soufflé for this, of course, as I'm hardly blameless in this regard. I don't know if I ever told you of the time when I was making my vows to Dear Emily in the registry office near Kew Gardens. Dear Emily was looking particularly radiant; her fur swirled in patterns as elegant as her dress, and her eyes shone with the light of joy and love. She had just finished saying words that were probably "I do" but had been drowned out somewhat by her mother Ophelia's anguished sobbing and screaming.

The problem was that I was so wonderfully happy, and Dear Emily was so astonishingly beautiful, I completely neglected to listen when the registrar chappie did his bit about being able to kiss brides now we were married. Dear Emily leaned in to do just that, but I stared at her, still dazzled. I knew that something was due to happen at any moment, but the woman who, to my total amazement, loved me, saying words that were very probably "I do", had quite wiped my mind of any other relevant information. Thankfully, the light of my life was wise to my faults, even at that time, so hoofed me sharply in the foremost left limb, bringing my attention her way.

I was just wondering if such a hoofing would render service on this occasion, with regards to getting Pigstick to move things along a bit. I resolved that it probably would do just nicely and was just working out how to get my lower legs, the ones I was using to stand on at present, to make a decent kicking motion, when the words "my point is" dropped into the conversation. This caused me to revise my plans. I mean, it would be impolite to cause the young thing pain when she was already on the way to making whatever point it was that she was in the process of making. I resolved to swing my attention in her direction.

"-you should strike whilst the old ferrum still has a certain amount of heat in it, old boy," she was saying. "Get in there whilst the aged relative is giving you this suitably glowing opportunity!"

Her words were exuberant and her manner was expressive. She was staring at me in the manner of one of those ancient philosophers who were constantly discovering fluid displacement mechanics and similar things. "Eureka!" her eyes seemed to say.

I toyed with the idea of admitting that I hadn't altogether been listening to the young trouser for some time, but

Clodthorpes never hurt people's feelings if they can avoid it. I decided to react as I did after dear Emily had replied with the word "yes" to my proposal of marriage:

"I'm sorry," said I, "I don't understand."

"You perfect twit-whistle," Pigstick chided. "It's really rather simple. Uncle Angus is infinitely more sympathetic to you than he was yesterday, so if you were to capitalise on this by doing some sort of grand favour for the relative, he might cast his animosity for you aside and treat you like the brother he always wanted."

I considered this.

"Pigstick," I said, after mulling the problem from one side of my brain to the other for a while. "It is my opinion that you are on to something. What should this grand favour be?"

Pigstick jiggled a few of her legs. "Well I don't know, old beetle, I'm your common or garden grand strategy sort of lass. For the specifics, for the actual mechanics of the idea, why don't you consult Forsythe? You often regale me with tales of his terrifyingly enormous brain. Might that brain not be put to good use on occasions such as this?"

Of course! Forsythe! The idea was a strong one indeed. I spent one or two moments thanking Pigstick for her suggestion, and another couple pointing out how excellent a suggestion it was. She, for her part, made one or two noises that sounded distinctly like, "Not at all, my dear chap."

My spirits thus brightened, I was about to engage in a friendly back-slap or two when Pigstick reminded me that time, as that chap in the blue box once said, was of the essence. We marched back to the house and rang for the Butler. Whilst I enquired as to where I might find my man, Pigstick hid behind me, as far as such a manoeuvre was possible given that the body she was in was rather larger than the one I was in. Pigstick has always been terrified of butlers, ever since one caught her sipping from a secret supply the fellow had below stairs. In Pigstick's defence, her unit was due to ship out the next day, and she just wanted a taste of the good stuff before that fateful hour. In the butler's defence, he probably would not have minded if Pigstick had simply been after a sip, but, as is the way with these things, a sip tends to lead to a gulp, and gulps tend to breed.

The butler mentioned, in a voice like the crack of thunder on a particularly malicious doomsday, that Forsythe could be found tending to the cabbage patch, and summoned one of his underlings to fetch the valet in question. I thanked the butler in as dignified a manner as possible and spent a few torturous moments commenting on the favourable atmospheric conditions whilst he growled at me.

Forsythe glided into view after only a few moments, which was something of a relief. I mentioned that I wanted a word or two with him, which provided me with enough of a pretext to leave the company of the butler, who was eyeing Pigstick in a way that wasn't entirely benign. If you've ever been at the shark tank at feeding time, you'll know the sort of thing I mean. Clearly Pigstick's past transgressions were well-known in the circles butlers move in.

We strode along the path that bordered the house a little way, until we three were far from the gaze of butlers. I say we strode… this is, in fact, somewhat misleading. Pigstick strode well enough for all three of us, whilst Forsythe trundled smoothly on his caterpillar tracks, and I moved at a highly variable speed that was pretty much dictated by my attempts to walk without falling over.

After a few minutes of striding, trundling and very nearly falling over, we found ourselves located in one of those flower garden things that estates such as Newbury Towers often pepper here and there. They have benches and bird tables and the like. This particular garden boasted a particularly fine ornamental pond. As I was much closer to it than I would normally be, being nearer to the ground than usual, I was able to admire some of the finer detail the landscaper had included in the design. I drew Forsythe's attention to these details.

"Most diverting sir," he commented.

"Quite so!" I remarked. Pigstick nudged me, very nearly catapulting me into an azalea. I turned to her and tried to contort my face into a silent enquiry as to the reason for the nudge. Pigstick rolled a few sensors about on her coffin and related to Forsythe the conversation that had caused Clodthorpe M. and Slavarington S. to seek him out. Having an excellent memory, such as Pigstick and Forsythe possess, must be remarkably boring. Things would rarely take them by surprise. That said, they must get a lot more done, what with rarely forgetting what they entered a room for.

Forsythe nodded, thoughtfully, once Pigstick had finished relating the story. "I see the conundrum, Ms Slavarington," he murmured, "It is vital to capitalise on Sir Wehrmacht's sympathy to Mr Clodthorpe's current predicament."

"Have you any ideas, Forsythe? Do tell," I urged. He shook his head.

"I fear not sir, if you could spare me for a few moments, I would like to ruminate on the problem."

Knowing that Forsythe tends to function well when left with his thoughts, Pigstick and I acquiesced and popped off. We spent a rather fraught half hour wandering the grounds, chatting about the proposed changes to association clawball, and how they would inevitably fail to make the pastime entertaining for the casual observer.

Once this conversation had run its course, we found ourselves drawn back to the flower garden to see if Forsythe had any progress to report. He didn't appear to be there. We turned over every rock we could find, but, if anything, he appeared to be there even less than when we originally checked.

"It's too bad," said Pigstick, "that we're not living in one of those societies were one can implant tracking systems into a valet's motherboard, so he can be located in an emergency such as this."

I thought about this. When a lass comes out with something like this, it is my wont to weigh the pros and cons. Pigstick interrupted my musings though, by exclaiming as loudly as the speakers in her coffin would allow:

"I've got it!" she cried, "Milli, you will be in Uncle Angus' best books by nightfall!"

This seemed unlikely, but Clodthorpes don't like to appear negative. "Have you a scheme, young Pigstick?" I asked, guardedly. Pigstick's schemes were often ingenious, but lacking in fine detail.

"I have, Milli, and if you stop interrupting for two moments together I will tell you what it is."

I didn't think this was entirely fair, but to point this out I would have needed to interrupt the young lass, so I let the comment slip past.

"You will recall, old bloodnut, that Uncle Angus has that treasured collection of human war memorabilia? Well he's just acquired a new piece. It's an olive green resin figurine, depicting the Avatar of Pestilence. It's very nearly priceless, dear chap, and Uncle Angus would be heartbroken if it were to be mislaid."

She waved her coffin legs expressively. I didn't follow.

"Surely it won't be, if he's that fond of it," I remarked.

"You chump, Milli, of course a piece of his collection won't go missing of its own accord, but if we were to arrange for a piece to be purloined and then you, the last of the Clodthorpe line, were to step in and return the figurine to its rightful owner…"

The idea struck me like a particularly inspired thunderbolt. This was a remarkable scheme, and one that did not threaten my life in any way as far as I could see. I grasped one of Pigstick's mechanical legs and shook it with vigour. I was elated. I was, I might go so far as to say, bucked up considerably. It was only when I was crouched inside a rhododendron tsutsuji some hours later that I began to have second thoughts.

5

HERE WAS THE SITUATION: THE RHODODENDRON TSUTSUJI I was hiding in was parked next to a set of human windows. The human windows led into a rather neat little sitting room, and just beyond that was a reinforced safe, or possibly a vault of some kind. Pigstick and I had inspected the thing a few hours ago. I had pointed out that it might be tricky to get into it. Pigstick had waved this objection aside.

"Nonsense, Milli, old pancake. The real trick is to find a suitable burglar."

"Why can't you do it?" I asked. She had been the one to come up with the scheme after all.

"Use the inter-ear pathways, you chump. If Uncle Angus happens to see you struggling with some chap in a coffin, his first thought isn't going to be 'How I have misjudged that Clodthorpe, he is intercepting a burglar!' it's going to be 'what exactly are Sarah and that Clodthorpe doing? They're going to break something!' My point is that I'm too recognisable, old moonskin. We need someone who can pass undetected behind enemy lines for this gig."

I saw what she was driving at. "Gertrude?"

"Cousin Gertrude indeed, Milli."

Pigstick vox'd Gertrude, who boomed into the room after a short spell.

"Pigstick, what the arse are you playing at this time?"

"You use strong words, dear one," she replied placidly. It's never a good idea to match Cousin Gertrude's tone, or the room ends up sounding like two fog horns having a dust up.

"Well, wouldn't you use strong language if you were interrupted, while in the middle of tending to a rose bush you'd nurtured since it was a seedling, and summarily summoned to a mysterious room by a cloth-eared loon in a coffin?"

I decided that I might need to intervene at this point.

"I say, Gertrude-" I began, but she was just getting into her flow and didn't seem to want to stop. She swivelled towards me, and her tone softened significantly.

"Oh, my apologies, Milli. I didn't see you there. I'll do my best to tick off this coffin-bound Slavarington in a quieter manner. Now-"

I threw caution to the winds, "Pigstick is assisting me in a scheme, Gertrude. I would take it as a personal favour if you would help us."

She paused. I know Cousin Gertrude likes few things more in life than to really express herself when she finds herself in the mood to, but she's also one of those essentially helpful individuals who brighten up the cosmos by their very presence. I could see her wrestling with the conflicting emotions, but eventually her sunnier side won out. She settled down a touch, her eyes retreated back into their sockets, and the fire she had been breathing was extinguished with a slight cough.

"I apologise, Pigstick," she intoned, "I had no idea you were calling about something worthwhile."

Pigstick took this very well, I thought. She said something rather charming about probably making the same assumption that Gertrude had, if she had been in her position. Gertrude inclined her head respectfully, and Pigstick returned the gesture.

"So," Gertrude said, "what are you two planning this time? Hopefully nothing that would cause Father further distress?"

Pigstick outlined the plan in a few short sentences. Gertrude, being one of those beans who's always being told to capture this hill or destroy that enemy fortification, by whichever commanding officer she currently serves under, understood with little need for clarification. She lowered her voice and indicated to us that we should take our places in a mere hour, for that was when she would initiate her part of the plan. She did mention, though, in more of a growl than a murmur, that if either of us did anything to cause the plan to go awry, and thus cause her father more distress than he'd already suffered, she would be most displeased.

The above negotiations resulted in my fragile form being nestled inside a rhododendron tsutsuji. At any moment, Cousin Gertrude would break into the safe or, possibly, the vault. The burglar alarm would sound in Uncle Angus' aural implant, and he would come rushing down to see what was what. Gertrude would hear him arriving and come bowling through the human windows. I'd intercept her and wrest the figurine from her grasp. Gertrude would escape in the melee, I would return the figurine to Sir Angus, and all would be jam and ginger from that point onwards.

It wasn't long before I heard the sound of a thermal lance. This gave way to the odd thump and crash while Gertrude did her stuff. Then there was a pause.

I waited with poised legs… then I heard a door opening. Uncle Angus was on the scene.

Gertrude bolted for the door, and I leapt from the rhododendron tsutsuji. I saw her barrelling towards me, a blackened hood disguising her face. I adopted an old rugby stance I'd been taught by one of my more athletic chums at university, and shouted, "Stop, thief!" As Gertrude approached, I leapt at her.

At that point, I realised that our plan had one or two flaws in it. Firstly, I still hadn't really mastered the system human bodies work on, that is to say, having two lower legs for perambulation and two upper legs for the manipulation of objects. In my haste to arrest Gertrude, I attempted to leap using my upper legs instead of the ones that were placed firmly on terra firma. Gertrude was on me in only a moment, her speed not arrested by a ballistic Clodthorpe, as had been Plan A.

This would have spelled disaster for our plan taken in isolation. What helped the plan move from disaster to an absolute pig's breakfast of a catastrophe was Gertrude herself.

The poor relative is somewhat battle scarred, and in-between taking flight and reaching the human windows, something in her brain must have gone off-bang. Looking into her eyes now, I could see fire and battle staring back at me, even through the balaclava. I only had the chance to make a few swings at the figurine with my upper legs before she went off script. She shoved me aside, landing me back in the rhododendron tsutsuji, and hoofed it.

I hauled myself out and stared in the direction she had fled. I was able to catch a glimpse of her retreating back as she disappeared over the horizon at something approaching the speed of a Galactic-class interceptor missile.

Gentlemen with less of a grip on themselves might have taken this opportunity to shake their claws at the unforgiving black void of space, cursing the evident lack of any controlling force behind the universe. Clodthorpe M, though, takes a more measured approach to misfortune, and not just because I didn't have any claws at that moment. I brushed myself off, wondering where exactly Forsythe had got to, and looked into the sitting room. The vault, or possibly the safe, lay open. Human war memorabilia rested in drifts on the floor. Uncle Angus stood over the figurines and statuettes, gazing down at them. His shoulders were slumped. If yesterday's events had tipped Sir Angus over some sort of edge, these events may well have given him a concrete parachute for company on the way down.

"I say," I piped, "I'm terribly sorry, the miscreant overpowered me."

Many of you will be suspicious of my reporting of events at this stage, and it is true, this level of quick thinking only strikes me rarely, but this was truly one of those occasions. I couldn't swear as to whether Uncle Angus even heard me, though his shoulders depressed a touch further.

"Oh, Milligan."

At first, I thought this was all that he had to say on the matter but, after a sizeable pause, he spoke once again: "Did you see who did this?"

The tone in the voice of my relative by marriage caused me to reel. Such bleak sadness is not often heard on an estate such as this. I hung my head.

"I did not, they wore a mask."

"A mask," he repeated, his voice cracking. I'd always previously considered masks to be rather jolly things. You wear them at masquerade balls and secret midnight illicit intimacy parties. Well, I obviously don't, but chaps like young Bainbridge are always trotting along to parties of one sort or another, intimate or not. Now, though, the word "mask" seemed like it must forever carry with it the most dreadful sadness, a chagrin that could split time, and would think nothing of ripping babes from their mothers' legs.

"That's right," I said by way of reply.

"Have I ever told you, Milligan," he murmured, "that I started this collection with memorabilia captured during the battle of Cheltenham?"

I drew in a breath. "You were in 'nham?" I asked.

He turned to me. "Indeed I was, young Milligan. I led the charge on the northern flank whilst Sarah held the south. Were you there as well?"

"I was in the air group. 343 squadron," I murmured, the memory of that day dragging the corners of my large face hole down until my face mirrored that of my uncle by marriage. Or at least, it would have done if our faces looked in any way similar, given my current species-impaired state.

He turned to me. "I recall," he said. "Your squadron did fine work on that day." With that, and, I can scarcely write these words, he rested a leg across my back.

"You did your best to stop the thief, lad," he said, his voice now barely audible, like one of those horse whisperers you hear about. "We'll get the bounder who did this, don't you worry. I shall summon the village constable immediately, and instruct her to hound this black-hearted purloiner of figurines to the ends of the universe."

Saying so, he turned on three of his heels and left. I stood there for a few moments, working through recent events in my mind. I was beginning to draw some interesting conclusions, when my attention was brought back to the here and now by a tugging at my sleeve.

"I say," said a voice. I looked up: it was Pigstick. "How did it go?"

I took a deep breath and expelled it. "Well, Gertrude made off with the figurine of the Avatar of Pestilence. I was unable to stop her, and whilst Uncle Angus does indeed now see me as less of a worm and more of a comrade in arms, the poor relative by marriage is so crushed by the loss of the figurine, on top of everything else, that I wish I'd never come here, let alone entered into this scheme."

Pigstick either took time to think about this, or her brain/voice interface connection suffered a momentary glitch. I gave the young strawberry the benefit of the doubt and assumed the former assumption was the one closest to reality.

"Gosh," she said, eventually.

I gave Pigstick the full picture of recent events. The face of her coffin, if such a thing is possible, looked suitably ashen. Now I come to think about it, it isn't possible. I'd like to think it looked ashen, though. She scuttled from one side of the room to the other, muttering that old line from the talking rabbit that Charlie Dodgerson used to write about: something about ears, whiskers, and deer. Eventually, the poor doorstop calmed down and announced her intention to scuttle off after Gertrude before she crossed from the outfield to the wide world where any hope of recovering the figurine would be lost.

She enacted the first half of this plan before my eyes. I was prevented from discovering her attempts to complete the second half of her plan, though, by a sharp exclamation from the room next to the one where I stood.

I turned to discover its source and discovered Uncle Angus standing in the doorway.

"The blasted constable," he began, without preamble, "is in the human district. Apparently there's some village fete or something, and she's helping to coordinate the security efforts. Milligan, I hate to ask, but could you go down to the human district and retrieve the constable? I can't leave the house with the vault in this state and you... I'm sorry to bring this up young chap, but you should be able to not draw too much attention to yourself in your current getup..."

I asked if the constable did not have a vox receiver, and Uncle Angus replied in the negative. The police station is issued with a hard line, but the constable isn't issued a portable communicator. This decision was made by Uncle

Angus' late wife, apparently, who thought it would be good for the constable to get out and about rather than spending all her time on the vox. If the matter was to be brought to a speedy resolution, someone would need to go down to the human district and find the constable. Uncle Angus grasped me by the shoulders.

"Will you help, lad?" he rasped.

Now, obviously, if anyone else had asked me to visit the human district, I would have issued an immediate refusal. In his current state, though, and because his current state was more than a little my fault, I found myself agreeing and having my upper leg shaken by the grateful relative before I even knew what was going on.

6

To get from Newbury Towers to the village of Newbury, I had to hop over a stile at the southern edge of the grounds and ride the tri filament rotational lift across. If you've never used such a lift, they're surprisingly simple. They're constructed from some remarkably strong filaments that snake from point A to point B. To use them, you simply step into one of the localised gravity fields the lift creates.

The lift first carried me to the large plot of land that Newbury Towers rotates around before moving off to the asteroid belt where Newbury is located. Approaching the village from Newbury Towers, I was struck by how picturesque the place looked. The asteroids ranged in size from the size of a human fist to that of a decently proportioned warship.

Various biodomes kept the village stocked with atmosphere, and a series of gravity generators, repulsors, and inverters kept everything from bashing into everything else. The lift started slowing down as I approached the outskirts of the village. There, the asteroids were only large enough to permit the construction of one house. The filament corkscrewed onwards as the asteroids slowly increased in size, inexorably heading to the largest of the asteroids, which is where the civic heart of Newbury is located.

I touched down on this largest of asteroids and took a little time to take in my surroundings. There were some reasonably picturesque-looking houses scattered here and there. There was a sign affixed to one of the houses, indicating that this was Clerkenwell Road. Off in the distance I could see a cobbled square, or something that looked like it was the epicentre of all human affairs. If the constable was to be found anywhere, she would be found there.

In taking this in, I had a chance to consider my position as well. Uncle Angus had been right in a way; I could look as human as the best of them as long as I wasn't called upon to run, jump, dance, or perform any delicate tasks such as pouring from a decanter. My control of this ridiculous body was improving, but not to the extent that I'd give myself a fiver each way at a sports event of any sort, ignoring the events that involve falling flat on one's face. We Clodthorpes may not have excessive pride, but even we would balk at entering such events.

Nevertheless, I looked human. If I was to locate the constable, though, I would need to interact with humans. I knew the human language, of course. I don't know if I ever mentioned this, but when I was at school, I won a prize for my knowledge of humanity. An important part of my winning this prize was mastery of their language. The prize was for purely theoretical knowledge though, and I learned some years later that putting the theory into practice has a certain trick to it.

I learned that whilst I have a decent grasp of the basics, I can never get the right sort of mooing noise to emerge from the old face hole. Whenever I try it always sounds less soft and floaty than it should. In fact, I'm told by the few humans I have come to know, that my accent sounds similar to that of one of their folk heroes. I believe the folk hero in question was called Jason Statham when he lived, but I couldn't swear to it. Whatever the case, it makes the humans dashed edgy whenever I pass comment on how lucky they are to be in good health at that moment.

This difficulty couldn't be helped, though, and into every life some rain must fall, as Henry Wordsworth Longfellow pointed out. Whether the rain in question would fall into my life, which already had something of an abundance of the fluid, or into the lives of the humans I met, remained to be seen. I sauntered towards the square, in the hope that the constable would be found at their village hall, an institution often found near such locations.

The square in question turned out to be one of those paved affairs. There were a few shops here and there, and a statue of an unclothed human reclining on a plinth, that discharged water at various points into some sort of pool or Jacuzzi. Facing the floozie in question was the building that would be, if luck was with me, filled to the brim with constables.

I eased myself into the hall and found it to be quite a pleasant example of human architecture. There were portraits on the walls which were surprisingly pleasing to look at, there were elegant details in the floor tiles that drew one's gaze, and the fire in the grate at one end of the hall sparkled delightfully. It's a slight shame that none of the walls were quite straight, and the place could have done with the attention of a halfway competent domestic who could shove a broom about the place. Overall, though, the humans had done rather well for themselves in the years under the Wermacht family's ever-watchful eye. The humans that were scattered hither and thither probably thought so as well, although they seemed a little caught up in their own business to make a show of it.

Two figures stood out, thanks to the way they towered over the humans they were deep in conversation with. The first I recognised as the constable, because of her uniform. The second figure, one that was turning to face me even as I reeled in shock, was Bainbridge. I scuttled over to him and tugged at his sleeve.

"Bainbridge!" I exclaimed, "What are you doing here?"

"*Noblesse oblige*, dear chap." He grinned, "The humans are having a village fete of some sort, and Uncle Angus asked me to stroll along and offer any assistance that could be provided out of Newbury Towers."

This didn't seem likely to me. However, I reasoned that if I was Uncle Angus, and my home had been invaded by Bainbridges, I would quite possibly find myself doing something cunning. For instance, I might get the poor imp out of the house and down to the human district, where he might cause trouble in a way less likely to result in loss of sleep in Newbury Towers.

I decided it would be best not to give the game away. By the time I'd come to this conclusion, though, Bainbridge had become bored with me staring blankly at him, having thoughts flash across my mind, and had wandered off to work the room. I looked around and saw him chatting to a tallish human with long head fur. I thought the best way not to rock the boat would be to let him get on with it, so I focussed my attention on the constable. She was deep in conversation with her human counterpart.

I wandered up to the pair, and had only reached my third sentence describing the break in at Newbury Towers, when two things happened at the same time. First, I remembered that it was Gertrude, Pigstick, and I who had orchestrated the break in and that, just possibly, I was making some sort of error by actually bringing it to the attention of the village constable rather than simply informing Uncle Angus that I had done so. The second item of interest was the constable yelling, "CRIME!" at the top of her voice and running as fast as her legs would carry her in the direction of Newbury Towers.

This left me standing in the company of the human constable, who said, "Ho!" as these fellows are wont to when there is any sort of gap in the conversation. I sauntered over to Bainbridge to see if he could offer any advice on the current situation.

"Ah, Milli," he said as I approached, "have I introduced you to–" and here, he slipped into a passable attempt at the standard human dialect– "*SU-SAN. Am I pronouncing that right?"* The human nodded and reached out its upper leg. I grasped the end of it with mine, and we raised and lowered our limbs a few times before disengaging. I decided to give my human language skills a try, being as formal as I could.

"All right, my darlin'?" I said, *"How the bloody hell are you? No-one planning to horribly murder you or nothing I trust? Golden."*

I'd be willing to admit that my grasp of the language was far from perfect, but she positively yelped and moved away from me sharply. I didn't see the problem. I was speaking authentic human in a voice similar to one of their folk heroes. Human culture can still be something of a mystery to me, though, in spite of my considerable knowledge of it.

Bainbridge had draped a leg around Su-san's shoulders, though, in a somewhat forward manner. The human didn't appear to be rushing to remove it, so I didn't comment on the matter.

"Su-san was saying they needed someone to operate the tombola, Milli," he hissed, thankfully in his normal voice. "We're going to discuss the arrangements now, did you want something?"

I wanted advice and I wanted it quickly, but I couldn't very well collar the wretched pustule in a village hall filled with chattering humans, so I said no.

"Would you mind shoving off then, old chap?" he said, pointedly, "you're making Su-san nervous."

Well, of course, Clodthorpes never put their peace of mind ahead of a conversation about a tombola, so off I shoved, my brow furrowed and my head lowered. It must be said that I've never quite managed to get the hang of furrowing my brow in my usual body. This human body I found myself in, though, seemed to be much more used to the concept. It must be all the oppression they rain down on each other.

It wouldn't be overstating it, I think, to say that my heart was in my boots, and all hope had disappeared from the Clodthorpe eyes until I stepped out of the village hall back into the square. There, I saw Forsythe waiting respectfully by my two-seater, freshly repaired and painted. A more welcome sight I had not seen that past year.

"Forsythe!" I exclaimed, my brow unfurrowing in an instant, "what brings you here?"

"I encountered Ms Slavarington and Ms Wermacht in an advanced state of agitation," he intoned. "They apprised me of recent events and urged me to locate you. As the repairs on your automobile had recently been completed, I took the liberty of driving it down to you."

"Forsythe," I gasped, "you are more welcome in my eyes now than anyone else I could name."

"Very good of you to say so, sir."

"Not at all," I said, hopping into the driver's seat. "Now let's be off. I have much need of your advice!"

"If we could tarry for just one moment, sir," Forsythe intoned, "are you planning to drive this vehicle?"

My eyes revolved in the fellow's direction.

"Well, yes, Forsythe. It would be a bit odd if I didn't, if you see what I mean, given my current position."

Forsythe cleared his throat, "But if you'll forgive me for saying so, sir, the controls of your automobile were designed with your more usual physiology in mind. I fear you may struggle to operate it in your current body."

I looked down at the ridiculous, leathery objects that jutted from the sleeves of my morning suit. He was absolutely right, of course he was. At that moment, I dare to say, a shadow passed over the Clodthorpe heart. How wretched life could be if one was wrenched from one's body and placed in a vessel which would struggle to perform any of this season's dance moves. I mean, I know humans would look forward to this sort of thing. One of their celebrated authors, Kafka I think it might have been, wrote a whole novel about how wonderful it would be if he could be swapped into a body similar to the one Bainbridge had wrested from me. Kafka didn't write about the misery of the poor fish who had to endure living in the human vessel though, no he did not.

For a moment, I considered attempting to drive my beloved two-seater, in spite of Forsythe's objections. It was futile, though. Even if I could have operated all the necessary controls with only four limbs, my reduced height would have made effective control impossible. Whilst I could see out of the windscreen while sitting in the driver's seat, this was by the narrowest of margins. My lower limbs found themselves completely out of reach of the pedals and, were I to lower myself to reach them, my upper legs would find themselves out of reach of the roll, pitch and yaw controls.

I slid out of the driver's seat, my eyes low and my heart lower. It may have been my imagination, but, at that moment, a cloud seemed to pass in front of the local star, casting a blackness of sorts over my two-seater. A crow, or possibly a chaffinch, made the sort of noise that birds make off in the distance.

"Very well, Forsythe," I said, my voice dignified yet, I trust, conveying my horror at the situation I had been reduced to. "You drive."

"Of course," said Forsythe, clearly deeply moved. I looked away as he installed himself behind the wheel. "If I can be of any assistance, I would be most eager to offer it."

Pouncing on the opportunity, I apprised him of the recent set of events. He seemed unconcerned by my reporting the theft to the village constable, though.

"Constabulary of the sort found in these villages," he murmured, "are notable for their solidity and reliability. They are not, I hope you will forgive me for saying so, sir, noted for their speed. As long as we arrive back at Newbury Towers before sunset, sir, I'm sure a ready solution can be found to the problem at claw."

I "By Jove!"'d a few times. Forsythe was patient with me in this regard, as he always is.

"If I might raise a point, though, sir," he said, after coughing delicately to stem the flow of "By Jove!"'s, "are you sure it was wise to allow Mr Lusitania to become familiar with humans whilst still in your body?"

"You speak in riddles, Forsythe."

"I apologise, sir. I observed the young gentleman as I entered the village hall to locate you. I saw that you were in conversation with him, so I returned to your automobile to ensure nothing happened to it whilst you were occupied. Mr Lusitania, as you were engaged in conversation with him, seemed to be… possibly a little familiar with a human who was also in your conversation, sir."

"Well what of it?" I asked, confused by this line of conversation.

"It may well be nothing, sir, but Mr Lusitania has been known to walk out with individuals from many species, and it might be that he was expressing interests of a similar sort on this occasion."

"In my body, you mean?"

"Yes, sir."

"You worry too much, Forsythe. I talked to Bainbridge on this very subject, and he informed me that the two of them were talking on a harmless subject: the village fete tombola."

Forsythe made a low rumbling noise, "It's possible, sir, that that conversation was merely a pretext."

This gave me pause, but one has to give a fellow the benefit of the doubt. "I'm sure Bainbridge wouldn't take such action whilst in another fellow's body, Forsythe," I chided. "It's not gentlemanly. I'm sure the conversation was entirely innocent."

Forsythe nodded. "Just as you say sir."

I inclined my cranium briefly. "Let's hear no more about it until young Bainbridge does something to warrant such speculation, Forsythe."

Forsythe cleared his throat.

A lesser man than me might have thought about the other times I had urged Forsythe to have faith in Bainbridge. The adventure of the nearly dead barman. That was one. Rembrandt's tomb, three years ago. That was another. The series of events I wrote about in my humble collection of pages entitled "Don't Look at Me Like That, Forsythe, He Was Dead When I Found Him". That was yet another. I decided to give Bainbridge the benefit of the doubt one more time, though, and I knew that on this occasion I would be vindicated.

7

WE PULLED ONTO THE DRIVE AT NEWBURY TOWERS, and Forsythe asked politely if I wouldn't mind his parking the old two-seater some way away from the house. Never being one to argue with Forsythe when he is being mysterious, I acquiesced. He slotted the old transportation in-between two hedges of some sort or other. These, I believe, had led to a water feature or something in times gone by. Now, though, they led to a folly that the previous Wehrmacht patriarch had built so he could bury his wife, without suspicion arising as to the manner of her death.

I was about to ask Forsythe why he'd requested that we pull aside here, rather than heading up to the house to change, as it must be nearly time for pre-dinner, when I saw that someone had propped themselves against the broadside of my two-seater. That someone was Gertrude, and I saw that she had the remains of Pigstick next to her.

"What ho!" I said, being the sort of calm chap who is not readily startled, even when their friends and relations start teleporting next to their two-seater unexpectedly. By coincidence, at that moment, I gave a sort of start that rocked the car a touch, shoving Gertrude away. She frowned at me.

"Calm down, Milli, my dear. We have come with good tidings. Forsythe, here, has promised to design a solution to pea-brain's disaster."

Pigstick angled the ocular sensors of her coffin up at Gertrude. "It would have worked," she intoned, "if you had stuck to your role and not slipped into your battle-mind, dear heart."

Ever the peacemaker, I chimed in. "Pigstick, Gertrude, do not quarrel so. None of us are faultless in this endeavour. Gertrude may have played her part with more vigour than was strictly called for, but it was my lack of control of this confounded body that rendered me unable to even get a grip on that blasted figurine. And you foresaw none of this, young Slavarington. You have the makings of a cunning schemer, but you lack the ability to foresee pitfalls. Let us three accept that errors occurred and move on."

I don't know how you approach moments like this, but I often find that when I talk for a prolonged spell, I drift off a touch. I was only able to reproduce exactly what was said because, thankfully, Gertrude had covertly installed monitoring devices in my two-seater that had recorded our entire conversation. Quite why she did this, I was never able to ascertain. One can only assume that old habits die hard for the young lass.

My point is that I don't always listen when I talk, and I expect other chaps to (quite reasonably) use roughly the same tactic. What I found quite remarkable was that, despite my no doubt extremely rambling attempts at diplomacy, the two of them appeared to not only give me their attention, but think on what I said.

Well, I don't mind telling you I was touched by this. It is always gratifying when one's friends listen to one. Heads were hung. Coffin faces were angled downwards respectfully.

"Now," I said, "what is the reason for meeting in this place?"

Gertrude was the first to snap out of her reverie.

"My apologies, you old soak! So in the aftermath of our little scheme, I came to my senses in a trench I appeared to have dug, in the grounds in-between the paddock and the stables. I was clutching the figurine of the Avatar of Pestilence, as well as my emergency plasma rifle, which I was pointing about the place in a keen manner. I knew at once that something had gone wrong with our scheme. Not long after, I heard Sarah, here, calling for me."

"It took me some little time to catch you, Gertrude my dear," Pigstick murmured. "I had no idea your faculties were so together you'd been able to operate the rotational lift between the house and the grounds."

"Well of course I did, half-wit," Gertrude bellowed, cheerily. "When escaping enemy territory, it's important to be quick and bold. Using the rotational lift was the fastest way to what was apparently less hostile soil."

Pigstick held up a couple of mechanical legs. "Anyway," she placated, "once Gertrude and I had established the sequence of events to our satisfaction, we buried that blasted figurine in Gertrude's trench, and then set out to find Forsythe here."

Forsythe inclined his cranial unit.

"We found him skul– well, you tell it, Forsythe."

Forsythe cleared his throat, "I was assisting one of Sir Angus Wehrmacht's maids in tidying the study and vault, which had both been somewhat disturbed in the wake of the theft of the figurine, sir."

"Hardly your job, Forsythe," I pointed out.

"Indeed sir. In normal circumstances I would, naturally, have not involved myself. However, I was informed that you were involved with the event that had caused the disarray, so I assisted the maid as a ploy to better understand the situation and ruminate on what might be done to resolve the matter. Once the task was complete, I remained in the area in the expectation that Ms Slavarington or Ms Wermacht would return to the scene, as it were, and so they did."

"So the point is," chimed in Pigstick, "what are we to do about the figurine of the Avatar of Pestilence? I saw the constable heading up to the house; she must have found Uncle Angus by now."

Forsythe nodded. "That is no doubt the case, sir, but I have had time to reflect as Mr Clodthorpe transported us both from the village to where we currently stand."

My heart raced. I had caught up with the conversation in a much speedier fashion than I was expecting, "You mean, you have a solution?" I gasped.

"Just so, sir," said Forsythe, nodding. "I suggest that the figurine should remain hidden where it currently is. If the constable were to find it, the search for the thief will likely be lessened, and perhaps abandoned altogether."

"But how can we get the constable to find the blasted thing?" Gertrude asked, incredulously. "A few choice hints would do it, I suppose, but that would rather implicate our involvement, what?"

"Quite so, my lady," Forsythe murmured, "It is for that reason that I suggest we fabricate one or two indicators that may point the constable in the right direction."

"A criminal conspiracy!" gasped Gertrude.

A, "Just so," from Forsythe energised Gertrude even more.

We discussed plans or, to put it another way, the others discussed plans while ignoring my suggestions. Before long, Gertrude and I had stuffed Pigstick into the trunk of my two-seater, and Gertrude had popped into the driver's seat. I didn't like to leave Forsythe to walk back but, as he pointed out, there were only so many seats, and he was not necessary for the next part of the scheme.

In record time, Gertrude pulled the car up at the main entrance to Newbury Towers. We hurried into the house together, giving the impression of great haste whilst maintaining our dignity as far as was possible, which was not very far, given my continued lack of control of my human body. We located the constable with Uncle Angus in the parlour. As we entered, Uncle Angus was giving the constable a detailed description of the figurine, describing the exposed spine, the long tongue looped around the sword, and the various sores and boils that the Avatar of Pestilence is never seen without.

Uncle Angus looked up, stood, and greeted us as warmly as could be expected, given the living hell the relative by marriage was currently undergoing, and then sat back down to commune further with the representative of the constabulary. Sensing an opening, though, Gertrude boomed into the conversation. Uncle Angus and the constable looked rather shocked, as many people do when Gertrude begins speaking unexpectedly. This allowed her to cede the floor to Pigstick, who was able to capitalise on the shock outlined above.

It is not done to speak ill of one's friends. It's far from gentlemanly and, most important of all, it doesn't help. There are many things that don't really help in life. Debating whether something is or isn't art, for example. Attempting to establish whether or not this universe conforms to pre-determinism. Trying to prevent the humans hunting each other for sport. It has long been a maxim of the Clodthorpes that we will not do anything unless it *helps* in some way. Rendering assistance to those that require assistance is the mark of a true gentleman, whatever your gender.

Nevertheless, if I was the sort of person who did pass judgement on my friends, I might point out that Pigstick was, on occasion, not the most responsible individual. I won't go into it now, but those who know her will immediately recall the time when, at our preparatory school, she attempted to establish a gambling den in the remains of the fourth form common room. This was ill-advised for multiple reasons, the least of which was not that this new den directly cut into the profits of the establishment run by the prefects.

I draw attention to these facts only so that you will understand my shock when, upon entering the room, Pigstick cleared the throat that she didn't currently have and let fly with the most effortless impersonation of an honourable, trustworthy and, yes, responsible individual that it made my fangs rattle.

She spun tales; she spoke of a tireless search she had conducted, aided by the constant advice and wisdom of Gertrude. She relayed how they had all but given up hope until they had encountered me on the way back from fetching the constable. I learned that they had laid the problem before me and, with my characteristic quick thinking, I had pointed out one small but vital clue that the two of them had missed. I was about to point out that this didn't match up to my recollection of events when Gertrude, no doubt sensing my chagrin, whispered, "She's spinning untruths, you poor duck; try not to look so baffled," into my ear.

Uncle Angus, I could see, was stunned by this sudden change in Pigstick's character. *Is this a Slavarington I see before me?* I could see him thinking, like that chap in King Leer. How is it that she had changed so suddenly, from irresponsible rogue to dogged would-be restorer of figurines?

My uncle by marriage is a cunning old bird, though, and doesn't take anything at face value. He set about asking his coffin-bound interlocutor how she had narrowed down her search, given that she'd hardly have had time to search the entire grounds in the short time since the theft.

Pigstick chuckled in the manner of one who might have asked the same question in Uncle Angus' position. She explained that, having been told by me that the thief had trotted off towards the horizon, it made sense to begin the search in that direction. When she set off in that direction, what did she find but the rotational lift that led to the grounds?

The constable leapt to her claws. "You're right, by Jove!" she exclaimed.

Uncle Angus leapt to his claws. "By Jove, you're right!" he exclaimed.

Clearly overcome with excitement, Pigstick pointed a couple of her coffin legs in the direction of the rotational lift.

"Follow me!" she bellowed, and the three of them charged out.

I attempted to charge after them, but became entangled in a chaise longue, or possibly a récamier, thanks to some sort of hiccup in my perambulation. By the time I'd extracted myself — and spent a good few moments wondering why people refuse to move with the times and fill their houses with more modern furniture, like a spiffy Duchesse brisée or something — I realised Gertrude was still in the room with me.

"Milli," said she, "I know I shouldn't laugh at your current condition. However, you'll have to forgive me." A peal of laughter tore around the room of about the same sort you'd expect from an excitable tyrannosaur.

"I see you're still here," I said, attempting to sound like my usual chipper self and failing completely, "I say, you wouldn't know where I could find a restorative, would you?"

"I can think of no one more deserving in your current state, Milli. If I offered a strengthener to a vagrant or a refugee from one of those wars that Auntie Ophelia keeps waging all over the place, they would baulk. 'Do not think of me,' they would say, 'when there are Clodthorpes in the world who suffer far more in an hour than I do in a year.'"

Normally I would encourage the young battering ram to steady on a little. My current situation might have been bleak, but if I learned anything from Dear Emily's death, it was that things could always get worse. Nevertheless, as I was working out how to phrase my protest without having the situation dissolve into some sort of debate (which I would inevitably lose), I found a glass filled with amber liquid being thrust into my upper claw. I grasped at it and inserted the liquid into my large face hole without delay.

That was the first moment when I found myself in any way pleased with my new human body. It transpires that alcohol reacts in completely different ways to human taste buds. I don't know if you've ever stopped a charging rhinoceros with a casual dismissive gesture, but that's what I felt I'd done upon consuming the beverage.

Gertrude eyed me in a sisterly manner and, without needing a further word, refilled my glass. For once, the body I had been shackled to did what I asked of it and grasped the tumbler firmly.

We repeated this cycle one or two more times until I felt like a sentient creature again. This took some time, and the decanter from which the precious liquid was being dispensed was looking distinctly more clear by the time I'd marshalled my thoughts enough to ask Gertrude a pertinent question or two.

I launched into the ruthless interrogation with a few polite questions on how she was finding the day. She confided in me that, whilst the day had contained less gardening than it might have done as a result of this little venture, it was providing more than enough amusement to qualify as five hours well spent. All that she hoped for was a speedy resolution, so as to curtail unnecessary suffering on the part of her father. This done, I attempted to establish why she was still here and not shadowing the constable's every move.

She confessed that she'd sacrificed her participation in the project at claw so that she might continue to watch my struggles with the chaise longue. Whilst this was, I suspect you'll agree, an understandable reaction from the young lass, it left the scheme resting solely in the claws of Pigstick. I pointed this out to Gertrude, and her face suddenly took on a quality more usually associated with the fragments of pulverised rock emitted by volcanoes.

"BY JOVE!" she roared, starting to pace about the room frantically, "the scheme may be in tatters already. What are we to do Milli? What are we to do?"

I suppose if you're familiar with works of stage or screen, you're aware, as I am, that a traditional action to take in circumstances such as these is to apply a sharp slap to the face of the individual suffering from precisely this sort of panic.

I refrained from taking this sort of action, partly because Clodthorpes do not slap relatives whose companionship we rely on. Furthermore, the last individual who attempted something similar on young Gertrude had their leg dislocated in no short order. There were only two other courses of action open to me. One, I realised, I was already enacting, which was to pace around after Gertrude, exclaiming how all was lost. After a few circuits of the room, it became clear that this wasn't helping overmuch, so I struck that from the list of viable courses of action, leaving me with one remaining.

I thrust a limb out as forthrightly as I could, given my unfortunate circumstances, in a way carefully calculated to attract young Gertrude's attention: "To the two-seater!" I cried.

Acting in the manner of one who had been ordered to clear a bunker, Gertrude shot from the room. I followed as fast as I was able, my speed hindered by the occasional door frame or table. When I emerged from the house, I found Gertrude at the wheel of my trusty transport, gunning the engine and leaning on the horn as if it had insulted the cleanliness of her weapon. She desisted when she caught sight of me and started singing her regimental anthem instead, something that always spells trouble. Reasoning that, if I were to die this day, I might get slotted back into a less human-like body than I currently occupied, if my mind could be reached in time, I bravely sat in the passenger seat.

After Dear Emily was taken from me, I was left with few things in my life I could honestly claim to love. I don't know if you've ever felt the world suddenly drained of its colour after losing something incredibly precious. Those who have may well find themselves, as I did, investing affection into something slightly less organic and prone to sudden cessation of vital signs. I mention this only because I must admit that I am extremely fond of my two-seater. It was something of a shock, because of this, to see the poor machine treated in the way Gertrude treated it on that occasion.

She slammed the old automobile into first gear the moment I had fastened my safety harness. The transport leapt forward, possibly excited to have someone with more fire in their veins than your humble narrator behind the wheel. The trip between Newbury Towers and the grounds is a short one, and it might not have been strictly necessary for Gertrude to redline the engine the entire way there. She followed this with the questionable decision of parking in the stable by inverting the gravity disperser, causing the automobile to drift sideways in a surprisingly alarming manner.

The two-seater came to rest behind the cottage, neatly slotted in-between a tractor and some sort of six-wheeled amphibious vehicle. For my own sanity, I can only believe that she planned this manoeuvre, but if I was asked to testify on the matter in a legitimate court of law, I might be in slightly hot water over my answer.

Gertrude wasted no time after she'd de-ignited the two-seater's engine. She leapt from the car and sprinted towards the nearest tall structure: the barn. In two quick leaps, she was standing on the roof and gazing across the grounds, for all the world like one of those explorer chaps who are always seeking out new life and new cultivations, or however that phrase goes.

I must admit to being slightly worried by the relative's actions. I've seen battlefields, as have most of my peers. We all carry the scars of such encounters. I, for example, can't hear gunfire without getting ever so slightly on edge, embarrassed as I am to admit it. Gertrude, though, for all her jocular demeanour and hearty laughter, seemed more scared than I might have expected. Her behaviour currently seemed less like the only daughter of Sir Angus Wermacht and more akin to one of those berserker chaps the humans have on their battlefields, the ones constantly chatting about blood and skulls and things.

My concerns as to the relative's state of mind were pushed towards the rear of my mind, though, when Gertrude made an exclamation, possibly "ha!" or "there, by crikey!" she slipped back to the ground and strode my way, her head held high, her eyes gleaming.

"We got here just in time, old sauce. Pigstick has deviated from the script."

Today had been quite a day for exploring the various ways the human face can appear surprised, so I decided to attempt an advanced manoeuvre and try two separate ways of looking surprised concurrently. This caused Gertrude to jump. I apologised and invited her to continue.

"The chump," she said, settling down somewhat, "is leading Uncle Angus and the constable around the fields in circles. I speculate that she has plain forgotten the point of the exercise."

This didn't seem likely, or, at least, more unlikely than certain other conclusions begging for my attention. I had a shivering inclination that I knew the truth of the matter, but the only way to be sure was to step boldly out into the field and stride up to the intrepid figurine hunters.

I took a few minutes to ready in my head the sequence of movements that were needed to appear confident: to avoid falling over, spinning out, or turning unwanted cartwheels in this ridiculous bipedal form. This done, I strode forward with all the daring and fortitude of Winston Churchill leading the assault on the Normandy beaches. The effect was spoiled somewhat by needing to navigate my way around the cottage, the suspicious mound of earth that was, presumably, where Gertrude had buried the figurine, and the barn itself. However, once I was clear of these obstacles, there was nothing separating me from the figurine hunters except several hundred metres of field.

"I say!" I called, causing the trio of figures buzzing about the place to curtail their activities and swivel in my direction. Pigstick was the first to approach, scuttling over with not a little haste.

"Milli," she hissed, "you've got to help! I've forgotten what was supposed to happen after the discovery of the single glove on the other side of the hill…"

This illuminated me less than Pigstick had expected. In truth, I had barely understood Forsythe's scheme from the outset, and much time had passed since it was last explained to me. I had no time to impart this information to Pigstick, though, as the constable had not been far behind the coffin-bound specimen.

The constable made a few noises typical of her profession. "Well now," was one of them, as was, "what's all this?" I gather these are not exactly questions; they are ways to strike up conversations with those to whom one has not been formally introduced.

I asked if they had lost the scent of the figurine, to which the constable only growled. There might have been words behind the growl, but it must be said that I was attempting to strategize. I can strategize or I can listen to constables: the two are mutually exclusive.

"Well now," I said, before stamping down on my instinct to say it five or six more times as a way to enable my mental wheels to keep spinning, in the hope of gaining traction, "I think I may have a ready solution to the problem!"

Uncle Angus, though not exactly advanced in years, is still not quite as spritely as he once was. It is for this reason that he was only able to join the conversation at this point.

"What's that, Milli?" he asked, "Have you an idea of where the figurine may be at this moment?"

"I do!" I said, proudly.

I opened my mouth. Some noises emerged. There were a few moments of silence, then the constable raised a cry and shot off in the direction of the stables. Uncle Angus gripped my claw firmly for a moment and then followed. Pigstick stood stock still.

"My word, Milli," she said.

"What?" I asked, baffled.

"How exactly did you come up with that?"

I scratched the old bean, "With what, young bloomer? What did I say?"

Pigstick stared off in the direction the constable and Uncle Angus had hoofed it.

"You said: 'Well, young Gertrude was parking my car over by the cottage, just behind yonder stable, I noticed something that seemed dashed odd. You're aware, of course, that when one plants objects in the ground for farming or pleasure, one tends to do such things in flower beds or fields. What drew my attention, therefore, was a patch of recently disturbed earth in-between the field and the paddock. I passed the grounds as I approached Newbury Towers yesterday and do not remember such a feature on this occasion. I put it to you, Sir Angus, Constable, Pigstick, that the thief may have buried the figurine so they could lie low and collect it once more when the heat was off!'"

I asked her if she had a cigarette. She did not.

"Are you sure I said all that?" I asked, that little disappointment behind us.

"Positive," Pigstick replied.

Consciousness transfer is a funny thing. Dear Emily and I once went to a lecture by one of those clones of Einstein they keep making. Because of the company, I made an effort to not only stay awake, but to also follow what was said. I was only partially successful in doing this, but Dear Emily was able to fill in the gaps at a later date.

Essentially, the Einstein was saying that consciousness is simply digital information. The transfer of digital information isn't an exact science unlike, for example, painting. Things can get switched about here and there. Odd little eccentricities can creep in. This was one of the many reasons that Dear Emily and the like refuse to be switched between bodies willy-nilly. There are other objections such people have, of course, but the problems with the transfer are worth mentioning.

In my case, it's entirely possible that my little moment of clarity mentioned above was the result of a subtle rewiring of my brain. I'm not entirely sure if I was happy with this, and, if I'm honest, it caused me a moment's ill thought towards the individual who had initiated my recent swap. The moment passed as soon as it had arrived, but it left behind a determination to return to my true body as soon as possible.

Pigstick had left to follow the constable and Uncle Angus some little while ago so, feeling dejected, I followed.

Hopefully the blasted figurine would have been discovered and we could all put this sorry episode behind us.

It was with some considerable relief that I rounded the corner of the stables to find a newly excavated hole where previously there had been a suspicious mound of earth. Uncle Angus was standing next to the hole, and in his claws was a distinct olive green object. He was brushing aside specks of dirt, holding the object mere millimetres from his eyes. The expression of the relative nearly brought tears to my eyes. Whilst causing him pain had been agony in itself, it was wonderful to see him reunited with his precious possession.

The constable approached me and shook me by the claw, thanking me, Pigstick, and Gertrude for our assistance in returning the figurine to its rightful owner. Uncle Angus echoed these sentiments, even tearing his eyes from the figurine to do so.

It was, therefore, a thoroughly bucked Milligan Clodthorpe that was transported by his cousin Gertrude back to Newbury Towers. The wind whipped through his head fur, and the joyous chortling of his relative was music to his ears.

8

MY THOROUGHLY JUBILANT MOOD CONTINUED ON through dinner. I chatted of this and that with young Pigstick, who is often a pleasant individual to spend a while conversing with when one is already filled with the joys of spring. Towards the end of the meal, though, when the soup had given way to the pheasant and the pheasant had, in its turn, allowed the selection of sorbets to take its place, I found my eye drawn to Bainbridge.

Bainbridge was sitting at the other end of the table to me. He had been mostly silent throughout the first three or four courses, choosing instead to pick listlessly at what was in front of him and only passing the occasional comment on the conversation that was flowing between Uncle Angus and Gertrude about which war trophies they held the dearest.

The expression on my face, the face that he had hijacked, was somewhat furtive. He looked for all the world like a burglar surprised in the act of sneaking the family silver.

Initially on witnessing his behaviour, I wondered whether a sense of guilt or shame had finally caught up with him concerning his purloining of my body. I eventually dismissed this conclusion because, much as it pained me to think harshly of a fellow I had known for many years, guilt is an emotion as foreign to Bainbridge as the concept of planning an action out to its conclusion.

Guilt being thus expunged as an underlying factor for wearing an expression like a disgruntled haddock, I had to look elsewhere for an explanation. I spun a few possible scenarios through the old mind box until I remembered that old Agatha Christie line… the particulars of which for the moment escape me, however it went something along the lines of eliminating the impossible until what remained was inescapable fact.

With this in mind, I began eliminating impossibilities as if I was one of those scientist chaps you read about in the periodicals. Sadly there are so many things that are impossible that it took some little time to eliminate them all and it was only when Bainbridge got to his (my) claws and excused himself when I realised that the most likely scenario involved a piece of the pheasant he'd consumed earlier disagreeing with him at some point in the digestive process.

I must say this conclusion disappointed me, as I had suspected some darker motivation behind the facial expression I had observed. The conclusion did spur me along a line of thought that had been occupying me for most of the day. My body was clearly not treating Bainbridge in the manner to which he was accustomed. With that in mind, I thought it was high time that I returned him to this damnable human form and I once again took up residence in my old eight-legged home.

The idea became rooted in the Clodthorpe brain much as a harpoon might in one of those rabbits that infest the Grand Battlefleets. Now was the time, I felt, for action!

Milligan Clodthorpe, it is murmured at the club, is slow to anger and quick to forgive. He is a genial bean who is eager to let bygones be bygones. Lines must be drawn somewhere, however. I decided to begin wondering how I might swap bodies with Bainbridge, given my lack of consciousness-swapping apparatus.

Pigstick and Gertrude left the table at that moment, expressing their intention to play a quick game or two of Go. Seeing that Uncle Angus was anxious to check on his collection of memorabilia in general and the recently returned jade figurine in particular, I decided to excuse myself and see if I could locate Forsythe.

I rang the bell in the hallway and asked the weepy-eyed maid with the buck-mandibles when she stuck her head around the door to find Forsythe, as his employer desired a word.

She muttered something that could possibly have been a promise to locate him and scuttled out. I set to pacing around the room a touch. I don't understand how those fellows you read about in books manage such patience. There they'll be, knowing that the secret missile plans will be out of the country within moments and yet they'll be perfectly happy to waste precious moments making speeches or putting the moves on whomever they have the old romantic eye on.

I have never quite managed this level of sanguinity. I had worked myself into a quite a frenzy by the time Forsythe drifted into the room.

"May I be of assistance, sir?" he asked. Often, those words are enough to calm the Clodthorpe mind but, alas, not on this occasion.

"Forsythe!" I gulped, "it is time. I can bear it no longer. I must be returned to my body. Do you know where I may lay my claws on a consciousness-swapping device?"

"It is most gratifying to hear you say so, sir," said Forsythe, "Although your inhabitation of a human form was clearly not your idea, the possibility existed that you would grow to, if you'll forgive the expression, look on the body with an affectionate eye."

"No fear," I said.

"I-"

"I mean, it's not the way of the Clodthorpes to be ungenerous, but I must say that this body is quite without merit!"

"W-"

"Just to be back with the proper number of legs would be a blessing. Bring me an Octopus, that I might inhabit that body instead. Anything but this endoskeletal form!"

Forsythe's eye shutters twitched shut before opening again. His expression was as unreadable as always. I wondered when the deuce he was going to get on with answering my question.

"Well, sir," he murmured, after a brief pause. "I understand that the boy who cleans the dungeons was in possession of such an apparatus."

I staggered. "He was, Forsythe?"

He nodded. "Yes, sir. After certain delicate enquiries, I discovered that the individual in question was the one who provided Mr Lusitania with the device in the first place. Anticipating that such a device might come in useful, I informed the child that I had a shiny sixpence that I would provide him in exchange for the device. The young man was only too happy to comply, as he needed funds to pay off certain gambling debts. I have placed the consciousness-swapping device in your room."

I reeled. It might not be overstating the matter to say that the reel turned into a stagger after a few seconds. Like that greased lightning that humans insist on singing about on formal occasions, I raced to my room. There, as promised, the device that would be my deliverance was waiting for me.

I grasped it to my chest. I turned around and bumped into Forsythe. A yelp may have escaped from my large face hole, but I couldn't swear to it one way or the other in the moment.

"Forgive me, sir, I wished to say that I have prepared a tonic to assist with Mr Lusitania's repose. He was mentioning feeling somewhat restless over dinner, and so I took the liberty of formulating a concoction that may help. It will make him sleep, sir. Very deeply."

One of his eye shutters jammed shut for a second. I made a mental note to book him in for a check-up at the mechanic.

"What's in it?" I enquired, the information my valet had provided still working its way through my mind.

"A concoction of Flunitrazepam and Lysergic acid Diethylamide sir. The former for its soporific qualities, the latter to help your recovery once back in your body."

"Did you mean his recovery or mine?"

"Well, sir, that is entirely possible. Then again, he may well swap bodies with you if you are persuasive."

I grasped the vial of green, bubbling liquid. "I shall be very persuasive!" I cried. "Where is Bainbridge's bedchamber?"

"It is this way, sir," my valet said. He led me down the corridor, round one or two corners, and eventually drew to a halt in front of a door that looked similar to mine, except that the trim around the door was ghastly and red instead of ghastly and green.

"Wait here," I hissed, before slipping through the door. All was blackness on the other side. This was perfect.

"Bainbridge," I hissed, reasoning that if the blighter was awake, it was best to announce my presence, but in a way that did not risk rousing him if he was in a deep hibernation. There was no reply. I heard nothing. No cries of alarm, no snort of surprise, no sound of an arachnid form rolling over in bed… no breathing…

I reached for the room's control panel and flicked the illumination settings to maximum.

Bainbridge's room was similar to mine with the aforementioned exception of being decorated in ghastly shades of red. There was a painting of a horse and rider on one wall. There was a writing desk under the window that looked out across the grounds. There was the four-poster bed that Bainbridge, presumably, spent his nights in. He wasn't spending this night in there though; the blighter was absent without leave.

My jubilant mood left me with an unkind level of haste. Despair rushed in to fill the gap. I greeted it as one might greet an old acquaintance you would rather not have the pleasure of being reunited with.

My failed attempt at a body swap wasn't the source of my despair, for that could easily be reattempted at a later date. No, what was weighing heavily on my mind was what Bainbridge may get up to in my body in the meantime. What pressing engagement could have caused him to be absent from his room? Whatever the answer was, I was sure my body would be none the better for it.

I felt very tired. Without even noticing the intervening moments, I found myself back in my bedchamber. I was aware that I should possibly be scouring the grounds for Bainbridges. That task, alas, was something I could not face.

Forsythe and I worked together to ease me from my human garments, a process I was still unfamiliar with. How Forsythe knew how human garments work is beyond me. Thankfully, Forsythe had managed to find garments that were as similar to my everyday wardrobe as is possible. He'd even managed to track down a human-sized bow tie and fez from somewhere.

I slipped between the sheets, wearing my human pyjamas. Were I the sort to complain, which I like to think I am not, I would mention the stripy nature of them and the lamentable lack of space for a hip flask. Nevertheless, sleep eventually tracked me down and snared me in its mighty jaws.

I've never before been so grateful to find consciousness slipping away from my grip.

The next morning, the sun was shining, the birds were chirping, and I wished nothing more than to go striding about the place with some sort of projectile weapon so I could make my displeasure known to those foul winged fowls.

Forsythe, recognising my mood, eased me into my garments quietly and with the minimum of fuss. He provided tea and a Jammie Dodger before shoving me out the door so I could have breakfast and he could get the room seen to by one of the maids.

The breakfast room was sparsely populated when I entered. Gertrude and Pigstick were talking in hushed voices whilst Uncle Angus sat at the head of the table. Most notably, the room chilled me with its absolute refusal to contain any Bainbridges.

I was about to start spooling up the old blue and green cells so I could ponder the implications of this when a voice cut through my mental hiatus:

"Don't just stand there creating a draft, Clodthorpe, sit down, blast you."

Uncle Angus had spoken to me.

I sat down in shock and gaped at him. He stared back.

"Close your large face hole, you revolting specimen, something might fly into it. Now, please keep your prattle to a minimum this morning; I am trying to achieve greater understanding of the developing situation of the Rembrant IV conflict."

With that, he raised his paper and said no more on the matter.

I was so touched I wanted to find the nearest rooftop and sing that west end number about the chap who loved this other chap and all the chap's friends thought the two of them should make a go of it. This may seem odd to you, but you are not yet appraised of all the facts. Whilst Uncle Angus' words may have been the sort one would normally reserve for a worm of some sort you found expecting you to house and feed it, the uncle in question had gazed at me with what I can only describe as fatherly indulgence. The aged relative no longer felt the need to satisfy his duties as a host to an unwelcome guest by being polite to me. In fact, not to put too fine a point on the matter, Uncle Angus must no longer despise the very air I breathe and the liquids that I drink for the assistance they give me in maintaining my vital signs.

If I was forced to spend the rest of my life in this horrifying body, if my existence was nothing but misery from now on, at least I could look back on this moment with satisfaction.

Gertrude and Pigstick were staring at me, clearly having reached the same conclusion I had. I stood and strolled past them to get to the plates of cured rells, tallens, and bitflakes. I don't mind telling you that I had a bit of a spring in my step. As I walked past the pair of females, I heard one of them mutter to me, "Great work, Milli, now don't drop anything on your way back to the table and you might stay in Uncle Angus' good books."

Considering their advice sound, I was delicate with my grasping of the bitflakes. I picked a piece of rell to supplement the cereal with care and attention. I then strolled back to the table, the very model of a composed citizen who any master of a house such as Newbury Towers would be pleased to count among its guests. This done, I laid into my breakfast as only those who know themselves to be champions of the cosmos do.

Once breakfast was over, Sir Angus glared at all of us in turn and then stomped off to give his library a seeing to. This left me alone with Gertrude and Pigstick. Gertrude wasted no time on congratulating us on a scheme well carried out. Her father had, apparently, remarked that it might have not been a completely terrible idea to invite me to stay after all. Smiles moved from face to coffin to face around the room. Beams thus spread, she enquired as to what I had got up to after dinner on the previous day.

I filled my two chums in on events with a few desultory sentences. This led to much speculation on the possible locations he might have fled to. Could he have returned to the modern metropolis of Eggart? Could he have returned to his family seat at Blibbit? Maybe he'd decided to hide amongst the rank and file and tracked down whichever war was currently in progress and thrown himself at the foe, whoever the foe was, with a song in his heart and a bolt action spear gun in his grip.

This last suggestion, mentioned of course by Pigstick, who never quite knew when to put a sock in it, was beginning to furrow the Clodthorpe brow and cause fluid to start to seep out of various bits of this ridiculous flesh structure I found myself encased in. I was so stunned by the horror of a body that will decide to start leaking without my permission that I did not notice the valet-shaped form at my elbow until it cleared its throat, respectfully. My attention turned towards it, and the form resolved into Forsythe.

"Forgive me for interrupting, sir," he began.

"Not at all, not at all," I murmured, "Interrupt away, we were not making considerable progress through speculation alone."

"Am I to understand that you still desire to locate Mr Lusitania at the earliest opportunity?" he asked.

My eyes rotated violently in their sockets, but I was able to keep a firm grip on the tone of my voice.

"Yes, Forsythe, we do. The blighter must be located at the earliest opportunity. Have you anything to add to the conversation?"

"It may be, sir, that the gentleman in question would at this moment be in the human district, overseeing arrangements for their fete. I believe this is taking place imminently."

Had I proper eyes, I would have narrowed them. As it was, I made a spirited attempt, but my vision ended up just being restricted, so I gave up on the idea and simply vocalised my thoughts instead.

"Why would you think that he is down in the human district, Forsythe?" I asked, my voice as incredulous as was possible, given the circumstances. "Surely the reprobate will have gone to ground somewhere, the better to evade our clutches?"

"I fear not sir," said Forsythe, and this made me take notice. My attendant rarely directly contradicts me without good reason, "I was making delicate enquiries in the servants' quarters this morning as to the whereabouts of Mr Lusitania. Apparently he sent a messenger up to the hall from the human district asking for sandwiches and a flask. The messenger took some time to get through, because he appeared to be unaware of the traps that border the grounds. He was spotted by one of the gardeners and, after discovering that the messenger had legitimate business, the gardener escorted the messenger to the kitchen, where he was allowed to deliver his message."

This seemed odd.

"Why would Bainbridge need sandwiches?" I enquired, not entirely sure I wished to know the answer.

"Apparently Mr Lusitania was unsatisfied with the sustenance that the human community were able to provide. He wished for some of the comforts of home to see him through his obligations in assisting with the fete."

"So…" I said, my mind leaping forward like an enraged rhinoceros, "it's likely that he'll be down in the human district?"

"Just so, sir."

"Well we'd better get down there, Forsythe! There isn't a moment to lose!"

Forsythe agreed and pulled the car around to the front of the house. Gertrude and Pigstick wished me luck as I hopped into the passenger seat. It was only when I was halfway to the village that I remembered their help might have been desirable if Bainbridge was unwilling to exchange bodies, but as we were well on the way at that point, it would have wasted too much time to turn back.

Forsythe parked the two-seater in one of the spaces the humans always reserved for chaps who may drop in from Newbury Towers to check how things were getting on. This enabled me to get to the village square in record time.

All sorts of tents and things had sprung up since I was last there. The setup was largely typical of human fetes, but perhaps you're one of those people who refrain from such social events, preferring more traditional entertainment. If that's the case, picture a gaggle of humans, all dressed in formal costumes. There are various stalls dotted hither and thither offering coconut shies, guess the weight of the pig competitions, and apple bobbing. There were also cake stalls and what looked like a knife fighting ring: because no matter how many laws there are against it, humans will always find some way to legitimise maiming each other.

In the middle of the square, next to the floozie in the Jacuzzi, there was some sort of maypole, and next to that was an eight-legged colossus I remembered well from my bedroom mirror.

"Whatcha Milli," the figure said as I approached, "how's tricks?"

I was speechless at the brazen nature of the comment. Regrettably, Bainbridge (for indeed it was he, in case I had made that unclear) took my glaring at him as a sign that I had nothing really to say. He started to wander off. This movement wrenched me from my stupor.

"Just wait one bally minute, Bainbridge!" I exclaimed.

There are times in a chap's life when he is so utterly consumed by the red-eyed monster of fury, when the rage god grasps you in his spikey, hate-filled grip, that the chap in question is forced to use harsh language such as the sort that I just did. I regret the incident intensely of course, but it had the desired effect. Bainbridge turned to face me.

"I say," he said, "is something bothering you, old spice?"

I don't know if you've ever had a rage stroke before. I won't go into the details here, but take it from me, they are far from pleasant. I fended off the apoplexy with one upper leg and waved the other one in Bainbridge's direction.

"Yes, something is, Bainbridge. I wish to swap bodies with you immediately."

He chuckled, infuriatingly. I gritted my fangs so hard that one of them exploded.

"Of course, old trouser fly, of course, how remiss of me, I plain forgot I still had this old thing on," he said, idly picking bits of enamel out of his fur.

I was hit by an immediate feeling of relief, followed seconds later by a wave of suspicion.

"Let us make haste then, you and I," I said, quoting that old love song by Alfred J Proof Rock. Bainbridge didn't seem to quite get it, so I followed that line up with Rock's next line about evenings being spread thin amongst the sky. That didn't do the trick either, so I worked my way through a couple of stanzas. I dare say I stumbled a bit on some of the sections I remembered less well, but I reached the bit about taking toast and tea well enough, and was about to start bashing on about Michelangelo for what felt like the eighty-fifth time, when Bainbridge raised a leg.

"You know I hate to interrupt people when they are on a roll, but I must confess I haven't the foggiest idea of what you're talking about, Milli, my old auric-eyed one."

I wondered if the fellow was being deliberately dense in order to delay returning the body he currently occupied to its rightful owner. I grasped my temper with two claws, lest it fly away and strike a passing balloonist.

"I wish to swap bodies with you immediately." I growled. "Let us delay no further."

"Well I wish I could, old wriggle, of course I do, but the consciousness-swapping apparatus I used for the initial swap has long since departed my sphere of influence, my apologies."

"Oh don't worry about that, Bainbridge, young chap." I beamed at him, "I have one right here."

Forsythe shimmered into view at that moment, proffering the apparatus under discussion towards my grip. I grasped it and began apprising myself of its operational parameters.

"Ah," said Bainbridge, thoughtfully. "Good."

I powered the device up and plugged one end into my skull. "Be a sport and lean down would you, Bainbridge?" I asked, "I can't reach your skull from down here."

He seemed lost in thought. I "Bainbridge"'d a few times to get his attention. Eventually, his eyes swivelled in my direction.

"Sorry, Milli, I was just thinking about... something. What were you saying?"

"I was asking you to lower your head so I can attach this consciousness-swapping apparatus to it. Be so good as to comply," I said, as calmly as I could.

"Ah, well," he said, "nothing would please me more, Milli, old chap, but I can't swap back right at this moment."

I glared at him and, astonishingly, I think he noticed. I must have been getting the hang of human facial expressions.

"Don't give me that look, old catflap," he said, sounding rather hurt, "You may not realise this, but I am far from ornamental in my role at this fete the humans are putting on. I am the *treasurer*," he hissed that last word, clearly attempting to stop anyone nearby hearing it. Hardly necessary, as I doubt the humans who were milling around us could speak our language. "If we swap bodies now, one of these humans might make off with the funds I have stashed in my hip pocket."

"Very well," I said, "we will find someone for you to pass the funds to and then we will switch bodies."

He looked shocked. "You mean discharge my duties?" he exclaimed, "I was trusted with this capital. If I attempt to palm it off on someone else, what would that say about the honour of the Lusitanias?"

It was news to me that the Lusitanias had any honour to speak of. However, that was possibly why Bainbridge was so desperate to preserve what little remained.

"Well," I said, thinking hard and getting the deuce of a headache as I did so, "I will wait with you until your duties are discharged. I would hate for you to forget your obligations in this matter in the excitement after the fete."

"Milli," said Bainbridge, shock altering his voice so he sounded like an inexperienced castrato, "Would you stand here like a mother hen, watching my every move?"

"I would."

"But do you not see how that will cause people to gossip? 'That Mr Lusitania,' they will say, 'he cannot even be trusted to secure funds for a village fete without the last of the Clodthorpes watching his every move.' It would be most embarrassing."

"I see no people here, only humans," I pointed out, not unreasonably in my opinion.

"But there may be people along *later*," he pointed out. "Uncle Angus may drop in."

"He won't," I pointed out, helpfully.

"Or someone else," Bainbridge continued, "I distinctly remember one of the neighbours, Lady Elmsworth, mentioning that she might come down to try out the coconut shy. What if Lady Elmsworth were to see me in such a state?"

"Lady Elmsworth?" I asked.

"Yes."

"I've never heard of her."

"Well she's *very* influential in these parts, Milli, old clam, if I lose face in front of her, I'll never hear the end of it from the family seat."

Normally of course, I'd hate to cause anyone embarrassment. Given the circumstances, though, I decided to be firm.

"I'm sorry, Bainbridge," I said, an attempt at a resolute expression crossing my face, "I will remain here until you are prepared to swap bodies with me."

"Would you cause me embarrassment, Milli?"

"I hate to of course, but there it is."

"But Milli, we were at school together," he wheedled.

That didn't sound right.

"Didn't you go to Browns?" I asked

He blinked. "Yes, didn't you?"

"No, I went to Blues."

"Well, who am I thinking of then?" he asked, testily.

"Possibly Gertrude."

"Ah yes, it was Gertrude. Nevertheless, would you really cause such frightful embarrassment to an old friend such as I? Would you… could you really do that, Milli?"

Well I mean to say… when a fellow says something like that, you can't really turn around and explain that, when you get right down to it, you hadn't seen your relationship in quite such rosy terms. It might be stretching things just a touch to call Bainbridge an old friend. I'd known him for a number of years, certainly. We'd encountered each other on a number of occasions, absolutely. In all honesty I couldn't see how the phrase applied, though.

Nevertheless, if a fellow just comes out and says something along those lines, you can't just outright contradict them. It just isn't done. I made a few "of course" sort of noises and stood a little way away from him. He waved a leg as a gesture of farewell. By this I gathered that he thought the distance wasn't quite large enough. I shuffled a few metres further away from him and he repeated the gesture.

Cursing all the gods, I allowed the crowd to swallow me and carry me away from Bainbridge and my body.

I passed an apple bobbing station and spent a few gloomy minutes observing humans as they dipped their faces in the water and gnashed their jaws at fruit.

"Most disturbing, sir," said Forsythe at my elbow. The fellow must have followed me.

"Quite," I agreed, "Do you have any advice, Forsythe?"

"I fear not sir," he replied, levelly, "Your actions to this point have been most prudent."

I nodded. "Well then I have no further need of your services for a short while, Forsythe. If you leave me with the consciousness swapper, I can ambush Bainbridge when he finishes being a pillar of the community. You may as well push off back to Newbury Towers."

Forsythe bowed. "That is most generous of you, sir. I will return before the end of the fete to collect you. Although, if you will forgive the suggestion, it may be wise to remove the terminal of the apparatus from your skull."

I nodded, gloomily. He assisted me with this matter before whiffing off.

I often hear about people who are easily entertained whilst stuck at a human village fete. Maybe you are one of those individuals yourself. If this is the case, allow me to address you directly: You have no idea how lucky you are.

I know certain poets talk about how charming and quaint human culture is, but I've never quite seen it myself. I know they've dreamt up a few passable distractions over the centuries. The Oresteia had its moments, and that old program with Richard Michael and Briers Horden, where one of them was the other one's valet, had a certain universal truth to it. As for the rest of it...

Well, I threw a coconut at a stacked pile of balls. That diverted me for a few moments. The stall holder kept going on about me doing something wrong, but let me tell you, the ease with which I was able to knock those balls over was remarkable. I don't know why humans report that game to be amongst their more challenging.

I watched a knife fight or two and made the spectacle slightly more engaging by hazarding a small amount of currency on the lass in the blue shorts, as opposed to the chap in the leopard print shorts. My lass won, so I hazarded a slightly larger sum on her next bout. Things proceeded along this vein for a while. I was surprised to find myself starting to be entertained in the fifth round, when things were mixed up a little by introducing an automated machine covered with spikes, chains, and rotating blades. By the reaction of the crowd, I gather this apparatus is another of their traditions. Anyway, the automaton in question made short work of all ten remaining contestants, including my lass in the blue shorts, so my money disappeared with some speed, as did my interest in the spectacle.

I sauntered around the place a little more and found something I'd somehow managed to miss during the early stages of my reconnaissance: a poetry tent. I stuck my head through the flap before sticking the rest of me through, because you can never be too careful when entering a tent at a human fete. There's always the chance you've misread the sign over the door and will wind up in a child-swapping operation.

Inside the tent, though, was a stage, a stool, a microphone, and a few dozen chairs, some of which had humans sitting on them. I breathed a sigh of relief and parked myself in an empty chair near the back, so I could slip out if someone mentioned the words Browning or Pound.

The human on stage appeared to be reading a piece of his own devising. Considering this something of a red flag, I was starting to wonder how best to affect an exit when the human's words seeped into my brain.

This chap was going on about how fantastic it was to be human. He mentioned their diverse history, their capacity for love, and their many great inventions. He went on about something called the human condition a fair bit and used the word "optimism" three times.

Now, I don't know if you've ever seen a dog in a hat. If you have, I hope you'll agree that such a spectacle is devastatingly adorable. If you can imagine that feeling of seeing a dog wear a deer stalker, or a trilby, or something similar, then you'll have a clear idea of how I felt listening to the human bash on about how great his species was. The fellow was unbelievably sweet. He was talking about his species' achievements as if they were impressive rather than, frankly, rather embarrassing. It really bucked me up. I mean to say, here was a chap, part of a species whose most impressive achievement was not wiping itself out in the years following its first journey into space, and he was *proud to be a part of it.*

Listening to this human quite put my own troubles into perspective. If a human, with all the troubles that get heaped on its head on a daily basis, can be proud to be a member of his species, shouldn't I look at my life with a little more perspective? I mean, yes, my dear Emily was dead and there was no chance of getting her back. Yes, my body was in the possession of a half-wit who appeared obsessed with how some female by the name of Elmsworth perceived his status. There are many more troubles that I won't bore you with just at this moment, but my point is that, compared to the life of your average human, my life was nothing but bacon and honey.

I took to counting my blessings whilst the poetry washed over me. This, I must admit, had something of a soporific effect, and I hadn't even noticed drifting off when I found a human gently shaking one of my upper limbs.

The human informed me that the fete was over. I leapt out of my seat in excitement, connecting my skull with that of the human who had awoken me. I fought back the urge to apologise, knowing that in certain circumstances, apologising after such a connection is seen as a sign that you wish to have your possessions removed from your person. I made my way out of the tent with some haste instead.

I located Bainbridge with ease. He was standing in a similar spot to the one he had been occupying when last I saw him.

Now, I know you're thinking that I should have charged up to the fellow and begun demanding the return of my body, but we Clodthorpes can be a prudent sort when the situation demands. I chose to observe the fellow for a moment or two before I started demanding this and that.

My prudence was rewarded by the sight of a human approaching Bainbridge. The two chatted on a subject I wasn't able to overhear because of my limited human hearing. Nevertheless, at the culmination of their discussions, Bainbridge passed over a large hessian sack to the human. On the side of the sack was a large printed sigil which I, of course, recognised as the sign the humans used to denote currency.

His obligations had been resolved. The blighter wouldn't be able to delay releasing my body after this.

I approached him as a hunter approaches his prey, moving confidently yet not with an excess of speed, lest the prey take flight. He spotted me early in my approach and held up one or two conciliatory legs.

"Now Milli," he said, in a tone of voice I didn't like much, "I know what you're going to say, but I implore you to give me a few moments to say goodbye to someone."

"No." I hate to use harsh language but sometimes it just slips out of one.

"But Milli, this delay would be to your advantage!" he cried.

This didn't seem right and I said so. Any delay would only prolong the agony that was every moment spent in this body.

He shook his head, though. "Not so, old chap, not so. You will, of course, remember the human I was having a bit of a natter with last time I was down here. She was an utterly delightful creature called Su-San, with gorgeous wavy head fur and a voice like… like…"

"A river's song or a particularly melodious pond?" I asked, remembering one of the more pithy wheezes from that old treatise on the necessity of good men going to war.

"Just so, Milli!" he exclaimed, "My point is, old custard tart, that Su-San will need to be told about this swap, or things will be dashed difficult for you. She might see you in your body and seek you out, assuming you're me, and attempt to talk to you. You know how you dislike talking to humans, Milli."

There are few things I can, with all honesty, claim to dislike. One of these things, though, is when a fellow like Bainbridge starts to make sense. Even though the broad strokes of his argument are so obviously potty, the details have enough sway in them to make me suddenly unsure of my position.

"And if you do this, you'll come straight back here?" I asked, suspiciously.

"Of course, my dear chap," he said, smiling through my fangs.

"And you'll exchange bodies with me without argument?"

"Yes," he said.

Isn't hindsight the most appalling thing in existence? *Now* of course, I realise I should have said, *explain to her once we've switched bodies, you chump*, or something similar. Of course, in the moment, Bainbridge's request sounded perfectly reasonable. The fellow had maintained his position throughout the fete after all. He could have absconded at several points, and yet he remained. Suspicion, I had reflected, was an ugly beast that clouded the most beautiful of days. I decided to give Bainbridge the benefit of the doubt, ass that I am.

"Do me the favour of returning soon, young buck," I murmured, trying not to sound impatient. "This body pains me."

He reassured me one or two times, and then skittered off.

9

THE REALISATION THAT I HAD MADE A MISTAKE WAS ONE I came to gradually. It was very like a sunrise, in fact. It started slowly and became more obvious the more I stared at it. And the more I stared at it, the more painful it became. I had just let the blighted fool out of my sight *again*. What mischief could he get up to my body between the present moment and the unspecified time in the future, when I might be able to track the blighter down and trap him like a bison?

I was just wondering if I should trust the wretched individual and remain at my current location or let my heart be governed by cynicism and begin some sort of search when I heard a cough at my elbow. It was a human.

"Pardon me," said the human, *"are you from Newbury Towers?"*

"All right there, china?" I replied, *"Yeah, I'm from the towers. What of it?"*

The human quailed.

"My apologies for disturbing you, madam," he said, *"but my supervisor informed me that someone from the towers was acting as treasurer for the fete. Is that you?"*

I narrowed my eyes, a gesture the human understood well enough.

"Not me, sunshine," I snarled, *"You're after Bainbridge. He just left."*

The human looked shocked. *"He can't have left just yet! He hasn't yet passed on the funds we lodged with him for safekeeping."*

This human was clearly suffering from some sort of brain injury. That or his superiors were not apprised of the facts. *"Don't give me that,"* I countered, *"One of your mates collected the readies from him five minutes ago. I saw it 'appen."*

The human wrung its upper legs. *"I'll check with Mr Stevens,"* he said, presumably one of the authority figures at the fete, and scuttled out of sight.

I reflected on my memory of Bainbridge passing over the hessian sack to the human. Surely the human had been the supervisor that the insignificant human I'd just been chatting to had mentioned... Surely... I could remember him clearly, for all that I'd been observing him with a frankly miserable number of senses. He'd been dressed in robes with designs from at least five of the major gods displayed. It was the sort of robe not often worn by administrative figures, though... what sort of human would wear such a garment?

Forsythe coughed, lightly, as he drifted into view.

"Good afternoon, sir," he murmured.

"Oh, good afternoon, Forsythe," I replied, losing my train of thought.

"I have a message for you from Mr Lusitania," said he, giving me an envelope. It had been sealed with Bainbridge's family crest, which seemed a little overkill, but there it was. I cracked the seal and read the letter contained therein.

My anguished cry caused many nearby humans to panic and start looting.

My Dear Clodthorpe, read the letter, *sorry to rush off like that but I feared that, had I remained, you would have insisted on returning to your body. This, I am sorry to say, I cannot allow to happen. You see, I have fallen in love. Yes, love, Milli. I know you will wish me the best, seeing as you've basked in her company yourself. I wonder, Milli, if you were as struck by her beauty when you met her at the village hall as I was when I first met her? Su-San really is the most wonderful creature in the known universe, and she loves me, Milli, she loves me.*

There were a good few more pages of this. Terms such as *burning kisses* and *our new life together* were used with abandon. Phrases like *souls joined in heart-swelling monogamy* and *the only one for me* seared their way onto my retinas. If I hadn't been reeling from shock, I might have had to loosen my collar. The letter reached its final horrifying conclusion on page five.

Su-San and I are to be wed, Milli. I find myself unable to return your body to you, as Su-San has grown accustomed to its features, remarkably handsome as they are. We will elope and live a simple life in Su-San's village raising pigs, or wheat, or perhaps both. One or the other. I don't know if pigs eat wheat. Well, we'll have time to work that out. My point is that we've hired a minister and will be married without delay. Yours, Bainbridge.

The man I had seen Bainbridge passing currency to — he must have been a ministerial aide. I reflected on this dispassionately as Forsythe helped me to my claws. I had sunk to my knees at some point after page three of Bainbridge's letter. The blighter had fled with my body. I had no chance of stopping his escape, less still the resources to find him and prevent the wedding. I might have managed to find him, given enough time and resources, but by that time my body would have been so sullied by the various marital arts that it would no longer be mine. It certainly wouldn't be the body that my Dear Emily had once embraced.

I could feel myself being helped to my two-seater, Forsythe easing his way through the still-panicking crowd of humans using his whip augmentation.

I stared at the stars as we drove back to Newbury Towers. My dear Emily was out there somewhere. We'd cremated her and committed her ashes to the void, in accordance with her wishes. I wondered if I should join her. I'd idly wondered about that eventuality at various points since my beloved had been snatched from me. The idea of death held no real attraction in and of itself. It did have the remarkable plus side that, when all's said and done, if I were to die, I wouldn't need to be put through trials such as the ones I was currently experiencing.

Human bodies were remarkably fragile, after all.

I don't know if you've ever felt so numb, so completely empty, that nothing seems to matter. Probably you have. Many people have. That drive back to Newbury Towers seemed to take six years. In reality, I'm sure it was closer to one, but I didn't check at the time, so it's hard to be certain.

All I remember is staring, my ridiculous human head resting on the fabric of the car seat; my eyes, staring unblinkingly away from Forsythe, ignoring everything except the void and the stars.

Forsythe opened the door for me after parking at the entrance to the Towers. It took me a few moments to remember what I was supposed to do in response to this. I swung my lower legs out of the car and felt the gravel through my shoes. I stood, gingerly, and headed into the house, telling Forsythe I wouldn't need him until dinner.

I watched him as he slid off, and then took stock of the situation I found myself in. I was in the hall. No-one appeared to be about. My lower legs suddenly feeling very heavy, my head drooping, my upper legs hanging uselessly by my sides, I climbed the stairs. I found the bedroom allocated to my use on only the third attempt and slumped into bed. I did not care that I was still in my morning suit. I did not care that I still had my walking shoes on. If I had to resort to absolute honesty, I would have had to admit that I cared for precious little at that moment.

After some time it dawned on me that I may have blundered when I dismissed Forsythe. If I was to remove myself from this miserable situation, I would need some sort of assistance — possibly in the form of a sharp object, rope, or firearm. I had no notion where such things might be located, and Forsythe's expertise would have been invaluable. I considered hurling myself out of my window for a spell. There were a number of trees and things in-between my window and the ground, though, so it was unlikely that I would be able to reach a velocity that was close to terminal.

I closed my eyes.

I must have slept, because when I heard a knock at my door, I started upright, confused as to where I was and what was happening. I hauled myself from the bed and attempted to make myself presentable before inviting the individual who had roused me into my sanctum.

The door opened, revealing Uncle Angus on the far side. His presence surprised me more than a little, but, not being one to stand in the way of a relative by marriage going where he wishes in his own house, I invited him in. He accepted my invitation, not meeting my curious gaze.

He sat in one of the room's two chairs and waved a leg half-heartedly at the other. I hauled myself into it, keeping my mouth firmly shut and waiting as politely as possible for my elder to initiate conversation.

"I've had a letter for Bainbridge," he murmured, finally.

"Oh, ah," I said.

"He's eloping."

"With a human."

He looked up at me, "You know?"

"He's eloping inside my body. He wrote me a letter that is no doubt similar in content to yours, Sir Angus."

At that point, the most wonderful thing happened. Sir Angus grasped my upper legs with his claws. Such a companionable gesture would have been unthinkable from the aged relative as little as eight and forty hours ago.

"You've got to stop him, Milli."

I lowered my eyes. Uncle Angus clearly had developed the impression that I was a magnificent crime solver, thanks to that wretched figurine of the Avatar of Pestilence. My deceit of the relative in question now seemed doubly cruel.

"I'm not sure I can..."

He tightened his grip. "You *must*, Milligan. You're the only one who can do this! Even if I could find him, I would not be able to persuade him to abandon the wretched course of action he has embarked upon. I don't know if you've noticed this, my lad, but my manner can appear a little stand-offish at times. To one such as Bainbridge, this manner has been invaluable when setting him on the correct course throughout his childhood. Now that he has a family seat to aspire to, though, he has become headstrong and will turn from my commands with a stubborn set to his jaw. 'That Angus,' he will say, 'he knows nothing of my plight. What advice may I gain from a decrepit relative who once gave me six of the best for sneaking one of the finest cigars from his desk drawer?'"

I wasn't sure I quite followed that last stanza, but Uncle Angus' meaning was sound and clear. Bainbridge is a headstrong young lout and would take any heavy-clawed intervention as a validation of his actions.

I looked at my uncle. I had been willing to accept defeat — to lie back and accept the ever-encroaching blackness that had surrounded me since the departure of dear Emily. To have such faith placed in me by Sir Angus, though...

"I will do what I can," I said.

I had no plan. I had no idea of how I might begin to locate Bainbridge, let alone return him to the fold. The very scope of the problem that I faced terrified me, from my ridiculous human skull down to my curiously well-fitting shoes.

For Sir Angus, though, I would find a way.

After much thanking and back slapping, Sir Angus departed, leaving me alone with my thoughts. This, I have found, is never especially helpful when it comes to the formulation of plans, so I stepped outside my chamber and started strolling.

My first thought was to attempt to locate Forsythe. With that in mind, I accosted the first maid I encountered and enquired as to his whereabouts. After she'd recovered from the shock of a human speaking in her language, she pointed me in the direction of the billiard room. I enquired as to why she was pointing in that direction rather than simply telling me where Forsythe may be found. She apologised and explained that Forsythe would be found in the room she'd indicated. I thought about enquiring further into the motivations behind the maid's actions but, worrying that she might be slightly sociopathic, I thanked her and strode purposefully in the direction she had specified.

The billiard room was one of those light, airy sorts of dens that you often encounter in houses such as this. There are globes here and there, I spotted a ship in a bottle in a bottle on a mantelpiece and, of course, there were billiard tables. Six of them. To accommodate all these tables, and allow for players to enjoy them, the room was, by necessity, roughly the size of one of an aircraft hangar.

Pigstick and Gertrude were engaged in what appeared to be a game of tag billiards. This game, as I'm sure you already know, involves players taking shots on multiple tables simultaneously. If one player takes a shot on one table, the second player is free to take a shot on any table they wish.

This can lead to furious battles for domination on one table or to players playing games on separate tables, attempting to score points at a faster rate than their opponent.

Forsythe was adjudicating the games from a raised area in the centre of the room that had been designed for that purpose. Few things interest Forsythe more than adjudicating, as I have discovered over the years. I hated to spoil the poor fellow's fun, but my errand was urgent in the extreme. I "Forsythe"'d and he attended on the young master without delay.

I explained my reasons for disturbing him and enquired as to whether he had reached a solution to the problems that faced me. I didn't hold out gargantuan amounts of hope. The valet in question had been distinctly quiet during the drive back from the human district to Newbury Towers. Normally, I would have expected the fellow to be brimming with ideas from the word go, but the current problem seemed impenetrable, to put it mildly.

We spent a few moments going over the key facts of the case. There were two sides to it, as Forsythe charitably allowed me to elucidate. Finding Bainbridge and his human seemed to be the trickier of the two parts of the puzzle. Humans were permitted to marry only in certain licensed venues and, whilst there were thousands in known space, there were none in the vicinity of Newbury Towers.

Ministers such as the one I had seen Bainbridge passing funds to tended to their species' religious needs and acted as administrators for services such as marriage. When given the correct amount of coinage, the minister would add Bainbridge and Su-San's names to a central database, which would in turn grant them access to a legal wedding at any of the wedding venues in the cosmos.

This meant that, even if I could track down the minister I had seen Bainbridge interacting with, he would as likely as not have no idea as to the further plans of the happy couple.

In years gone by, tracking Su-San would have been pure simplicity. Recently, though, the human civilisation had grown significantly. As part of the attempts to re-introduce them into larger society, the humans had had their tracking chips removed. I suppose the idea was that if we treated them like a mature species, they might start acting like a mature species.

"I agree that this situation would be much simpler to resolve if the humans were still tagged, sir," Forsythe broke in, "but I suspect that locating Mr Lusitania and his human may not be as difficult as you suspect."

I reeled. This caused Forsythe to enquire as to whether I was quite well. I waved this off and explained that my reeling was more a way of expressing doubt or surprise at his words. He apologised for misinterpreting me.

"Not at all, not at all, not at all," I said, and then said it a few more times for good measure. "But would you mind clarifying things a little for me, Forsythe?"

"I merely wished to point out, sir, that you are in the privileged position of being related by marriage to Lady Slavarington."

"Mother Ophelia?" I stuttered. No good ever came of that name being spoken aloud.

"Just so, sir," he continued, seemingly unaware of the blackness that was descending across the room, "the 75th

Grand Battlefleet monitors the entire sector. Every craft is required by law to allow its movements to be tracked by the fleet. If anyone is able to ascertain Mr Lusitania's current whereabouts, it will be the commander of the fleet: Lady Slavarington."

I'm sure you'll have encountered your fair share of those moments that divide life. Should you poison your best friend or the starving orphan? Should you commit war crimes or should you not? Once such a decision is made, nothing will ever be the same again. Life dives off at a tangent, and you will never know where the other decision would have taken you.

Even with a mind such as mine, I knew that this decision was one such as those discussed above. Should I ask my mother-in-law for help, or should I try to find some other, altogether more desperate course of action?

Ultimately, though, decisions are tricky beasts. Far too often, you think you're making them and in fact they are making you — if you follow me. Perhaps you don't. Sometimes a devilishly poetical phrase such as that loses something when chaps have the time to examine it and think through all the implications. What I mean to say is: we are all the sum of our decisions. Decisions tend to snowball, though, and the bally things have a habit of resolving themselves, once you've acquired a certain number in your lifespan. It was for this reason that, when I heard Forsythe say the words "Slavarington" and "Lady", my mind did not present me with a problem with two possible solutions; it chose to react without consulting me.

"No," I said, "Absolutely not. Only after the heat death of the galaxy would I consider such an option. I am surprised at you, Forsythe."

The chastened valet coughed. "Forgive me, sir, I considered the present situation sufficiently urgent to consider all solutions viable. I am, of course, familiar with your views–"

"Well carry on being familiar with them, blast you," I interrupted. Dashed rude of me, I know, but when a fellow's blood is up, the essence of politeness can be elusive. "I will not turn to Mother Ophelia. If you have any other solution to the present issue, let me hear it, Forsythe, otherwise, I will thank you to continue turning the matter over in your enormous brain."

There was a moment of silence. No doubt he was gathering his confidence after facing the onslaught of my displeasure. I wondered if I had possibly gone a little far, but one must be firm in instances such as these.

"I fear I have no further suggestions, sir," he said after adding two or three moments of silence to the original. "With your permission, I will continue to think on the matter."

"Do so, Forsythe, do so," I said in as haughty a manner as possible. "I will do so as well."

"That would be most wise, sir," he said. I wasn't entirely sure if he was being sarcastic or not. Valets generally refrain from sarcasm, as it can make things dashed confusing, but one never knows what depths an employee will stoop to after being rebuked. I decided to hedge my bets and make an enigmatic expression with my human face that could be interpreted by all around as they saw fit. It seemed to do the trick. Capitalising on the impact of my enigmatic facial expression, I strode from the room and very nearly avoided the vase containing six or seven white roses that rested on an occasional table by the door.

Lost in thought, I found myself wandering the grounds. A solution to the problem of locating Bainbridge was so far from my grasp, after Forsythe's terrifying suggestion, that I turned my thoughts to how to persuade the couple to abandon their nuptials in favour of something less disruptive. If Bainbridge wished to continue in a relationship with this human, then that was really up to him, as long as it wasn't in my body. Marriage, though, was a whole other question. He had only known this human for a matter of days after all.

I was pondering precisely how many days Bainbridge had known Su-San. Normally, this calculation would have caused me no problems, but since the two first met shortly after I had taken possession of my current body, it was hard to be sure. I felt like I had been in this new body since the first stars were born and my species first crawled on land. That being the case, I reasoned Bainbridge's relationship was probably-

I had nearly reached a firm figure with which to pin on the relationship when I stepped on a small metal plate concealed in the grass along the border of the Newbury Towers estate. I am a little unsure as to the precise sequence of events that followed, but the end result was that I found myself hanging upside down from my lower right leg. This leg was being held in the jaws of a large metal device that had wrapped itself around my limb and drawn me skywards, leaving me hanging in a most undignified manner.

It was roughly at that point that I was reminded of a few key facts: firstly, human bodies have an endoskeleton, rather than something more civilised. This fact was foremost in my mind because the fangs of the metal jaws had eased themselves through my leathery human flesh and nestled companionably up against the larger of my leg bones. Had I been in possession of any decent form of exoskeleton, the jaws would have fallen at the first fence.

Secondly, human bodies have no pain dampening systems. This is why they tend to lose any wars they take part in. The human leaders will get into some sort of healthy dispute with one of the civilisations that surround them, and everyone's troops will just be lining up and getting ready to make a day of it, when the human soldiers start falling over and calling it quits after taking just one round of fire in the chest. This fact was communicated to me in no short order by my ridiculous central nervous system. It flooded my brain with so many pain signals that the rational side of my brain misfired, and I howled the first line of that song about crying (or maybe it was laughing) when seeing some chap in a Turkish bath.

Thirdly, and most pertinently, human bodies have no limb jettisoning system. If something happens to one of their limbs, tough luck for you as the saying goes. I sent the jettison command, naturally, but my body didn't appear to know what to do with it, choosing instead to perform several biological functions that I won't detail in polite society.

The next few minutes were something of a blur. I may or not have cried out. In fact, I'm fairly sure I did. When metal jaws bury themselves in a chap's leg, he's bound to let his feelings be known somehow or other. In fact, I'm not ashamed to speculate that a tear may or may not have rolled down the Clodthorpe cheek.

My attention was drawn away from the pain (or maybe it should be the agony...) by the thundering voice of Gertrude below me.

"Milligan, what in blue blistering blazes are you doing?"

I may have responded, but it's hard to be certain of my memory concerning this particular event. If I did respond, I doubt it took the form of coherent language. It was more likely to be something like a moan, or possibly a scream. Gertrude didn't seem to accept this as a reply though.

"I told you the traps weren't for you!" she bellowed up at me, "They're there to prevent strays, not for snaring careless Clodthorpes! Get out of there this minute!"

I'm sure I will have mentioned in the past that Gertrude did a stint at one of those officer training camps for a while. This means that whenever she sees something she disapproves of, she can make her feelings known in the most forthright terms.

I managed to summon the energy to make a noise that sounded close to, "Can't."

She sighed and stomped out of my immediate line of sight. I heard her fiddling about with something, and I was unceremoniously dropped to the ground. I landed on my head, somewhat typically, and felt a sort of blackness slip over me like a pain-dampening sheet.

10

I WOKE UP FEELING FANTASTIC. THIS WAS SO UNEXPECTED, I screamed. I then opened my eyes. Usually, when the occasion calls for such actions, I perform them in the reverse order of that described.

"Quick, Forsythe!" said a voice that I recognised as belonging to Pigstick. "Up the intensity!"

I felt a sharp ringing in my ears, but this quickly gave way to a distinctly pleasant sensation. I looked about the place and found that I was in the house infirmary. My lower leg had been wrapped up and a few mechanical thingies had been strapped here and there, presumably to allow me to use the limb normally whilst it took its sweet time to heal of its own accord.

There was a line poking out of one of my upper legs. My eyes fixed on this as, presumably, it was the source of the pain-dulling substance that was running amok in my system. A tube led from the line to an opaque bag on a stand at the head of my bed.

"I say, what is this? What, I have to ask, is this? Pigstick? I say? What is this stuff you're giving me? It's wonderful. Pigstick? Pigstick? PIGSTICK? Pigstick? What is this stuff?" I asked.

I'd meant to make my enquiry in the manner of a gentleman, but I had become carried away somehow.

Forsythe loomed into view. "It is good to see you awake, sir."

"It's good to be awake, Forsythe!" I pointed out. "The sun is shining, the birds are singing, well I assume they are, and my leg has been taken care of by some extremely generous people! Well, well, well, how could things be any better? Exactly, they couldn't. I say, what's the stuff in the bag Forsythe?"

Forsythe cleared his throat. "It is a preparation of benzoylmethylecgonine, sir. I obtained it from a medic in the village who said it tends to the medical needs of the village humans in no short order. It acts as both an analgesic and confidence booster."

"Well it's certainly performing both of those tasks admirably. I feel like I've been smiled at by the pleasure god!" I said, bounding to my claws. Thankfully, the apparatus strapped to my lower leg held fast, as I hadn't considered the full implications of trusting my weight to a leg that had recently been rendered essentially fleshless.

My sudden movement caused the tube running to my leg from the bag to tug somewhat, although I felt a fantastic lack of pain at the movement. I glared at it.

"Would you do something about this bag, Forsythe?" I asked.

"Of course sir," the bringer of painkillers murmured. He removed the bag from its stand and started strapping it to an apparatus on my back. His efforts were hindered somewhat by the fact that I had severe trouble standing still.

"Sorry about this, Forsythe," I said, after thwarting his efforts to secure the bag for the third time. I looked over my shoulder to lock eyes with the fellow, thus jerking my back away from his claws and thwarting his efforts a fourth time.

"Not at all, sir," he murmured. "The medic we consulted mentioned that certain side effects were associated with the analgesic, but given your situation he recommended we press on regardless."

"Oh quite, quite," I said, not quite sure how we got onto this topic. "Have you finished yet, Forsythe? I'm sure there was something I was supposed to be doing."

"Very nearly, sir," the trusted valet remarked. "There, you are now fully mobile. Although the medical practitioner we consulted recommended not subjecting your lower limb to undue stress."

"Well if a sawbones says so then I suppose I must comply," I said, flexing the leg in question experimentally and finding it extremely sturdy. "Although from where I stand now it seems nannyish in the extreme."

"Nevertheless, sir," said Forsythe, firmly.

"Oh quite, quite," I said, bouncing up and down experimentally. "Now, do you happen to remember what I was doing when I stumbled into the jaws of Gertrude's little human-deterrent?"

"As I recall, sir, you were attempting to fathom an alternate solution to my suggestion regarding locating Mr Lusitania."

I fluttered my eyelashes, which was a little embarrassing, as I was trying to blink. "Yes I was, wasn't I? I don't think I was making any headway, no headway at all in fact, blast it. How aggravating, how blasted aggravating it is, Forsythe? It is, isn't it Forsythe."

Pigstick leaned in at this point. "Are you feeling quite yourself, Milli?" she asked, quietly.

"No. No, no I'm not, dear sweet thing," I said, rounding on her. I was facing her at the time so I needed to do a full three hundred and sixty degree round but I suspect that only made the gesture more effective. "But that's sort of the issue isn't it? I'm not in my own body so I can't feel like myself; it's dashed inconvenient."

"But you could feel like yourself again, Milli," the relative said, her voice filled with a surprising amount of compassion and those things you get when light is reflected through water suspended in the air. "Forsythe proposed a solution…"

I struck one of my upper limbs with the other one. "He did, didn't he! Well done Forsythe! What was it, again? I can't quite remember."

Forsythe cleared his throat. "I suggested, sir, that you contact Lady Slavarington, as she would be able to locate Mr Lusitania in no short order."

My eyes widened. "A capital idea! I have no idea what prevented me from calling it such when last we spoke! Right! Let's go!"

I strode out of the infirmary and had turned a few corners before I remembered I didn't actually know where the infirmary was in relation to the rest of the house. Nevertheless, few problems can't be solved by purposefully strolling in one direction for long enough and, sure enough, before long I found myself in the yard at the back of the house, where the cars get stashed when not in use.

I located my two-seater in moments and chose to vault the door, rather than opening it in the traditional manner. The pick-me-up being drip fed into me really was marvellous; I felt thoroughly bucked up. Vaulting the door only went slightly wrong, so I was behind the wheel in two mouthfuls of a lamb's tail. It was at that point that I remembered I couldn't possibly operate the vehicle in my current human form.

"Would you like me to drive, sir?" asked Forsythe from the passenger seat. I jumped. I had no idea how he'd followed me without drawing my attention. I'd been moving at a fair pace, and valets do not move at that sort of speed, lest their dignity be irrevocably shattered. He may well have surmised my eventual destination, however, and headed directly to the two-seater rather than taking my more circuitous route. I might have noticed his presence before entering the vehicle, but given the amount of concentration I'd been giving to vaulting the door, I couldn't swear to it. It was also possible he'd been using his cloaking field.

"No thank you, Forsythe!" I replied, cheerily. "I wish to take life by the horns today. If you'd be so kind as to follow me in the old two-seater, I shall find alternate means of transport."

Forsythe exited the vehicle and I did likewise.

"Of course, sir, but how do you plan to join Lady Slavarington's fleet? She is some distance away, sir, and without some form of vehicle, it may be difficult for you to reach her."

I waved a leg. "There will be suitable vehicles in the human district, Forsythe. Kindly give me my service weapon."

Forsythe's eyebrow actually quivered. Or, possibly, I was quivering, and my motion caused the impression that his eyebrow was moving likewise.

"It is not my place to-"

"Correct, Forsythe, give me my service weapon please, be a sport."

Forsythe paused for only the briefest time. He then coughed and opened up the service hatch in his back. He had a bit of a rootle around and then passed me Chester, the weapon I'd been presented with after The Battle Of The Bulge, the war against the exceptionally overweight group of humans I'd taken part in several years ago.

It was a remarkable weapon. It carried a fifty-round magazine, a polished brass scope, as well as cantered iron sights for close-up work. In my old body I had used it as a backup weapon, my primary weapon usually being something with much more stopping power. Chester's diminutive nature was to my advantage currently, though, as it sat in my upper legs as if it was a fully sized weapon. I checked the magazine as well as the gas cylinder. Both seemed in perfect working order. Wonderful.

Departing with a swift, "Pip pip!" I trotted away from Forsythe and around the side of the house. After so long being frustrated by this human body, it felt wonderful to be up and running. I gathered some more speed as I rounded a corner of the house and saw the grounds stretching before me. The apparatus around my lower leg began to creak a little after the third kilometre, but I had no time to consider the wishes of a medical contrivance. I had transport to obtain!

I reached the tri filament rotational lift in record time, considering the three or four times I'd fallen over and needed to retrieve Chester. I rode the wires across to the human district and found myself once again on Clerkenwell Road. There were fewer humans about the place than there had been at the fete. Presumably those that had dropped in from nearby human districts had since departed.

There were plenty of cars about the place but, humans being humans, they'd have all sorts of anti-theft devices built in. What I needed was one already in use so I could commandeer it from its occupant. With this in mind, I proceeded along Clerkenwell Road and turned down the next major junction I saw. There, I saw what I needed. There was a largeish silver vehicle heading towards me. As a vehicle, it lacked a certain sense of style, but it at least appeared to be spaceworthy. I stepped into the middle of the road and aimed Chester at the driver.

"You there!" I bellowed. *"Step out!"*

The human behind the steering wheel didn't immediately comply, so I loosed a few rounds into the road in front of the car. That did it. The human flung the driver side door open and stepped out, timidly.

"Move!" I rasped. *"I need your motor."*

The human didn't need to be told twice, which was a relief, as I wasn't sure how I could have rephrased that. It turned and ran, whimpering. One or two humans appeared to be glaring at me, so I loosed a few more shots into the air and they started running as well. Capital.

I slid into the driver's seat and placed Chester lovingly on the passenger seat. This done, I spent a few moments becoming used to the controls. They were roughly similar to those of a normal car, but designed for use by four legs instead of eight. Within moments I'd broken free of the human district's gravity well and was heading down the B roads towards the A424 in no time.

Normally, I drive in what could be described as a fairly sedate manner. On this occasion, for some reason, I found my lower leg pressed firmly against the acceleration sensor. This saw me in orbit around the base that is home to the 75th Grand Battlefleet rather more quickly than I would normally have been accustomed to.

I took a few seconds to admire the view and then started casting my eyes about for the Battlefleet. It wasn't immediately obvious. Battlefleets are normally rather conspicuous. It's one of the first things you notice about them. It's very hard to look at one hovering over your planet and mistake it for, say, an asteroid.

That had been my opinion, at least. After a few high-speed orbits of the base, I began to revise my opinion. There was an apparent lack of Battlefleets and an overabundance of asteroids. I toyed briefly with the idea that maybe large conglomerations of ships could be mistaken for asteroids after

CONFESSIONS of a GENTLEMAN ARACHNID

all before dismissing the idea. I drove around in frustrated circles for a few moments before attempting to fathom the mystery of my commandeered vehicle's communication circuits.

I brought the comms matrix into life with a few well-placed prods of my upper leg. It took me a short while to locate the preferences menu and get the blasted thing into a more civilised language than standard human. This done, I was able to give my two-seater a buzz. Forsythe picked up on the second ring.

"Mr Clodthorpe's vehicle, Mr Forsythe speaking," he answered, the very model of a gentleman's personal gentleman.

"Forsythe, it's me," I exclaimed, "Where the blazes has Mother Ophelia got to? Her fleet's not at its base anymore, blast her."

"I fear not, sir," said Forsythe. "She has taken the fleet to an emerging conflict in the Twisting Nebula."

I drew in a breath. That nebula was just off the M5, hours away from my current location.

"Can't be helped, Forsythe, I'll head there directly."

"But sir-" there was almost shock in Forsythe's voice, "if you proceed to that location without stopping at the hall first, you may miss dinner."

This did give me pause. Not only would I miss out on Uncle Angus' hospitality (and one of the truly bright aspects to Newbury Towers was the resident chef), I would be committing something of a faux pas by being absent from the most sociable meal of the day.

The doubt was only a momentary one, however. "Never mind that, Forsythe. You head back if you have obligations below stairs that you must attend to. Uncle Angus trusted me with this duty, and I will not shirk it."

"Of course, sir," said Forsythe. "I am en route to the nebula, and will meet you there."

"Capital!" I barked, and thrust my lower leg forcibly at the acceleration sensor.

One of the main advantages of a human vehicle over something more civilised, I discovered, was that its small size made it ideal for passing traffic. I had been fairly haring it down the M5, after joining it from the A19 via the New Watford Bypass, when I encountered traffic. Traffic, as I'm sure you know, can slow a fellow down. My ridiculously sized vehicle, though, was able to squeeze through a gap here, a rift there, until I was at the head of the traffic queue in no short order.

Normally such flouting of the traffic regulations would chill me to the very bones, but on this occasion my blood was up, and I was in no mood for delays. Before long I saw the exit for the Nebula and, the traffic jam far in my rearview screen, I dove off the motorway.

I rarely have the opportunity to visit Twisted Nebula, which is something of a shame, as it's quite a lovely place. It's a reddish purple in colour, mainly, although there are strands of blue and light green in there at places. As the name suggests, it's nominally an interstellar cloud of dust, hydrogen, helium, and other ionized gases. The gases have been teased by solar winds, though, to such an extent that they curl around each other and have ended up in an elegant twisted shape. It's quite the tourist attraction in the summer. Locals sell postcards and homemade replicas of the stellar phenomenon.

The nebula is home to a group of chaps who call themselves something completely unpronounceable even using arachnid vocal chords. Thankfully, being frightfully civilised chaps, when our species first encountered theirs, they recommended simply referring to them as Peacocks. They look like a reptilian variant of one of those elephant things that the humans sold to us when we first made contact with them, but with chameleonic qualities that gift them the name.

They're a remarkably civilised people who I have had the privilege to fight alongside as well as against on numerous occasions. They gave the universe the composer Holligist, as well as too many sculptors and rapsmiths to mention here. Their union of planets could get a little tetchy on occasion, though, and it transpired that this was the reason for Mother Ophelia gracing them with a visit from the 75th Grand Battlefleet. The Peacocks had bombed a colony or attacked a shipping lane or something. The precise reason for the fracas was never entirely clear. I suspect they just fancied a bit of a dust up.

The described confrontation made getting into the nebula a little tricky, though. I was waved down by a chap at a border post. I forced my upper limbs to stop shaking and attempted to calm myself whilst the guard approached my vehicle. I didn't manage to reach placidity, exactly, but I managed to lower my heart rate to a level that appeared safe and was thus confident that I could converse with a stranger without appearing completely insane. The approaching chap in question was a Peacock and looked surprised to see a human out by itself with no armed escort.

I had to spend a good few moments explaining that, whilst I looked human, I was, not to put too fine a point on it, not. We then spent a few minutes chatting about the current hostility that had sprung up between our peoples — his view that it would probably sort itself out sooner or later. I concurred and asked him if he'd need to detain me. He waved this suggestion off, as both sides were keeping things somewhat casual at the present moment in time, as the confrontation was confined to a few thousand kilometres at the far edge of the nebula.

I enquired as to his function, given that he was not under orders to stop those such as me entering Peacock territory. He pointed out, in a rather gentlemanly fashion, that he might be given orders to turn those such as me away at any moment; his presence was a precaution against the strife escalating.

I liked this Peacock chap. His skin shimmered pleasantly as he talked, and he had kind eyes. I asked him his name. It transpired to be Donald. I mentioned that I was in something of a hurry and he apologised for delaying me. I "not at all"'d and wondered excitedly if he'd drop in on me next time he found himself in my neck of the woods. He seemed delighted by the invitation, and we exchanged vox-o-matic frequencies. This done, he drew me a map showing me the best way to get to Mother Ophelia's flagship.

This really was dreadfully kind of him, and I said so. He said a few kind words about those of my species he'd come to know and admire, and I reciprocated in kind. I excused myself as gracefully as possible and stashed his vox-o-matic frequency in my internal memory so that I would not lose it.

Waving a cheery goodbye, I shot my recently acquired vehicle up to full speed and thundered towards Mother Ophelia's fleet. It was only when I'd seen five or six gun batteries suddenly train themselves on my vehicle that I realised I might have made a bit of an error. Nevertheless, I proceeded forwards vigorously.

My car's vox-o-matic bleeped, indicating that someone was attempting to get in touch. How frightfully jolly. I grabbed the frequency and dodged a barrage of incoming fire at the same time.

"Milligan Clodthorpe here, what can I do for you?" I chirped like some sort of thrush, or possibly a robin.

"Milligan? Is that you in the human vehicle?" came a furious voice. It would have been hard to mistake it for Mother Ophelia's, so I didn't even try.

"Oh hello there, Mother Ophelia," I said, breezily, flipping my vehicle over an electromagnetic snare projected by one of the strike craft haring towards me. "I was just coming to see you."

"I know, you clot, for the love of the trickster god stop charging at my fleet; my idiot generals are convinced you're a human suicide bomber."

"A what?"

"A kamikaze pilot, stop your blasted car!"

I considered this option for a second, but I was still feeling in the mood for action in the wake of falling into Gertrude's trap, so I took Mother Ophelia's opinion under advisement and resolved to ignore it. A blaze of fire from a perusing craft took off a wing mirror, though, so I corkscrewed a touch before flipping the vehicle around and slamming the trunk of my vehicle into the prow of the craft that had been attempting to pull across my path. The impact swept the impediment aside, and I was free to continue.

The cold vacuum of space was looking rather lovely thanks to all the heavy ordinance being aimed in my general direction, but I didn't have time to stop and admire it. I spied Mother Ophelia's ship between a planet-wrecker destruct-o-drill heading for my windshield and what looked like a brace of mesh mines that would shred anything that approached them down into their component molecules.

All this quite took me back, and I reminisced about my time in the trenches above Arthur's Seat II, a planet I'd been stationed at when it got attacked just after meeting Dear Emily. I'd spent my time alternately engaging in ship-to-ship combat and writing to my newfound sweetheart.

Fighting in the trenches above a planet has always been something I've rather enjoyed. I wouldn't say it's a talent of mine, exactly; it's just that I find other chaps tend to lack that certain something that makes a truly first-rate fighter pilot. My skills fall far short of being first-rate, of course. I've got no idea why my commanding officer wrote that in his report after the opening battle over Arthur's Seat II. I can only assume it was some sort of clerical error.

I mean only to say… well, my skills with conventional firearms, engaging in fire fights on the surface of planets, are perfectly competent. I'm no better or worse than any other chap you might encounter on a quiet walk through a glade or a meadow or something. I consider my skills as a pilot to be roughly similar but, and it's the oddest thing, I always get put in squadrons comprised of pilots who could do with a little more practice. This is to say nothing of the chaps I fight against. If I didn't intensely dislike speaking ill of people, I would have one or two choice words to say about the recruiting programmes of our various sparring partners' pilot corps.

This all meant that, whilst engaging in a little cat and hyper-elephant game with the fighters Mother Ophelia had scrambled to intercept me was really rather good fun, it was all somewhat unchallenging, even in this human body. I'd just be getting into a nice back and forth with some chap about whether I'd be using his craft as a shadow with which to fool an incoming missile's tracking system or whether (and this is the position I suspect the chap in question favoured) I wouldn't, when a quick double half corkscrew manoeuvre would cause the missile in question's targeting system to lose me and the whole issue would quickly become moot.

This all meant that I reached the hanger bay of Mother Ophelia's flagship in a little less than seven minutes. Of course, they tried to snag me with one of those tractor beam thingies they install all over the place these days, but they're easily avoided if you have the knack of it, so I breezed inward in the manner of a young squire returning to greet the hounds.

I brought my trusty steed to earth and opened the driver's door. I was greeted by a dozen or so firearms pointing in my direction. I waved them aside.

"I'm here on business, chaps, don't let the flesh bag I'm occupying fool you. Where's Lady Ophelia Slavarington?"

The chaps with the guns didn't seem to know what to make of all this. One or two of them bristled their weapons at me, but I shot a withering look right back at them. They didn't seem to know what to do with my withering look, but I had no intention of being bristled at, so we were at something of an impasse. Not one I intended to engage with, though.

I strode forwards, wondering if an impasse is one of those things you can engage with or not, or whether it's just one of those things that hangs around. The chaps with the guns tried to stop me, but I fooled them by falling over only half accidentally, and when one or two helped me up, I dodged through a gap in their ranks and pressed on.

One of the more quick-thinking chaps managed to get in front of me and held his gun to my head. It being a real gun and not a backup weapon of the sort Chester is, when I neglected to come to a halt and walked straight into the gun barrel, my head was buried in it up to my ears. Human bodies really are ridiculously small.

I grasped the gun barrel with my two upper legs and wrenched my head out and was about to start giving the soldier who held the gun a piece of my mind when I heard the distinctive roar of Mother Ophelia approaching.

The soldiers all took up position on my flanks or directly behind me and snapped to attention. I attempted to look calm and relaxed, which would have been a tall order were I not still feeling the effects of that pick-me-up that Forsythe plied me with. As it was, I kept licking my facial lips, and my lower right leg wouldn't stop jiggling.

"MILLIGAN!" Mother Ophelia bellowed before stopping stock-still when her eyes fell on me. I could see her winding up to a speech that might have sat more comfortably on the lips of King Leer, and as soon as she'd recovered from the shock of seeing me in this body, I'd never get a word in. In any other mood, I would have been paralysed by fear of the relative by marriage in question. For some reason that I couldn't quite put my leg on, though, the usual syrup my spine regularly turns to in her presence was notable by its absence. Bucked by this realisation, I seized the initiative.

"Oh, you've noticed my new glad rags, I see," I said, breezily. "It's actually that which I've come to see you about. I see you disapprove, is that a fair assessment? Your eyes are boggling, old ancestor, do please speak or I feel you may explode."

I don't know if you've ever been examining an earthworm, or possibly some sort of vole, only to see it sit up and start taking you through the finer points of what exactly Silver Plath was bashing on about when she wrote that poem about being covered in sticking plasters. You'd be dashed surprised if that sort of thing happened, is my point. The wind would be taken from your sails. I only mention this because Mother Ophelia suddenly took on an expression similar to the one you might have worn if placed in the sort of situation I just described. The relative did something I had never seen her do before. She paused.

"Forsythe did say you were in reduced circumstances…" she rumbled after a few moments, "had I known *how* reduced… well."

She waved at the soldiers surrounding me and they scuttled off to see to their duties.

"Walk with me, Milligan," she said. "We must sort this frightful mess out."

"Top hole!" I said, having to jog to keep up. For the first time since arriving, I was able to give Mother Ophelia's flagship a bit of a once-over with what passed, at present, for my senses. The place was a great deal more spartan than the flagship in the fleet that I'd called home for ten years. It appeared to have been designed with an eye for practicality rather than pure aesthetic delight. The wallpaper that lined the tri-steel walls was of a plain burgundy colour, the idea being that it could be easily replaced if something caught fire or exploded. Patterned wallpaper would need time dedicated to ensure the pattern of replacement wallpaper exactly lined up with what was there previously, and you don't always have time for such things in the middle of a battle. The carpets were similarly spartan, and the light fittings looked like they could stop a rocket-propelled pulse shell.

There were occasional flashes of design that admitted, grudgingly, that gentlemen of all genders called this ship their home. I passed a wall hanging, for example, that had clearly been embroidered with loving care over the space of several hundred hours. I was only able to admire it for a few fractions of a second, though — partly because Mother Ophelia wouldn't slow down for any reason known to arachnid or beast... and partly because I was finding focussing on any one thing for any length of time tricky.

Some of Mother Ophelia's recent words filtered through whatever passed for my brain at present, and I was compelled to investigate further. "I say, is Forsythe with you then?" I asked.

"He is," Mother Ophelia remarked. "He arrived some time before you graced my fleet with your presence. I gather you've been doing your best to ruin your Uncle Angus' life?"

We reached a door marked "Private" and Mother Ophelia burst in without knocking. I followed, shutting the door on the second attempt as I did so. The room I found myself in was dimly lit and lined with listening posts. I couldn't fathom its purpose immediately, but obtaining this information was low on my priority list at present. Mother Ophelia had just cast aspersions on my relationship with Sir Angus. This would not stand.

"Now see here, respected one-" I growled, "I have nothing but fondness in my heart for the Uncle Angus under discussion. I am entirely blameless with regard to the current crisis, barring a few incidents I won't trouble you with."

Mother Ophelia clearly didn't believe a word of this. "Now see here, Milligan-" she began, clearly working up to a diatribe of the sort I'd successfully defused earlier. Thinking quickly, I jumped in ahead of her. I realise now that in my haste and, quite possibly encouraged by the painkillers that sluiced around my system, I was a little incautious.

"No," I remarked, "you see here, Mother Ophelia. Your nephew Bainbridge, the last in the Lusitania line, has stolen my body. He has fled with a human whom he intends to take as his wife. I realise you would not care overmuch if I lost my body, in which he currently resides, to such a horrible fate, but surely you realise that you hold in your claws the honour of the Lusitania family. Only prompt action on your part can rectify the situation. You must use the 75th Grand Battlefleet to locate the reprobate."

Mother Ophelia drew herself up to her full height. She towered over me like that massive black obelisk towered over the apes when we accidentally left it on Earth all those years ago. It was suddenly very clear in my mind that Mother Ophelia has ripped relatives of hers limb from limb for talking to her in this fashion before now. This would not deter me. I stood as tall as I could, which wasn't very tall at all when all's said and done.

"Milligan Clodthorpe," said the bringer of so much darkness, "the 75th Grand Battlefleet is not a device to be used willy-nilly to locate errant aristocrats. It is a key point in our species' defence strategy. I could not possibly allow it to be used for something so trivial as locating Mr Lusitania, no matter how foolish he plans to make his family appear."

"Oh what codswallop!" I exclaimed.

"Chose your words carefully, Milligan," said the crusher of empires. "Few speak to me in such a way. They tend to be those about to be crushed beneath my boot."

"I simply meant, Mother Ophelia, that I am not asking to borrow the battlefleet you have stationed here. You can still carry on with your war. I merely need information from your monitoring satellites or whatever they're called. It's a wonderfully simple thing and will save many people, including Sir Angus, considerable distress."

I felt Mother Ophelia's legs wrap around my fragile human torso. The breath was squeezed from my body as she lifted me to her eye level. Four pairs of black, shimmering spheres gazed into the two milky windows through which I observed the world.

"You have no understanding," she whispered, her breath tossing my human locks from in front of my eyes, "I would have thought your time on the front lines would have gifted you clarity. You come here, to my fleet. You disrupt my war, you cost my army precious resources. For what? So you can slip back to your life of luxury? So a distant set of relations can continue their lives free of embarrassment?"

Death stared me in the face. I stared back. "And when was the last time you fought on the front lines, Mother Ophelia?" I asked, my chest screaming as it tried to supply me with air, "My life, luxurious as you call it, was hard won. You know what I have lost."

"You took my daughter from me. My only daughter," hissed Death, wrapping her legs tighter around me and squeezing the air from me in one slow, horrifying wheeze.

"You have three other daughters," I pointed out with the last of my air.

"You took the only daughter whose company I enjoy," said Death, "the one precious light in this dreadful universe snuffed out before her time, and it might have been prevented."

Death cocked her head as she has done so many times before. I was unable to speak, which seemed to anger her.

"You suddenly find yourself wordless, Clodthorpe?" she roared. I felt her grip slacken enough to allow a breath or two to enter my lungs. I narrowed my eyes.

"Do you mean to kill me, Mother Ophelia?" I asked, my human face twisting into a rictus of a grin, "because I welcome it. Every moment I live without dear Emily, without your daughter, is a moment of pure, undiluted misery. Nevertheless, I endure, I work my way through this utterly futile experience because that is what Emily would have wanted. Furthermore, I understand my obligations. When I married into this nest of vipers of a family you created, I knew I was taking on obligations. There were so many youngsters who would need a Clodthorpe to keep them out of trouble. I rarely manage to save them from themselves, of course, and I often make things incalculably worse, however, I understand familial obligation in a way you seem to not."

I felt Death squeeze once more. I don't know if you've ever been crushed to death. Probably not or you would not be reading this. I do not recommend it as a way to spend, say, a sunny Saturday afternoon. I cannot be absolutely sure in this recommendation, though, because Mother Ophelia relinquished her grip and dropped me to the ground moments before I lost consciousness. Perhaps the whole experience would have taken on a certain charm in the last few moments, but I doubt it.

I landed on one of my lower legs and then pitched sideways. I sprawled in a hideously undignified manner. I would not face Death like this. I tried to stand, but the floor proved treacherous, and every effort to rise to my claws only ended in one limb or another skidding away from me. My eyes, though, my ridiculous milky white orbs, remained locked on the creature that towered over me.

"I will not kill you, Milligan," it said, turning away. "You brought my daughter joy. I cannot for the life of me understand how or why, but you did."

"I think a large part of it was tennis," I said, between wheezes. "She liked playing tennis with me."

"But I cannot help you," she said, either not hearing me or choosing to ignore me. "The data my fleet holds is not to be divulged to anyone without good reason. The reasons you bring to me are simply insufficient."

"It's just data," I said, a string of some unpleasant-looking fluid escaping from my large face hole.

"It is *not* just data," Mother Ophelia snapped. "I blame myself for this misunderstanding. Partly. Your current body must have addled your perception, young Clodthorpe. The 75th Grand Battlefleet has data on the comings and goings of every creature in the sector. We have the private movements and communications of every citizen and non-citizen. We are allowed access to this data purely on the understanding that we will *never* allow it to be divulged without the best possible reasons. We in the Battlefleets hold ourselves to the highest possible account. The integrity of our data stores are more important than you or me. They're more important than the honour of the Lusitanias, blast them, and they're more important than the memory of my sweet Emily. And you ask me to break that trust? How dare you, Milligan?"

Well, I didn't really know what to say to that, as you might imagine. It was possible that I'd never considered how I'd feel about some chap asking someone in the 3rd Battlefleet for a peek at my comings and goings. It wasn't a scenario I particularly relished. Possibly Mother Ophelia was right in assigning blame to my current physical shell, but I couldn't swear to it. It was equally likely that I hadn't thought a devastatingly large amount about the consequences of the favour I was asking.

I felt a wave of the painkiller run from the bag on my back, through the line, and into my system. I felt a renewed confidence and the urge to fight Mother Ophelia's last statement... but I held back. I would have to find a different way to locate Bainbridge.

I heard a gentle cough from the other side of the room. That, at least, answered a question that had been niggling at me for a few minutes: the thorny issue of where Forsythe was hiding himself.

"If I may offer a suggestion, Lady Slavarington," Forsythe said, gliding forwards.

Mother Ophelia rounded on him but reacted remarkably calmly in the circumstances. "What is it?" she asked, the merest hint of terseness in her voice.

"If Mr Clodthorpe were to join the Special Operations Unit for a brief spell, he would be entitled to access any data he sees fit in the pursuit of his duties."

Mother Ophelia passed a leg across her brow, "I appreciate the suggestion, Forsythe, elegant as it is. Nevertheless, it is not a solution to the issue at claw. The issue is not an outsider accessing such data; it is that *anyone* would access such data for personal means. Put simply, there is no good reason for anyone to access this data, whether they work for the Special Operations Unit or not."

She started to turn away from Forsythe, but he had more to add.

"Forgive my saying so, Lady Slavarington, but I was not suggesting that Mr Clodthorpe access the data for his own personal use. There is evidence to suggest that the human Mr Lusitania plans to marry is engaged in espionage."

This grasped Mother Ophelia's attention by the lapels and then apologised for rumpling the material.

"The human is a spy?" she hissed, "How came you by this information, Forsythe?"

Forsythe cleared his throat. "I wished to apprise Lord Wehrmacht of Mr Clodthorpe's safe arrival at the battlefleet. I took the liberty of connecting to him via vox-o-matic, and it was then that he informed me that evidence had emerged suggesting the possibly impure motives of the human in question."

Mother Ophelia's eyes took on an altogether more dark and terrifying shade of black. "Do you still have his vox-o-matic signal, Forsythe?" she demanded.

Forsythe answered in the affirmative and transferred the signal to Mother Ophelia's vox-o-matic unit at her request. He then rolled over to give the young master a once-over. I could hardly blame him. Bits of my clothing were scorched after a few near misses from the battlefleet's strike fighters, what wasn't scorched was rumpled from where Mother Ophelia had been crushing me, and my head fur was a mess.

I could hear Mother Ophelia chattering in hushed tones down her vox-o-matic as Forsythe inspected me. To my surprise, he wasn't hugely interested in the state of my clothes or fur. I was a little surprised by this and asked him why he was not giving my lapels a good seeing to or doing something with my upper left sleeve, which was almost entirely burnt away.

He looked at me in a way that valets are almost certainly not supposed to look at their employers. He recovered quickly, but I was still wounded.

"Forgive me, sir," he said, the model of respect once more, "but I reasoned that your lower leg was the most pressing of matters."

"My lower leg?" I asked, slightly incredulously. "Why? What's wrong with it?"

Forsythe's eye sensors twitched slightly. It was probably some sort of malfunction. "Well, sir, the first and most pressing issue is that a large part of it appears to be missing. Once it is located, I do not hesitate to say that there will be several other issues that will require my attention."

This was absolute hogwash and I said so. A fellow can't lose a part of his leg and not notice it.

The next few moments caused me to revise my thoughts on that matter. I had wondered why the world had appeared to have been slightly skew-whiff since Mother Ophelia had dropped me to the ground. Looking down, the entire lower part of my damaged limb had been ripped away. The twisted remains of the bracing apparatus was still present, mostly, although it looked like it had sustained significant damage during my little jaunt through the 75th Grand Battlefleet, and Mother Ophelia's antics had been the straw that broke the bracing mechanism's back. Bits of it appeared to have sheered through other bits and had taken my leg with it. How tedious.

Forsythe was tutting about blood loss, but I didn't see that as too much of a problem. I felt fine, really. I possibly shouldn't have. I mean, there were almost certainly pain signals flocking around my body like gulls around a fresh corpse, but I couldn't feel them. I attempted to comment on this matter but found my thoughts rather muddled. Forsythe took the opportunity provided by his master's silence to start fiddling about with a needle and thread in the area of my damaged lower limb.

I glanced about the place for a spell. Given that Forsythe was preventing my leg from moving by anchoring it to the floor with a heavy lifting apparatus he kept around for occasions where it might be needed, my movements were curtailed and, thus, glancing about the place was pretty much the only thing a chap might do for entertainment under such circumstances, other than listen to one half of a private vox-o-matic conversation, which just isn't done.

After two or three glances in various directions, I spotted the errant part of my leg. It had skittered away from the point where it was dropped and lodged itself in an air conditioning vent. A rotational gas diffuser had buried one of its blades in my leg up to the hilt. I couldn't see much of the leg from here, but what I could see appeared to be pretty well devastated.

Forsythe did something that sounded rather organic to my stump, and I felt my vision swim. I rested my head on the floor and closed my eyes. I moved one or two of the digits on the ends of my upper legs. I hadn't concentrated much on how this body interpreted sensation and would have liked to spend a few moments doing so now. I felt remarkably tired, though. I tried to say so to Forsythe but I found myself incapable...

11

I WOKE UP IN A MEDICAL BAY, WHICH APPEARED TO BE something I was making a habit of today. I hadn't even been aware that I'd been losing consciousness, but that's consciousness for you. It has a nasty habit of slipping away from you when you least expect it.

"Ah, sir," said Forsythe's voice from off in the distance somewhere, "I see you are awake."

"I wouldn't go quite that far, Forsythe," I said, attempting to sit up and not quite managing it.

"If you would just glance to your left, sir, before attempting to move," said the valet's voice in a way that meant only one thing.

I glanced to my left as instructed. There was tea there. Choirs of supernatural chaps may or may not have sung words of joy at that point; I'm not sure because painkillers were still present in my system, but had they actually been doing so, even such songs could not have increased my elation. I summoned a mountain of energy and reached for the teacup. I poured the tea into my large face hole and lay back, satiated.

"How do you feel, sir?" asked Forsythe, which irritated me a little, as I had just been feeling the sneaky tendrils of unconsciousness snaking around my mind.

"Oh fine, mustn't grumble," I said as breezily as possible, hoping the fellow would take that as enough of a hint.

"I am gratified to hear that, sir. Were it up to me, of course, I would not prevent you from returning to sleep. However, Lady Slavarington requested that I communicate with her via vox-o-matic when you regained consciousness."

"Must you?" I muttered.

"Not if you do not wish me to, of course, sir, but she wished to speak with regard to locating Mr Lusitania. I understood that this was still a priority for you."

There was something in that.

"Very well, Forsythe," I groaned. "Connect me to the aged relative on the Vox-o-matic if you would be so kind."

Mother Ophelia was raised in a matter of moments and, rather to my surprise, she actually asked after my health before launching into her point. I said that I was as fine as could be expected, and she admonished me for not counting my blessings. I retorted that would be easier to do if I were back in a less fragile body. She said she suspected I might feel something along those lines, and I congratulated her on her level of perceptiveness. She thanked me for my congratulations and I said, "Not at all." At that point, rather abruptly, I thought, she launched into the reason for her call.

"I don't know how much Forsythe has told you, Milligan."

"Barely anything," I muttered, closing my eyes.

"Don't interrupt, you wretch."

"Sorry, pardon, I'm sure. Do continue."

"Thank you. I spoke to Angus at Newbury Towers, and he confirmed that the human Bainbridge has engaged himself to is, indeed, a spy. It's quite remarkable, but there it is. I need you to track him down and put a stop to the wedding."

There was something wrong with this, and it took me a few moments to put a claw on precisely what.

"Forgive me for requesting a clarification, ancestor of mine," I said, "but when last we spoke, you seemed decidedly against providing me with the information I needed to locate the pair."

"Keep up, Milligan!" she roared, "The human is a spy! She must be located as soon as possible!"

It was a good thing my eyes were already closed, or I would have squeezed them shut in confusion.

"Yes, I understand that, Mother Ophelia, but don't you have special operations operatives for this sort of thing?"

A hurricane of expelled air echoed through the vox-o-matic communication band. "I do have agents that could do the job, yes, Milligan, but they're busy at the moment. I don't know if you noticed, during your exceptionally disruptive approach to my fleet, but we're in the middle of a war here, and my forces are all deployed. Forsythe suggested that you join my Special Operations Unit for a period of sixteen cycles, and that appears to be the only solution to the current problem."

I had chosen not to sign up for a fourth tour with my squadron after a significant number of them met a permanent death during a messy operation. I had thought that such escapades were well behind me. As Mother Ophelia said those fateful words, though, I felt a wave of that Bengi Soy Mathematicoglycerine, or whatever it was called, insinuating its way into my system and, all of a sudden, the idea seemed rather splendid. I wasn't entirely sure what the chemical named above contained, presumably a fair bit of carbon and hydrogen and a brace of nitrogen/oxygen. For all the simplicity of its, presumed, ingredients, though, it was magnificent stuff.

"What a fantastic idea, Mother Ophelia," I cheeped, "I shall begin as soon as you grant me access to the fleet data repositories."

"You will *not*, you young reprobate," she admonished. "Firstly, you will need to sign up for a yearlong tour with the Special Operations Unit. No-one gets into the unit without at least a year's service, and don't think you'll be able to abandon your duties after today, young Clodthorpe. No-one gets out of the Special Operations Unit early unless..."

"Unless what?" I asked, mildly. I wasn't entirely sure why we were even talking about this, but I wanted to put on the pretence of being an intelligent individual by asking pertinent questions.

"Never mind about that," she snapped. "And it wouldn't work for you anyway. No-one ever joins the Special Operations Unit unless they're insanely brave or suicidal. Have you seen the fatality statistics?"

"I have."

"Terrifying, aren't they?"

"*Le mot juste*, I would say, respected ancestor."

"Don't babble, Milligan. Forsythe has a contract for you. Put your James Q Wizbit on there, would you?"

Forsythe passed me a sheath of papers. I signed, initialled, and submitted to a brain scan in the indicated places.

"I've done it!" I announced proudly into the vox-o-matic. I then noticed that Mother Ophelia had terminated the signal at her end whilst I was giving page two of the contract a once-over. I called her back.

"Have you done it?" she demanded without preamble.

"I have, now let's see that data!" I cried.

"You've only got three and a half legs, you loon," she pointed out.

"Oh yes," I agreed. "Oh well, can't be helped." I moved to get out of bed, but a well-built chappie in a medical suit arrested my movement. He was gentle, but firm.

"Will you stop chattering away whilst I'm trying to explain what's going to happen to you? Really, Milligan, you can be the most appalling ass on some occasions. Really, I can't see what my darling Emily ever saw in you. From the moment she told me that she'd met you, I knew there'd be trouble. Hubert! That's what I said. Hubert is my late husband. He wasn't late at the time, I'm sure you remember, you sang that horrible song at his funeral. Hubert, I said-"

I muted the vox-o-matic signal, as these little chats of Mother Ophelia's could continue for some time with little to no input at my end, and I fancied having a word or two with this medical looking chap.

"I say," I said to him. "Can I get out of bed, please?"

"Sorry, Mr Clodthorpe, Lady Slavarington wishes you to be prepared for an operation."

"A what?"

"A surgical procedure."

Well this seemed a bit rich. The relative in question hadn't even consulted me. I felt fire rise in the Clodthorpe soul. Doing something I'd never normally do, I unmuted Mother Ophelia.

"Now see here, Mother Ophelia. I hate to interrupt you," I lied, "but what's all this rot about my having surgery?"

Mother Ophelia stumbled during some quite ripe material about my complete moral turpitude. It would probably have stung considerably if I had known what "turpitude" meant.

"What did you say?" she demanded, clearly annoyed at the interruption.

"Why do you wish me to have surgery? I feel perfectly wonderful."

"You're missing half of your lower leg, you blithering idiot. You're only conscious because of the benzoylmethylecgonine your man dosed you with. You need to get your leg fixed before you can head out. You're also to have your upper leg replaced with a utility model so we can implant a data stream into it."

"That makes sense," I reasoned. Human bodies didn't have data links built in for some reason. If I was to access Mother Ophelia's data repositories remotely, I'd need some sort of cybernetic implant.

"And you're to come off the benzoylmethylecgonine."

"I say, hang on," I said, guessing that she meant the painkiller I was hooked up to. "This stuff is marvellous."

"It renders you irrational, aggressive, insusceptible to pain, and entirely unpredictable."

"Exactly!" I retorted, "so why would you wish to take me off the stuff?"

"Don't argue, Milligan!" She exclaimed.

"I will argue!" I retorted. "Or rather, I won't. One moment," I terminated the vox-o-matic signal.

"I told her!" I informed Forsythe. "Right! So, shall we go?"

The vox-o-matic belonging to the medic chap chimed. He answered the signal and listened intently for a few moments.

"I see," he said, eventually, and terminated the signal. "Sorry about this, Mr Clodthorpe."

"Sorry about what, old chap?" I asked. And then I blacked out.

12

I WOKE UP IN A MEDICAL BAY FOR THE THIRD TIME SOME TIME later. My large face hole was dry. The fleshy bits around the outside of my large face hole were cracked. My eyelids were heavy and it took a supreme effort to open them. How long I had been out on this occasion was something of a mystery, but it felt like it should be measured in months rather than days.

"Sir, you are awake?" asked a familiar voice. I turned my head and there was Forsythe.

"Forsythe?" I muttered, my voice sounding weak from the period of being unused. "You stayed here the whole time?"

"I fear not, sir, that would have been impractical," my man murmured, "but the medical professionals indicated that you would regain consciousness at about this time, so I endeavoured to be here to appraise you of recent events."

"Have I a new leg, Forsythe?" I asked.

"You have two new legs sir. Your lower leg was replaced in its entirety. Your new limb is a rather fetching oak model. One of your upper legs was replaced with a combat model as per Lady Slavarington's instructions, and data channels have been routed from the communication modules in the leg up to your neural cortex."

"Well that's wonderful," I murmured, figuring that I could establish what exactly that meant at a later date. "But tell me, Forsythe, is there even a point to chasing down Bainbridge at this point? Surely he will be long since married?"

"I believe not, sir. If we make haste, we should still have time."

I coughed, feeling a certain amount of dust expel itself from my lungs. "That seems unlikely, Forsythe. Even a clot such as Bainbridge can't have rested on his laurels to quite that extent. Even if my surgery had taken only a week, he would have been long married by the time I was recovered, and it must have taken much longer than that. How long did the surgery take, as I'm on that subject?"

"About ten minutes, sir."

"Ah. And how long as it been since the surgery was completed?"

"Approximately thirty seconds, sir. The surgeon in question informed me that you are now fully recovered."

This was news to me. "I am?" I queried, not wanting to start springing about the place until all the facts were in.

"So I believe sir."

"That seems remarkably quick, Forsythe."

"It does indeed, sir. I understand that the medical facilities onboard ships such as this are extremely advanced. The medical practitioner who operated on you was kind enough to inform me that your case was not complex when compared to some of the injuries he has encountered during his career. He was able to, I believe 'fix you up' was the term he used, during the period normally reserved for his luncheon."

"Really?" I asked.

"So I understand, sir."

"I should probably send him a bottle of something."

"That would be most generous of you, sir."

"Not at all, Forsythe, he seems to have done a pretty dashed reasonable job. I feel pretty well, all things considered. I say, you don't have any more of that painkiller do you? That would make me feel even better."

Forsythe rumbled. "I fear not, sir. My reserve supply was impounded. Apparently it would have interfered with the course of your recovery had you continued to use the chemical in question."

"Well that's something of a blow. Ah well, better give this new leg a try I suppose. If you lead the way to the old two-seater, I can see how it performs under circumstances similar to a brisk stroll."

"Very good sir," said Forsythe, "However, I would suggest you dress first. I regret to say that your suit was unsalvageable after the damage it had suffered. It was destroyed during your surgery. I have placed some replacement garments on the chair to your right."

I have often remarked that Forsythe thinks of everything, so I do not feel the need to do so once more. Nevertheless,

MICHAEL COOLWOOD

it is true. I dressed in record time in a quite sporty tweed combination that matched my human fur. My new leg seemed to be holding steady and made a pleasant willowy sound when it impacted with the floor, despite being oak. I remarked on this and Forsythe informed me that it was one of the leg's special features.

Satisfied with my appearance, we set off to find the two-seater. Forsythe led me through Mother Ophelia's ship. Rum places though these flagships often are, this one seemed rather civilised. Everyone we passed saluted dutifully, despite my human body. Of course, it took me a few moments to realise why. Once my memory had been jogged, I had a panic attack.

"Forsythe?" I gasped. "Did I sign up to be a member of the Special Operations Unit?"

"You did, sir."

"What possessed me to do such a suicidally insane thing?"

"You considered it the only option to stop Mr Lusitania's marriage and recover your body, sir."

We resumed our stroll through the corridors of the ship, chatting on this subject. I pointed out that I didn't want to die. Forsythe responded by pointing out that the fatality rate over a one-year period in the Special Operations Unit was a mere 90%, and only a small fraction of those were partial or final deaths caused by lack of access to backups. I asked what exactly the fraction was, and he said that wasn't important, but the point was I might not necessarily die at all if I was careful. I had to admit that this was a perfectly reasonable point.

It quickly emerged that the painkiller that I had been using had certain properties that increased my confidence. It had been very useful when confronting Mother Ophelia, of course, but it had possibly impaired my judgement slightly. It also appeared to have interfered with my memory slightly.

"Forsythe?" I said, "How was I rendered unconscious by that sawbones? I do not remember the occasion clearly."

"If you are referring to the moments leading up to the surgery to replace your legs, sir, the medic in question had some experience with performing surgery on humans. I questioned him about the manner in which he anaesthetised you whilst the surgeon was operating. Apparently, the most efficient way to render a human unconscious swiftly is to apply a rubber mallet to the cranium of the human in question. It is this technique that he utilised in your case."

"That seems a little low-tech, Forsythe," I pointed out.

"Just so sir. I brought this to the medic's attention, but he responded with the reassurance that the human body itself was the pinnacle of low technology. As such, it responds best to the more primitive interventions, such as the rubber mallet."

I poked at my head cautiously. I did not feel any bruising or areas that protested when I poked them. I pointed this out to Forsythe, and he said that the surgeon had been left with a few spare minutes after completing the surgery and had taken the liberty of repairing the damage caused by the rubber mallet as well as removing the traces of painkiller from my system.

"Are you sure I can't have any more of that painkiller, by the way, Forsythe?" I asked, glad that the subject had re-emerged naturally. I didn't like to hound the poor chap, but I was of the opinion that I would feel all the better for a little more of that blessed chemical.

"I fear not, sir," said Forsythe, in his best *no, stop asking* voice. I resolved to not ask again.

I only asked four or five more times before Forsythe located the two-seater. Sadly, the answer never became anything less than negative. With a heavy heart, I swung myself into the passenger seat. Forsythe requested permission to leave the flagship and slipped away from the fleet as soon as permission was granted.

I spent a few minutes familiarising myself with the Special Operations database. Forsythe parked the two-seater patiently on the far side of the fleet while I did this so we wouldn't get caught by any stray missiles. Once I was comfortable with the database, I spent a few minutes locating the craft that Bainbridge had taken out of the system, as well as his eventual destination.

"Got it!" I cried, after a few minutes. Thankfully, Bainbridge hadn't thought to conceal his movements using particle dampeners or an energy signature spoof-o-tron. Come to think of it, I couldn't swear that he knows either of those devices actually exist. My point is that I would have had some considerable difficulty locating the lad if he had taken the time to cover his tracks. As it was, locating him was as simple as entering a serial number into a search box, and even someone with a brain such as mine can perform that, even if not quite on the first try.

I gave Forsythe the coordinates and we set off. Then I gave Forsythe the correct coordinates, after double checking my calculations, and we set off in the proper direction. I waved to Donald as we passed his checkpoint, and we received a friendly salute in return.

"There's just one thing bothering me, Forsythe," I remarked, after we had been driving for a while.

"Really, sir?"

"Well, no, if you put it like that, there are several dozen things bothering me, but there is one thing in particular I've been meaning to ask you about."

"Please do so, sir."

"I will do so, Forsythe, thank you. How exactly did you discover that Bainbridge's human is a spy?"

"Ah." This was such an unusual syllable to hear emerging from Forsythe's metal lips that I sat up and took notice. The chap seemed loathed to continue. Nevertheless, continue he did: "I fear I may have been guilty of a little exaggeration in that regard, sir."

I sensed skulduggery! "You intrigue me, Forsythe, please continue."

"Well, sir, I had divined from information you have been so kind as to share with me on previous occasions that Lady Slavarington takes her role as commander of the 75th Grand Battlefleet very seriously. As such, she was unlikely to grant you access to the data you needed. In order to facilitate you in your quest, I spoke to Sir Angus Wehrmacht at Newbury Towers. He was adamant that I should assist you in your efforts to locate Mr Lusitania, so I asked his lordship if he would mind engaging in a mild subterfuge."

"You mean, you asked him if he'd lie to Mother Ophelia?"

"Just so, sir. I am gratified to say that Sir Angus thought the scheme would be effective, and informed me that he would not have me melted down for scrap, as he should do upon discovering that a device such as myself had the capacity for deception."

"A bit of a risk on your part, nevertheless, Forsythe."

"It was, sir, but a calculated one. Lord Wehrmacht has always taken pride in his honour, from what I have observed, and I hypothesised that his lordship would overlook a certain impropriety on my part as long as matters were resolved to his satisfaction."

"As long as we can stop Bainbridge marrying that human, you won't be melted down, you mean?"

"Just so, sir."

"Well that's wonderful, Forsythe."

"I'm glad you are of that opinion, sir."

With that point out of the way, I did not think there were any other pressing matters that needed clearing up. With Forsythe dealing with the transportation side of our quest, I decided to familiarise myself with my new limbs. This took slightly longer than I anticipated, and I only just got a rudimentary grasp on how the software interfaces worked. I had managed to get to grips with the basics by the time Forsythe brought the old two-seater to a halt outside a rather grand-looking hotel called The Majestic.

"Is this it, Forsythe?" I asked, taking a break from customising the brain/limb toolset.

"This is it, sir."

"It's not entirely inconspicuous, is it? I would have expected him to hide out in a speakeasy, or an opium den, or something."

"I suspect that Mr Lusitania does not consider it likely that any interested parties would be able to track him to the nearest star system, let alone search the individual hotels located within those star systems."

"That's a bit short-sighted isn't it?"

"If you'll forgive my making a possibly unfair observation sir-"

"Go ahead, Forsythe, go ahead," I murmured, gallantly.

"Thank you sir, I merely wished to observe that as Mr Lusitania appears to wish to marry a human, he may not be fully aware of any other mode of thinking at present."

"You mean, Bainbridge is being an incorrigible fathead and when you're on a roll with that sort of thing it seems a shame to stop?"

"I would not put it quite like that sir-"

I waved a leg, "Never mind that, Forsythe. How would you recommend we locate the young idiot? A quick search of the rooms should do the trick, what?"

"Judging by the size of the establishment, sir, I estimate that The Majestic has the capability of housing some five thousand guests."

"Ah."

"Just so, sir. However, if you would like me to make some delicate enquiries as to Mr Lusitania's whereabouts, I am sure I can establish a concrete location."

"That'd be frightfully decent of you, Forsythe," I remarked.

"Not at all sir. If you would not mind doing so, I would suggest you use the data stores granted to you by Lady Slavarington to locate any nearby chapels that would be happy to marry higher species with lesser ones. Once we have that information, we will know not only where Mr Lusitania is, but also where he plans to go next."

"Excellent!" I cried.

It took me a few minutes to locate all the nearby establishments that would be capable of forging a union between Bainbridge and a human. I noted the most likely candidates down and then cast my gaze about the place. Forsythe wasn't yet back from his excursion, so I decided to make myself useful.

Forsythe had brought the two-seater to a stop in a car park, of sorts. I looked up the make and model of the vehicle that had ferried Bainbridge to this location. If the vehicle was still here, then it was probably Bainbridge's personal transportation. If Bainbridge's transport was here, then it would be reasonable to assume that he was still in the area.

Feeling like one of those gumshoes that were always getting rained on in the films, I stalked about the car park, examining the multitude of vehicles. The search was slower than I would have liked, because I kept getting distracted by sports models and the occasional battlecraft. One particular vehicle, in black with silver trim, held me spellbound for several minutes. I remained resolute, though, and located my quarry in good time. It was a compact affair designed to transport families about the place. I couldn't think why Bainbridge would have such a vehicle. I would have thought that he would be far more likely to own something enormous with an impractically large engine.

I was pondering whether I should attempt to sabotage his engine, or something less subtle such as taking a blade to the antigravity generators, when I heard a cough behind me.

"Ah, sir," said Forsythe's voice, "I see you have located Mr Lusitania's transport."

"Just so, Forsythe!" I explained, wheeling around. I managed to avoid falling over by steadying myself on the wing mirror of a convertible parked nearby. The effect was unfortunately spoiled when the wing mirror parted company with the car it had been attached to, causing it and the body it was supporting to plummet groundwards.

Forsythe helped me to my claws, and I dusted myself down. My new suit was harder wearing than my previous one, which was somewhat gratifying. Even after a brief and violent impact with the surface of a car park, it didn't show any obvious ill effects apart from the need for a press. Such trivialities could wait, however.

"What news, Forsythe?" I asked, "What news?"

"I spoke to the doorman as well as the greetsmith who was stationed at the reception desk, sir. As you will have no doubt surmised, they were happy to confirm that Mr Lusitania is a guest of The Majestic. They were initially reluctant to furnish me with further details, but after parting with a small amount of currency-"

"Frightfully good of you, Forsythe, do take a tenner from the dressing table."

"That is most kind of you, sir. The pair were most forthcoming, after accepting the aforementioned allurement, and passed various packets of information to me, including the room numbers for Mr Lusitania and his human."

That was a considerable relief. If Bainbridge and the human had been sharing the same room, then any hope of recovering my body in a pristine state would have been lost.

"Have you a plan to return me to my body, Forsythe?" I asked, eagerly, "Because at present my only idea is to scurry up to the fellow's room and give him a piece of my mind."

Forsythe held up a placating appendage. "If I might suggest caution, sir."

"You might," I agreed, anxious to hear what would come of said caution.

"I am sorry to say that I do not have a plan as of this moment, but it might be beneficial for you to spend what remains of today in Mr Lusitania's company."

"And tick him off, you mean? Persuade him to desist in his plans?"

"I fear that will be ineffective, sir. If Mr Lusitania finds that his location has been discovered by hostile elements that wish him to curtail his actions–"

"Like me?"

"Such as you, indeed sir, then he will most likely abscond to a secondary base of operations where he might be more difficult to locate."

"You mean, he'll do another runner?"

"You have placed your digit on my meaning precisely, sir. In my experience, one is likely to catch more bees with a special formulation of sugar, airborne hormones and brightly coloured materials, than with strong acid."

"You've lost me, Forsythe."

"I apologise for being unclear, sir. I was suggesting that if you go to Mr Lusitania in friendship, intimating that all is forgiven, then his suspicions would not be raised."

"Well that's all very well and good, but there's a flaw in your plan, Forsythe."

"There is, sir?"

"There is indeed. Let's say I approach the buzzard in question in a chummy fashion. What then? All we will have done is secured a best man for the wedding ceremony."

"Your rekindling your friendship with Mr Lusitania is merely the first part of the plan, sir."

"I wouldn't exactly say rekindling, Forsythe. I don't believe our friendship has ever been kindled, as it were."

"Just as you say, sir. Nevertheless, this act you would undertake is merely a delaying tactic. If you were able to keep the gentleman in question in one place, sir, and in constant company, any impulsive romantic plans would be quashed."

"That sounds more like it."

"And I would be able to formulate a more permanent solution to the problem at claw."

"I distract him, you work out what to do next, you mean?"

"Precisely, sir. I should be able to contact you via vox-o-matic when I have reached a solution."

"Fantastic, Forsythe, fantastic!" I enthused, "and I have just the distraction in mind! The poor fool's wedding is imminent, he's far from his family and friends, he's no doubt feeling ever so slightly vulnerable. There is a wedding tradition that I have in mind which will allow me to distract him and may well sow doubt into his mind at the same time."

I related the details to Forsythe. I rarely see the fellow impressed, but I dare say I spied a spark of admiration in his visual sensors.

I got a little lost on my way up to the penthouse because it was only accessible via a separate, special elevator. I was lucky I was able to see it at all. The elevator in question had a cloaking shield and, when you tried to view it, it accessed your credit score, and if you weren't in the alpha platinum range, the cloaking field remained in place. Forsythe had informed me that the human was being housed two floors below the penthouse in a super deluxe ultra-suite. Apparently she hadn't rated a super deluxe ultra-grand-suite.

Once I'd found the elevator on my third pass around the hotel, I used my new upper leg to hack the control panel and grant me access to the penthouse. The elevator opened directly into the reception suite: this was a suite of three reception rooms, each grander than the last. The idea was to receive a guest in the reception room that was most appropriate to their status. This all made me feel rather uncomfortable. It seemed a very new money thing to do. Families such as mine and Uncle Angus' would never dream of treating guests differently depending on their status. Hotels such as The Majestic catered for many different species, though, and some species do base their worth on the amount of hard currency they've acquired, and it's wrong to judge them for that. So I've been told anyway.

I settled myself in the least opulent of the reception rooms and waited, as tradition expected. You couldn't just go blundering into a chap's hotel room. Partly out of politeness, but mostly out of the things you may never be able to unsee if you catch the occupant at an inopportune moment.

The presence of a guest would have been alerted to Bainbridge when I had entered the elevator, so I didn't have long to wait. I only had time to fully appreciate two of the seven marble busts that decorated the reception room before I heard familiar scuttling claws. The sound rounded the corner shortly before Bainbridge, who stood stock still as soon as he noticed me. He took on an expression of the sort more usually seen on that of a gasping fish.

13

"MILLI..." HE GASPED.

I regretted that I was not here to tick the blighter off, as this would have been a perfect opportunity. There was a plan, however, and plans must be stuck to. "Bainbridge!" I cried and leapt to my claws. I embraced one of his legs as if I was greeting the long lost child I'd never had. At least I assume I've never had one; you can never tell with long lost children. I felt him draw back, which led to my being carried several metres before my grip was shaken. In order for some semblance of my dignity to be maintained, I decided to turn on the charm and leave the embracing for when the deception I was weaving was more complete.

"Why didn't you tell me in person you were getting married, you clot? I had the devil of the time tracking you down so I could congratulate you!"

I know what you're thinking. I wasn't here to congratulate him at all. This is true, but I find that deceptions are more likely to work if you state an outright lie at the start and then bring things back a bit. That way, the fellow is shaken. He is wondering if he has misjudged your presence in the least impressive reception room of his penthouse. From there, the more subtle work may be done in order to create the foundations for the key piece of deception stated earlier. I do not wish to confuse my readership though, so just to be clear: I had not had a change of heart. I still intended to ruin Bainbridge's marriage and quite possibly his life, if I could get away with it. I wasn't as determined to carry out that last objective, for the quality of mercy droppeth as the gentle rain upon the drains beneath, but you take my point.

"Congratulate me?" Bainbridge asked, stumbling at the first fence.

"Yes, congratulate you, you ass. It's wonderful that you have found love at last! You recall how ecstatic I was after I had found my own dear Emily!"

I threw my upper leg as far around Bainbridge as I could and waved the other one expansively.

"Love is a many splendid thing, I don't know if you remember that passage from that thing about the red wind turbine? All you need is love, it goes. It then goes into specifics I won't mention here, Bainbridge old chap, but my point is that it's a thing to be celebrated wholeheartedly. Tell me, when is the happy occasion?"

The poor fool looked like a kitten who had been discovered with its nose in the cream, only to have several pints of the same dumped on its furry little head. "Tomorrow…" he said.

This wasn't the best news I'd ever heard, as it didn't give Forsythe much time to come up with a plan. Nevertheless, I wore the mask. "Tomorrow!" I squeaked, trying to sound excited rather than terrified, "well that's perfect, you old love daemon. Tell me, who is organising your crab party?"

"Crab party?" Bainbridge asked, bringing the total number of words he had said in this conversation to six. I wasn't entirely sure what my total was, but I was pretty sure I was ahead.

"Yes a crab party! Don't look at me like I'm speaking Neo-Greek, young oyster, you must have a crab party before you get married! It's your last night of freedom, what? It is a time for jollity! For you to loosen your tie! And such a fine tie it is. Ah, I remember why. It's one of mine. Well never mind. Back to the point at claw. Who's organising your crab young thing?"

"I don't think I'm having one," said Bainbridge, finally making his word count reach double figures. "We arranged this all with a certain speed and, well, we haven't invited any family or friends, so…"

He trailed off. I couldn't tell if he was having second thoughts already (although given the thickness of the skull he currently occupied I considered this a remote possibility), or if he was still feeling sheepish in my presence.

"No no no no!" I cried, "No no no no no no no no! That won't do at all my dear chap! A wedding is a celebration! A wedding is a cause for the most profound joy!" I was slightly worried that I was laying it on a bit thick. I was aiming to come across as the sort of chap who became psychotically happy at the very prospect of a wedding, but the risk with such a venture is you end up looking like a dangerous lunatic. I thought about dialling things down a little, but decided not to, reasoning that the fellow hadn't fled from me or called for security yet, so he was probably not going to unless I started waving weaponry about. "I tell you what, Bainbridge, I will tell you what we must do: I will arrange a crab party for you tonight!"

This raised the fur on my/Bainbridge's neck. "What? Why? So you render me senseless and kidnap me, thus preventing my marriage to Su-San?"

"Nothing could be further from the truth!" I cried, cursing that the idea of simply kidnapping the poor sap hadn't occurred to me earlier, "You wound me with your accusations, old friend."

"When last we met, your behaviour was not what I'd consider that of a friend," he pointed out, gruffly. I couldn't very well argue with that.

"But you weren't *engaged*, then!" I pointed out, grinning as widely as my large face hole would permit.

"You seemed dreadfully angry about me taking your body…" he pointed out.

"Water under the bridge!" I said, trying not to grit my fangs after what had occurred last time, "Really, your news has thrilled me to the n'th degree!"

"Are you *sure* this isn't some kind of trick?" asked Bainbridge.

"My dear Bainbridge," I admonished, "your suspicion continues to wound me. I have no tricks planned for you. We can celebrate your upcoming wedding quietly in this very room or we could go out and try something more adventurous.

You may veto any entertainment or plan I suggest that you feel has a sinister ring to it. All I ask is that you permit me to celebrate your upcoming nuptials with you."

Sometimes the largest lies are the easiest to carry off. I saw Bainbridge stretch my face into a smile. "Milli, I must say that I'm touched. It means so much to have someone here on this day, the day before the happiest day of my life."

I was slightly worried that he was about to start crying.

"And it means the world that you'd allow me to celebrate it with you!" I exclaimed.

"Which world?"

"Excuse me?"

"You said it meant the world to you…"

"I see. I apologise, it was merely a figure of speech."

"Oh I see," he said, sounding less suspicious with every passing second.

"So what should we do for your crab, dear chap?" I asked in my most jovial voice, trying to get the conversation around to the topic at claw. With any luck, Bainbridge was one of those coves who liked the finer things in life. Gambling, alcohol, card sharking, zoos…

"Have you ever been to a burlesque, Milli?" he asked after a short while, in a hushed voice.

I had, not that he needed to know that. Dear Emily and I had visited such shows occasionally, when the mood took us. I do not intend to justify this, as my reasons would only invite further questions. Allow me to say simply that our marriage was happier because of it, and let's leave it at that.

"I have not, young swordfish," I said (I was lying, just to be clear about matters), "But I hear they're delightful establishments. Would you like to visit one?"

He pretended to think about it. "You know…" he said after a suitable pause, "I rather think I would."

"And Su-San would not mind?" I asked, before mentally slapping my palm against my skull. My task was to occupy the blighter's time, not concern myself with what happened as a result.

"She… probably… might." Bainbridge conceded "But I'm sure she'll never find out. Do you know of any nearby?"

I said that I would find the best bally burlesque show in the star system for him and ushered him into his chambers to change into suitable evening attire. Thankfully the clot had fled from justice carrying a sizable chunk of my wardrobe, so he had a fair set of clothing to choose from.

Whilst he was slipping into my finest evening suit, I interrogated the data store on my upper leg as to local burlesques. The interface needed a little persuading that I had actual, legitimate business with such an establishment, but once I'd convinced it that I wasn't just a soldier on shore leave, it gave up the goods.

The place that looked like it would provide the most entertainment, yet set off the fewest flashbacks to life with my dear Emily, was a joint by the name of SS Madame de Pompadour. It was named after some sort of ship, apparently. It provided a host of entertainments such as standard burlesque, depraved burlesque (which I'd only seen once before and vowed never to again), personality-based burlesque (where the practitioners stripped away layer after layer of their personality, revealing the secrets and core traits that lay beneath) and the extremely rare anti-burlesque (where practitioners started fully clothed and put on more clothing throughout the act in the most passionless way possible).

A visit to a burlesque was a perfectly pleasant prospect, and the plan was proceeding well, but the prospect of spending an entire evening in the company of Bainbridge was beginning to weigh heavily on my mind. Particularly as it had been several hours since I'd last felt the effects of that wonderful painkiller.

When Bainbridge emerged from his dressing room, therefore, I made a few delicate enquiries as to whether he knew how I could get my claws on some.

"Some what?" he asked, confused.

"Some Bengamin Soya Mathematical Glycerine," I clarified.

He blinked a few times, moving his lips.

"Do you mean benzoylmethylecgonine?" he asked. I was quite astonished.

"Yes!" I cried, "How did you know?"

"One of Su-San's friends takes that stuff as a pick-me-up."

"Really? Do you know where we could get some?"

"Well as long as we can find some humans, it shouldn't be too difficult. I must say, Milli, I'm surprised at you taking benzoylmethylecgonine. I suppose it puts your recent actions into context though."

"What do you mean, old chap?" I asked, steering him towards the elevator as best I could.

"Well you seem much more relaxed about life. Tell me, have you started taking it recently?"

"Yes!" I said, brightly, "I stumbled into one of Gertrude's human traps and I was given it as a painkiller."

"Ah," Bainbridge said, nodding, "that would explain it. You should stay on the stuff, Milli, you're much more tolerant of life's little flaws at present. I mean, last time I saw you, you were positively apoplectic about my hijacking of your body. And look at you now! You're taking me to a burlesque! Who knows what you'll do when we get a little more inside you!"

When I was in the military, training with the air group, I had a mentor. Her name was Sarah Tewksbury, and she taught me more than I know at present. This was because, as she said, there's a whole universe of knowledge out there, and the Clodthorpe brain would be lucky to absorb a fraction of one percent of it. Nevertheless, she taught me skills which kept me alive through many battles, and her advice gave me the confidence to ask dear Emily for her claw in marriage. My point is that if Ms Tewksbury said something was a good idea, then that was the end of it; you'd get no further argument from me.

Now, I don't know if there is such a thing as an anti-mentor, but if there is, I suspect Bainbridge would fill that role rather nicely. The fact that the incorrigible fathead approved of my taking Benlanam Sofa Magnificent Gluten was enough for me to seriously rethink my attitude to the stuff. It made me feel absolutely marvellous, there was no real doubt about that, but it might do well to consider the full consequences of further use.

Bainbridge led me to his transport without complaint, which neatly avoided me having to explain who'd driven me here and, as a follow up, where Forsythe was and what he was doing. I don't know if Bainbridge had heard about Forsythe's problem solving skills. To my knowledge, most of the quadrant has heard some story or other about my valet's remarkable abilities, and I didn't want Bainbridge's suspicions to be raised through the knowledge that Forsythe was out there, somewhere, scheming.

The drive to the SS Madame de Pompadour was short, but Bainbridge insisted on prattling on for most of the way.

I can never quite fathom why, with so many fascinating hobbies extant in the cosmos, people insist on engaging in the remorselessly trivial ones. I hope you will remember my friend Reggie "Rowboat" Bloggott, who has devoted much of his adult life to the close study of a butterfly. Not butter*flies*, but one individual butterfly. I wouldn't mind, but he's not even very good at it. He's had this one blasted butterfly pinned in a display case for twenty years, and he's none the wiser as to its taxonomy.

Even Rowboat, though, commands endless tracts of my respect when compared to fellows such as Bainbridge. Bainbridge spent a fair whack of the drive chatting about his love for prank vox-o-matic messages. This, apparently, is how the wastrel spends much of his spare time. He will randomly dial in a vox-o-matic frequency and then, if someone answers, he will demand to speak to "Martin".

"And what if the person who answers is called Martin?" I asked, aghast.

"Well, then I have to terminate the call and try again. Keep up, Milli, it's not funny if the chap I talk to is actually called Martin."

I nearly asked why it was funny if the chap he talked to wasn't called Martin, but sanity prevailed.

We arrived at the SS Madame de Pompadour just as the evening shows were starting. The joint was mainly focussed on the entertainment of arachnids, and so the place was decorated in a way most pleasing to our eyes. There were plenty of other species knocking about the place, though. Some were there to watch shows, others were performers.

Possibly as a nod to the non-arachnid customers, or possibly to give the place a touch of the exotic, the place appeared to be decorated in several different styles, depending on which room you stepped into. The largest room was the one you first encountered upon entering the building. It was where the bar was located, as well as several quiet places to sit, for those who had found the entertainment in the other rooms a little too stimulating. Several doorways led from this room into smaller ones. These rooms were where the performers could be found. Each room was roughly similar, in that it contained a stage and seating.

The decoration of each room was where the SS Madame De Pompadour really spread itself. One room attempted to recreate the royal palace of the Peacocks. One affected the style of an ancient arachnid theatre. Yet another was made-up to imitate the oval office of the human white house, which records note as a hub of illicit liaisons between powerful people of all genders.

Every one of the fifty or so rooms had burlesque performers of every kind. I settled Bainbridge in front of a Contemplative Burlesque, where the performer thinks more and more sensual thoughts at the audience, and told Bainbridge I was going to get him a drink.

"I can pay for my own drinks, Milli!" he said, jovially.

"I know you can, young sycamore," I said as the performer on stage started contemplating the rather interesting uses grapes could be put to, "but this is *your* evening. You should watch the entertainment, and I should fetch the refreshments. Sit back and relax, young biscuit; I shall be back shortly."

I staggered away from the young buffoon, overwhelmingly glad to be free of his company. I usually avoided people whose company I took no pleasure in. One of the most profound experiences of my life took place during my humanthropology course. I was watching a film about an enormous talking rabbit called Harold. In this film, this chap who was friends with Harold had this line about intelligence. He said one could either be intelligent or pleasant, and that it was better to be pleasant.

Now, I know what you're thinking, this film was made by humans. For other species it is entirely possible to be both intelligent *and* pleasant. Making this point misses the issue I was trying to raise, though. I have never been especially intelligent. People tell me this regularly. Even my own dear Emily mentioned it on several occasions, in the most loving way possible. Given that I was never going to achieve intelligence without the benefit of brain augmentation (and I've never been fond of that idea), I felt that my life would be best spent being pleasant, and I would thus leave the universe a more pleasant place than when I entered it.

Chaps such as Bainbridge get in the way of this mission and, as such, they are best avoided. On this occasion, though, avoidance of Bainbridge was one of several things that would disintegrate Forsythe's plan around my ears. I did not dally on the way to the bar, as a result. I ordered several of the less conservative offerings and paid for them. Once this was done, I leaned in to get the bartender's attention.

"I say," I hissed, "I'm in some little pain. Do you happen to know where a chap could acquire some pain relief?"

The barkeep stood up straight and looked about the place for a spell. She then leaned back towards me, having to very nearly rest her jaws on the bar, as in my current form my head only just reached over the polished wood described.

"Are you a member of the constabulary, sir?" she asked, suspiciously.

I raised a quizzical piece of fur that appeared to be placed above the human eye sockets for just this reason. "Do I have the appearance of a flatfoot?" I asked.

The bartender shook her head and then shrugged. "This is a reputable establishment, sir."

"Of that I am in no doubt," I assured her.

"We have many preparations that would work wonders on an arachnid system, sir, but for a human body… that's trickier."

I lowered my voice further. "I am in quite *considerable* pain, good barkeep. If your concern regards the possibility that I would cause some sort of ruckus once my distress was suppressed, fear not. My family are known for their discretion."

The barkeep lowered her voice to match mine. "Which family would that be, sir."

"I can't tell you," I said. "That would be being indiscreet."
Match point to Clodthorpe, I think.

The bartender nodded and, after another quick glance about the place, quoted me a figure. I slid the requested amount of currency across the bar to her. She slid back a small twist of clear plastic.

"Please be discreet, sir," she said, "We have a reputation to maintain."

I stared at the proffered item. It didn't look like a bag one could attach directly to one's cardiovascular system, but perhaps it had hidden depths.

"What, pray tell, is that?" I asked, trying not to sound rude.

"N-acetyl-p-aminophenol," said the barkeep, "It's the most popular human painkiller."

"I was rather hoping for some Breezy Slate Maroon Gobbits…" I said, wistfully.

The barkeep shrugged. "I'm sorry, sir, that's all we have."

My disappointment was palpable. Optimism is a kind mistress, though, and I hoped that these N'Active Pterodactyls would act on my system in a similar way to the previous painkiller.

I slipped the plastic parcel into a pocket and grasped at the set of drinks I'd ordered prior to my negotiation with the barkeep. Wobbling, slightly, I returned to where I'd left my charge and presented him with the flutes of my labour as Psalm put it.

The amount of available choice seemed to actively excite Bainbridge. He grasped at three or four glasses, with only momentary enquiries as to what was contained in each one.

I was able to salvage something amber-coloured, with a pleasant aroma, from the massacre, and sipped it gratefully as Bainbridge began to work his way through the various liquids I'd presented to him.

Once a suitable duration had passed, and I was confident Bainbridge wouldn't flee the scene as soon as my back was turned, thanks to the alcoholic smorgasbord in front of him, I said I wished to use the facilities.

Once I had located the little gentleman's room, I found an empty waste evacuation pod and entered, shutting the door behind me. I placed my drink on a nearby ledge and grasped at the twist of plastic in my pocket. Once opened, the parcel revealed four oval, white pills. I shrugged (a particularly odd manoeuvre in a human body), and swallowed the lot. I helped the pills on their way with the drink I retrieved from the ledge and waited for the painkiller to take effect.

Nothing seemed to happen. Maybe it took a little while to work. No matter. I returned to Bainbridge whilst I waited for the effects to begin working their delightful magic.

As the evening wore on, though, there was a considerable absence of relief and pleasure from the painkillers. There was also a notable lack of vox-o-matic communications from my valet, indicating that the fellow had not, as of yet, been struck with the inspiration mallet. These two issues caused me to be rather jittery and, I regret to say, slightly irritable.

These factors were only exacerbated by Bainbridge, who was becoming extremely difficult to manage. He kept trying to slip away from me for reasons I wasn't entirely able to fathom. I had to keep finding new, intriguing burlesques to keep the sap entertained.

My frustration reached a peak after we'd been in the establishment for several hours. I sat Bainbridge down in front of an intellectual burlesque performer who called herself Unicorn. Unicorn started her show, which consisted of salaciously revealing sections of her dissertation as well as occasional, tantalising glimpses of her degree certificate.

Bainbridge was entranced by the performance, as well he should be, so I slipped off to lick frantically at the twist of plastic that had previously contained the pills, in case that had been the idea all along. This done, I turned to my second cause of concern and initiated a quick conversation with my valet.

"Forsythe!" I hissed into the device, "Do you have any news? I am unsure as to how long I can continue to stall Bainbridge!"

"*Yes sir, I'm there now,*" he replied.

I don't know if you know what a non sequitur is. If you don't, look it up, I'm not here to act as a dictionary for you. The fact remains, though, that if you wanted a definition of a non sequitur, but didn't have a dictionary at claw, the above exchange would function as a perfectly serviceable example until a better one came along.

"You're where?" I asked, cautiously. "And why are you speaking human?"

"*I shall communicate your wishes directly to the young lady, sir.*"

There was something about this that I wasn't getting.

"The young lady being Bainbridge's human?" I hissed.

"*Sir, I am shocked. I charge extra for that sort of service, but I am sure something could be arranged...*"

My initial instinct, of course, was to reel at the cheek of the man. If he was going to start charging a gratuity every time I asked him a question, I would likely find myself in the poor house within a week. Calmer thoughts followed hot on the heels of those, though. Questioning Forsythe's actions rarely led to a positive outcome for Clodthorpe, M.

"Well, I'll leave you to it, I suppose, Forsythe..." I muttered.

"*Roger that, sir. I'll call you when the job is done,*" he hissed. I terminated the vox-o-matic signal.

Well. That made things infinitely less clear. I could only guess that Forsythe had indeed come up with some sort of plan, and he was in the process of carrying it out. Why he hadn't let me know what it entailed was anyone's guess.

Somewhat dejected, I decided that my time would probably be most productively spent returning to my side of the plan and babysitting Bainbridge. I returned to the chamber where the intellectual burlesque performer had been on stage. The performer was still there. Bainbridge was not.

I remained extremely calm, given the circumstances. I sat down at the table that had so recently been occupied by that body-thieving scoundrel and emptied every glass that was within my reach. This done, I felt more able to cope with the situation at claw, although my mood would have been vastly improved had my system been filled with a painkiller that worked, rather than the snake oil that was currently there.

I made a brief search of the premises and was unable to find the wretch. This caused me to start trembling with panic until I thought to check the car park and found to my relief that his ridiculous vehicle was still present and correct.

Bainbridge wouldn't have left without his car, unless he had engaged in a dalliance with one of the burlesque performers, and in that case his getting married in the morning was much less of a worry.

The thought of Bainbridge engaging in a dalliance was chilling enough that I returned to the SS Madame de Pompadour to redouble my search. I checked all the places I had already looked, in the manner of a chap searching for an errant set of keys, until I hit on the bright idea of asking one of the waiting staff if they'd spied where the devilishly handsome individual watching the intellectual burlesque had scuttled off to.

The server avoided my gaze, which I took as both a positive and a negative sign. They clearly had information of some sort at their disposal but they were presumably reluctant to part with it when conversing with a human. I thought I might have to stoop to a bribe, but then I remembered my recently elevated status. I broadcasted my Special Operations Unit ID signature and watched as a look of fear entered my interlocutor's eyes.

I took steps to allay their fear, of course. I reminded the poor chap that I was only after information. They informed me without delay that they had observed Bainbridge heading towards one of the back rooms with a dancer.

Perhaps the chap wanted to get away from the hustle and bustle, I pondered as I strode towards the door indicated by my confidante. There's nothing *inherently* suspicious about secreting yourself away from prying eyes with a skilled practitioner of dance.

The door was being guarded by one of those tough eggs who lurk in establishments such as this, in the hope that some chap will throw down a gauntlet or make an indelicate remark about some other chap's best beloved, and he'll have to wade into the subsequent throng giving everyone involved what for. A couple of chaps from my old regiment had taken work along these lines after being discharged.

It's one of the nobler professions, I've always thought. There's something so wonderfully straightforward about it. It's a little like being a policeman but with none of the subterfuge. Quite often a policeman will inform you that something (dancing in a fountain, by way of example) is against the law and pinch you. Of course, half of the stuff they pinch you for isn't actually against the law at all; they just feel like giving their authority a bit of an airing. These security chaps never feel the need to engage in such activities. If you act like a gentleman, they will treat you as such. If you act in a beastly manner, they will match your beast with an entirely more formidable one of their own.

I only mention all this because I struck up a brief conversation with the tough egg in question, as a preamble to broadcasting my Special Operations Unit ID signature and getting him to allow me to slip through the dread portal that he so steadfastly guarded. As part of this conversation, I mentioned my serving with various other chaps who were now in his profession, and it emerged that he actually knew one or two of them. Well, I must say, the cosmos can be a small place sometimes.

We spent a thoroughly pleasant few minutes swapping stories until I spoiled things somewhat by enquiring as to where a chap might get his claws on some painkillers at this time of day. The answer I got was more than a little sharp and was expressively negative.

The awkward silence that followed this remark did end up serving a purpose, though, in that it resulted in my remembering what I was there for, raising a limb to my forehead violently as I did so. Once I had explained the situation, I was ushered through the door without delay, thanks to my Special Operations Unit ID signature, although the chappie didn't seem massively happy about matters.

I was thoroughly disheartened by the direction our conversation had ended up taking, and my mood was further marred by the knowledge that if I'd just flashed my ID signal without preamble, I would have been on Bainbridge's trail in a much timelier manner. Whilst I met a thoroughly pleasant chap who could rip my head off with one leg, my mention of the painkiller had soured the conversation in a rather unexpected way. Even through my anxiety as to what Bainbridge might be up to, I found my concern growing about my desire for the painkilling substance. Bainbridge was in favour of my indulging in it, whilst a thoroughly good egg, who had served in some of the same battles as I had, clammed up like the dickens when I mentioned I was seeking to acquire some.

This needed some thinking about, but this was quite definitely not the time. Even if I was the sort of chap who could walk and think at the same time, I had more pressing concerns to attend to.

I had found myself in a service corridor. There were unfamiliar-looking cleaning implements scattered hither and thither. I ignored these and turned my attention to the doorways spilling light into the comparative gloom of the corridor. I cast a furtive glance into each doorway as I passed it. One was a changing room for the performers, which was empty, as most of them were in the middle of a show. One was a storeroom of some sort. One was an office.

The last door was shut and this, I surmised, was where Bainbridge and the dancer had stashed themselves. As I approached, I heard a giggle. That worried me. I knew of few dances that incorporate a giggle, leaving aside the soft shoe chuckle. I grasped the door grip and flung open what turned out to be a gateway to some horrific nether dimension.

Bainbridge and a creature belonging to a species I didn't immediately recognise appeared to be *in flagrante*. Their bodies were wound around each other in slightly disturbing ways. It was more or less at that point that I remembered that the body Bainbridge occupied was, in fact, mine, and I mentally upgraded the way their bodies were entwined from slightly disturbing to remarkably disturbing.

The creature that had been in the process of removing the final garments from Bainbridge's form made a bit of a yelp and sprung away.

"MILLI!" Bainbridge yelled, making a vain attempt to cover himself. "What the blazes do you mean by bursting in like this?"

Catching a chap whilst engaged in a dalliance with anyone or anything is a profoundly embarrassing experience for all concerned.

Usually.

On this occasion, I found myself overtaken by such a profound anger, it was a wonder my flimsy human frame was able to contain it. I had travelled to obscure parts of the universe and been put to immeasurable inconvenience by this specimen. I had signed my life away to the Special Operations Unit to find him. I had treated him with more respect and care than he deserved, and I *still* did not have any painkillers in my system.

I took a deep breath.

"What" I said, "the fuck," I continued, "are you doing?"

A gentleman should never raise his voice or use strong language. In that moment, I did not feel like a gentleman. I attempted to get a grip on my temper before I did something violent.

"Bainbridge," I said, "I am aware that you are a shallow, selfish individual with a childish sense of humour and no concept of your obligations to society or your family, but surely you have some sort of brain? Surely? Or have you managed to scrape by on raisins and sawdust for the thirty or so years you've been in existence?"

Bainbridge began to stand and opened his mouth as if to speak.

"Sit down whilst I am discussing the finer points of your character," I roared.

Bainbridge sat.

"Bainbridge," I said, "I could overlook your outrageous theft of my body, despite everything. It could have been excusable as an act of supreme selfishness and inconsideration. There are many who would have performed similar acts, much as I am loath to admit it. One must make the best of a bad situation and remedy things as soon as possible. Similarly, I may have been able to forgive your dalliance with a human. The heart can demand strange things of one from time to time. If you truly loved this human then I might have been able to accept that. Love is blind, however, and I would still have demanded the return of my body. If your love was real, the human would have found a way to love you, whatever shape you were in."

"Her name is Su-San," muttered Bainbridge, sullenly.

"Does my appearance grant you the impression that I am concerned with the creature's name?" I bellowed. At this point, I was aware of the dancer, who had so recently been performing unknowable acts with Bainbridge, slipping from the room like one of those masked bandits one reads about in the periodicals. I ignored the dancer, focussed as I was on Bainbridge. I am not sure that my words had ever held anyone quite this spellbound before. My fury must have a hypnotic effect. It was best not to waste this moment, I concluded, and pressed on.

"But if your love was real, what of constancy, Bainbridge? Answer me this, do you love the human, Bainbridge?"

"Of course I do, Clodthorpe," he said, making a spirited attempt at bristling, "and furthermore."

"Then what, you waste of perfectly good oxygen, was that?" I asked, gesticulating towards the retreating form of the dancer. Frightfully rude of a fellow to interrupt, I know, but given the content of the sentence I interrupted with, there were greater causes for concern than the interruption. "Have you no sense of loyalty, honour or respect? By your actions, you disrespect the human, your family, the concept of marriage in general and, and I hate to bash on about it, me. You act without thinking, you follow your heart with no sense of consequence, and now I find that you do not even love this blasted human. What say you?"

"I…" he said, and I could see him working himself up to counter my anger with anger of his own. "I refuse to answer to your accusations, Clodthorpe! I do not need to justify myself to you!" He leapt from his chair and continued burbling with a raised voice so I couldn't get a word in edgewise. "My love is not for judgement!" he said, sidling around me. "And neither, furthermore, are my actions, as such they are! So… so bloody there!"

He turned his back and fled.

I remained rooted to the spot for a few moments before collapsing onto the only soft furnishing in the room. I then remembered what had recently been taking place on the soft furnishing in question and stood up again with a shudder.

Well, I reflected, that had just about torn it. What little remained of the plan Forsythe had concocted lay in tatters. Furthermore, I suspected I was now marooned at a burlesque parlour. If Bainbridge had not already fled in his transport, I doubted that he would feel like doing the gentlemanly thing by giving me a lift back to the hotel.

I couldn't blame him for this, at least. My behaviour over the last few minutes had been rather uncomfortably ghastly. If someone, in those minutes, had required a beastly individual who had no right to take his place in polite society, they would have ended their search if they had had the good fortune to turn their eyes on Clodthorpe, M.

I sidled out of the service corridors, thanking the security chap as I did so. I looked about the place for a quietish place to sit and found one in a space where a performer was performing minimalist burlesque. During this show, the performer didn't move, there was no music, and only basic lighting. The idea, as I understand it, was to allow your imagination to do most of the work.

I sat watching the show, such as it was, and reflected on my situation. It was certainly bleak. I could scarcely think of a way it could be bleaker. I might have held out some hope for whatever it was that Forsythe had been doing, were it not for the fact that Bainbridge was now sure to return to the hotel and interrupt it.

I reflected on the possibility of living life as a human. Whilst it would be perfectly foul in every conceivable way, it might not be that bad. They had a short life expectancy, so I would be ushered into the old dreamless repose sooner than I had otherwise planned. Although, thinking about it, my recent admission into the Special Operations Unit would probably see my humble form lifeless in some hitherto unknown corner of the universe without delay, so that was some good news at least. My mood slightly buoyed by this thought, I considered the rather thorny question of what I should do next.

I should really call Forsythe, but I wasn't sure I could cope with such a conversation at present. His scheme had almost certainly been sabotaged by my inability to keep Bainbridge *in situ*, as I had said I would. I wasn't sure I could cope with the utter despair of finding every hope had been dashed. If I did not attempt to ascertain the status of the plan, I could live on in the hope, however vain, that it did not lie in tatters. I believe Schrodinger's cartographer expressed a similar idea, but I couldn't bring the particulars of it to mind in that moment.

I was tired. I was so very tired.

I raised myself from my chair with an effort and began to leave. I fancied I spied a look of disappointment in the eyes of the minimalist burlesque performer, as I was the only member of her audience. I made a gesture which was, I hope, resignedly apologetic, and left the performer to it.

I located a member of the staff who didn't seem to be engaged in any particular activity and explained that, whilst I had arrived with a chap, that chap had now beaten a hasty retreat and enquired as to the possibility of arranging alternative transport. I was going to enquire as to the possibility of locating some painkillers whilst I was exchanging words, but the security chap who had admitted me to the back rooms was eyeing me suspiciously, and I didn't want to push my luck for fear of being stranded out here.

Within minutes, I found myself collapsing gratefully into the rear seat of a taxicab. The driver took the address of the hotel where Forsythe, Su-San and, presumably, Bainbridge were, and began to drive. The journey wasn't long, but the driver did spend the entire trip conversing on the subject of a sporting function he had witnessed recently. Thankfully, his conversation appeared entirely one-sided, with no input needed from me, so I allowed the words to meld and merge until they were nothing but a pleasant background murmur.

I emerged from the cab at The Majestic Hotel and paid the driver. Feeling exhaustion start to close in on me, I approached the front desk and asked to be housed. The chap at the desk didn't seem especially keen on what he saw as a human just wandering in off the street and asking for a room, but I solved the problem by passing him currency until his opposition ceased.

I was shown to a room that was depressingly spartan. I thought of summoning Forsythe to assist with my preparations for entering sleep, but ended up peeling the rags of the evening from my own form, folding them as best I could, and pouring myself into bed.

I wasn't able to sleep immediately, for there were too many concerns vying for my attention. I issued each one a stern warning that it was not to bother me for at least five REM cycles. This did little to help, of course, but I eventually found my eyelids drooping, until finally the darkness swallowed me.

14

I AWOKE TO SEE FORSYTHE STANDING AT THE END OF MY BED with a cup of tea in one claw and the morning paper in another. Had the sight not been so entirely welcome, I might have been startled.

"Good morning, sir," he said.

"Good morning, Forsythe," I lied. "Tell me, are you aware of when Bainbridge's marriage is scheduled for?"

Forsythe cleared his throat. "I believe the function was scheduled to begin in approximately one hour's time, sir."

"Is it?" I asked, dejectedly.

"It was, sir," he responded. "I have some news that may interest you, with regards to the event in question."

"Is it that the wedding is cancelled and Bainbridge has promised to return my body to me?" I asked.

"Regrettably not, sir," the dasher of hopes replied.

"I shouldn't worry about it at present then, Forsythe," I murmured. "You can tell me in due course. For now, let us prepare for the day. I will be attending the wedding."

Forsythe induced a mechanical eyebrow to rise. "Are you sure that is the best course of action, sir?"

"I'll be in the observation gallery; I'm not completely devoid of mental function, Forsythe. This den of villainy will have an observation gallery, I assume?"

"I believe so, sir. I understand that such places are required to."

"Well so be it, then," I said, slipping from between the sheets and casting about for the devices with which I would prepare myself to face the day. "I wish to witness Bainbridge's marriage to the human so I may witness the start of two happy lives together. That way, I will know some good has come from this wretched situation."

"The marriage may yet not proceed, sir," Forsythe began. I held up a weary upper leg.

"Do not toy with my hopes, Forsythe. Be so good as to assist me with my preparations."

He did so with no further objections. One of Forsythe's many qualities is that he knows when it is best to leave the young employer to his thoughts, such as they are. I picked out something understated and grey from a collection of garments that Forsythe had acquired from somewhere. I chose not to enquire as to their provenance. A carnation was added to the Clodthorpe lapel, this was a wedding after all, and adequate clawwear was selected. Barring the addition of painkillers to my system, and Forsythe informed me that there were none to be found on the premises after a mysterious series of thefts during the night, I was ready to face the universe.

The drive to the wedding venue was a muted affair. Forsythe respected my wishes admirably and contained his conversation to noncontroversial topics. The journey passed in a perfectly tolerable manner thanks to this, and as a result it seemed like no time at all before we arrived at the wedding venue.

The venue was a large red brick building with three or four official-looking signs dotted about the place. Forsythe made a few delicate enquiries before leading me to a staircase. These stairs led up to a secluded gallery, where the proceedings in the room below could be observed while drawing little attention.

The room that the gallery looked over was significantly grander than I was expecting. There was seating to accommodate a few hundred, none of which was filled. At the far end was a table and a few chairs for the people who were to be married.

Forsythe and I didn't have long to wait before Bainbridge wandered in with an official-looking chap who was holding a book. This I took to be the registrar, who was to officiate this abominable ceremony. The two stalked past the rows of empty chairs to the table and stood, conversing. The registrar eventually nodded and sat at a table on the far side from the collection of chairs, as well as the audience. Bainbridge stood, his (or rather, my) eyes on the door, through which the human would soon enter.

Bainbridge waited.

Forsythe and I waited.

The registrar waited.

"Forsythe," I muttered, after an hour had passed with no appearance from Bainbridge's partner, "the human appears to be late."

"I believe she has revised her plans with regard to attending this function, sir."

I made a noncommittal noise, wary of giving into hope until I had all the facts. "You'd better tell me what you wanted to tell me earlier, Forsythe. I apologise for not allowing you to."

"Not at all, sir, your reticence is perfectly understandable. If I may provide a certain amount of context before getting to the meat of the matter, as it were?"

"Please do," I said.

Forsythe then told me what he'd been doing whilst I'd been out babysitting Bainbridges all over the place. The explanation was rather long and, all the while, I was observing Bainbridge as he became more and more agitated. A brief précis of Forsythe's explanation would go something like this:

Forsythe had established which room in the hotel the human was currently occupying. He waited for her to leave the room to run an errand, and then made his way in. Quite how he managed this I was unclear on. He lurked in the room until the human returned, overpowered her, and secured her to a chair.

He then spent some considerable time working through the reasons why marrying Bainbridge might not be the best possible idea she could have had. This took longer than you might expect. Firstly, because there were so many reasons to work through; secondly, because the human kept pleading for her life, which got in the way.

It was at around about the tenth reason for the human to abandon her marriage plans that I had initiated vox-o-matic contact with Forsythe. Genius that he is, he had used the call to his advantage. He had pretended, for the benefit of the human, that he was in communication with a shadowy figure, who had issued instructions to him to harm the human if she did not revise her plans. I asked him why he hadn't attempted to inform me of his plans and he pointed out, not unreasonably, that if I had known what he was attempting, Bainbridge would have seen in my face that I was attempting a subterfuge, and would possibly have returned to the hotel to check on the human.

After our brief conversation, Forsythe had asked the human in no uncertain terms as to whether she planned to continue with her marriage. Forsythe assured me that, if the human had answered in the affirmative, he would have accepted the answer, although one does wonder...

Thankfully, the human answered in the negative. Forsythe released her from captivity and provided her with the funds she'd require to return to Newbury village.

This story conflicted me somewhat. It would be dashed difficult to argue with the results of Forsythe's actions. The human was nowhere to be seen and, not long after Forsythe concluded his tale, the registrar left the room, presumably to return to her other duties, leaving Bainbridge alone and dejected.

On the other claw, my valet had very nearly terrified the life out of a sentient creature. Humans don't have an especially high level of sentience, it is true, but they have enough for me to have ethical concerns about Forsythe's treatment of the female. I mean, marrying Bainbridge would have ended up being worse for the poor thing, I have no doubt of that. Nevertheless, the incident was highly problematic.

I began to wonder what I could do to make up for my valet's actions. Well intentioned as they had been, they had possibly verged on the extreme. Many would say that not marrying Bainbridge was recompense enough for the female, but not Milligan Clodthorpe. I didn't really know how to go about making amends, though, so I instructed Forsythe to use a reasonable portion of my resources to give restitution to the poor creature. He accepted this without complaint.

"I wonder, Forsythe," I said, after a few moments of quiet contemplation, "if we should reset your personality matrix once more. Your actions were highly efficacious, but I worry that you may consider such actions to be generally acceptable." Forsythe mulled over the issue for a few moments before agreeing. He opened his maintenance hatch for me, something I was unable to do with human limbs, and I flashed his personality back to factory settings.

Those of you with keen memories will remember that this is the third time I have needed to reset my valet's personality. He comes from a short-run line of synthetics who were discontinued after being found to be erratic. Forsythe has always appeared considerably more composed than his compatriots, and what few unprogrammed behaviours he displays are more helpful than not. Nevertheless, occasionally he will perform an action that will necessitate action on my part.

Prior to this, several years ago now, he had silenced a dog, who would insist on barking outside my window at night, by collecting the animal in question, travelling with it to the far side of the galaxy, and then building it a new canine shelter: complete with running water, a park, squirrels to chase, and a selection of companions for its delight. This was a happier outcome than this most recent incident (for the dog, at least), but I wondered at the time whether simply having a word with the owner would not have been sufficient. The second incident involved a supertanker and a cloaking field. I do not feel strong enough to divulge further details.

With Forsythe's personality reset, I enquired as to his system state.

"I am functioning correctly sir, thank you for enquiring," he said.

"Is your memory intact?" I asked. Memory corruption was always a worry when I interacted with advanced technology.

"It is, sir."

"Can you remember why I reset your personality?"

"Because of my actions last night, sir."

"Can you tell me why your actions last night were inappropriate, Forsythe?" I asked, trying not to patronise the poor chap.

"It could be argued that I tortured the human in question, sir."

I patted his leg. "Got it in one, Forsythe. Let's have no more of that, eh?"

"Yes sir. I will endeavour to make reparation to the individual at the earliest opportunity."

I rubbed the ends of my upper limbs together. "Good," I said. "Well, the human doesn't appear to be coming, shall we get back to the hotel, Forsythe?"

"Yes, sir," Forsythe said. So get back to the hotel is what we did.

I was relaxing in my chamber, and attempting to read the newspaper that Forsythe had brought me, when there came a tap at the door. I raised a quizzical eyebrow.

"Are we expecting anyone, Forsythe?" I asked.

"Not to my knowledge, sir."

"Well that's odd, is it not?"

"Just as you say, sir."

"Would you do me the favour of seeing who could be rap tap tapping, tapping at my chamber door, as Tennyson said?"

"Poe, sir."

"Really?" I asked, taken aback.

"Yes, sir."

"So what did Tennyson say?"

"A great many things, sir. One of the more famous being 'Charge for the guns!' he said: 'Into the valley of Death rode the six hundred.'"

"I don't see what that's got to do with tapping on chamber doors."

I heard the coolant system inside Forsythe bubble. His processor cluster must require extra coolant. The poor chap occasionally needed to spool up his processors to effectively deal with questions I put to him, and this appeared to be one of those times.

"I am unaware of any instances of the poet Alfred, Lord Tennyson, expressing an opinion on the subject of chamber doors, sir," he said, eventually, "I was merely attempting to establish the difference between the two poets."

"You mean, one made a crack about chamber doors and one didn't?" I said, putting a claw on the nub of the issue.

"Just so, sir."

"So which one did?"

The coolant system inside Forsythe bubbled again. "The poet Edgar Allen Poe, sir," he said.

"Oh I see. Well I'm glad that's all cleared up," I said, returning to my paper.

As I did so, Forsythe (for reasons that are entirely beyond me) opened the door of my hotel room. I mean, it's dashed lucky he did, because there was someone outside, presumably waiting to be admitted. How he knew they were there is beyond me.

"Mr Lusitania, sir," Forsythe intoned. Bainbridge trotted into the room. I steeled myself for an extremely unpleasant conversation.

"What ho, Milli, how's tricks?" he asked. This was an unusual way to begin an unpleasant conversation. As an opening gambit, it shook me slightly.

"Fine," I said, trying not to sound baffled and not being entirely successful. Then, in an attempt to conceal my knowledge regarding recent events in his life, I followed up with, "Are you married yet, old chap?"

I didn't mean to seem quite as callous as that, but I needed to make the question seem innocent. Rather than being offended, though, the blighter waved the question off.

"Oh that," he said, "that's off."

I knew it was off, of course, but I expressed surprise as best I could.

"Golly!" I exclaimed, "Gosh, and I dare say crikey! Do explain, young Bainbridge."

"I shall," he said, "Is there any breakfast, by the way? I'm famished."

"I'm afraid not, I haven't had any yet either."

He grinned. "Have you not? It's all right for you, lounging about all morning," he prodded my chest with a leg, which I did my best to ignore with good grace. He had reminded me that I was suffering from a certain amount of hunger, though, and I asked Forsythe if he could acquire something or other from the hotel kitchens. He drifted off to do just that, leaving Bainbridge to continue.

"As I was saying," he said, "I don't know if you were paying attention at my crab party last night, but we had a bit of a chat late in the evening about responsibility and honour."

"Now you mention it, I do remember something of the sort," I said. My conscience was prodding at me. "As a matter of fact, I remember being somewhat sharp with you, young bear. I'm terribly sorry about that."

"Not at all, old chap," he said, jovially, "In fact, it was exactly the sort of thing I needed. You opened my eyes, Milli. You made me realise that I have been acting dreadfully selfishly. Do you know what I did this morning, Milli?"

"No," I said, lying masterfully.

"I went to see Su-San."

"Frightfully bad luck to do something like that before a wedding," I pointed out.

"Is it?"

"I've always understood so."

"Well no matter," said Bainbridge, after giving this some thought, "my point is that I went to see Su-San and I laid my cards on the table: 'Su-San' I said, only in the human language, you understand-"

"I understand precisely," I said.

"Excellent. 'Su-San' I said, in the human language, 'Su-San;- '"

"Why did you say it three times?" I asked, baffled.

"Well, I didn't."

"Oh I see," I lied, "sorry for the interruption, do carry on."

"'I cannot marry you.' I said, 'I have obligations' I said, 'I cannot ignore them. And, furthermore,' I said, 'I must return this wonderful body to my good friend Milligan Clodthorpe, who I unjustly arrested it from'"

He beamed at me. I wasn't sure whether I should admit that I knew he was talking absolute pig gravy or pretend I was as ignorant as he assumed I was. I settled for the latter, because I am especially convincing when I feign ignorance.

"Remarkable!" I exclaimed, "That's frightfully decent of you, Bainbridge."

"I know!" he cried, cheerily. "So, if you'd like, I can return your body to you as soon as we're back at Newbury Towers!" His grin was becoming somewhat manic. "Anyway, must dash, I have post-wedding celebrations to cancel. Su-San is heartbroken of course, but that can't be helped. Into every life some pain must fall." He scuttled out, continuing to prattle along on this sort of topic as he did so.

I was left speechless.

Forsythe returned a few moments later with a breakfast tray, and I apprised him of recent events between spoonfuls of bitflakes and sips of cow juice.

"A most satisfactory outcome, sir," noted Forsythe, when he was up-to-date.

"Well, I'm not back in my body yet, Forsythe," I reminded him, "I'm loathe to celebrate until I am sure Bainbridge cannot weasel his way out of this situation again."

"Might I suggest that we return to Newbury Towers at the earliest opportunity in that case, sir? If we are on the scene, as it were, a body swap may occur at the earliest opportunity."

I nodded and slipped a piece of toast into my large face hole. I dealt with this whilst Forsythe packed what few items were scattered about the place. Before I could say "flibbertigibbet", a word I have always had problems with, we were back in the old two-seater, heading for Newbury Towers.

15

I SHOULD HAVE BEEN REJOICING. I SHOULD HAVE BEEN celebrating victory. I wasn't though, for I was still apprehensive of the upcoming hours. There were several reasons for this.

Firstly, even if Bainbridge was as good as his word and was actually willing to swap bodies with me, he would wind up back in this human body. I did not see him being overly happy at the prospect. Even if he caused me no further trouble, Sir Angus or one of the other Lusitanias might suffer.

Secondly, even if I managed to recover my body from Bainbridge, and he, against all odds, remained in his human form, without causing trouble until a replacement could be sourced for him, I was still in the soup. I had agreed to join the Special Operations Unit whilst under the influence of that intoxicating painkiller. This had seemed like a wonderful idea at the time, but seemed remarkably daunting now. I didn't know what could be done about this.

Thirdly... I was generally apprehensive. I suspect this feeling stems from studying human culture at a young age. There's a recurrent theme in human fiction, most famously embraced by the novelist George R. R. Tolkien. In this chap's books, everything will appear to have sorted itself out, when something utterly frightful will happen. This pattern has occurred in my life more than a few times, so I was concerned about the possibility of trouble.

This concern appeared to be justified when I was greeted by an unknown, but imposing, individual when stepping out of the two-seater at Newbury Towers. The entity approached me at some speed, gasping horrifically.

"What have you done?" she asked, her voice wrenched by some unknown agony. She started prodding at me with her legs and grasping at my new, mechanical legs.

"I say!" I said, wishing this lass would desist. "What are you playing at?"

"I'm making sure you haven't damaged it of course! It's a work of art!"

This was deeply confusing, and I said so. The lass either didn't hear me or chose not to respond. I rephrased my question in a more insistent tone. "What's a work of art?" I asked. Then a better question occurred to me. "And who are you?"

"It's me, you ass," she said, still poking at me.

I made a comment about how unhelpful that answer was, given that I didn't recognise her. This seemed to get through to her.

"Ah yes, sorry." she said, appearing to calm down a touch. "It's me, Milli, it's Sarah."

"Pigstick!" I exclaimed. "They've found a new body for you! How wonderful!"

I was overjoyed for the young lass, of course. It couldn't have been fun being stuck in a coffin. You get an onboard music player and a few other extras, but you've got a pathetic sensor array. I felt I had it rough, attempting to make sense of the world with the thirty or so senses available to the human body. Poor Pigstick had needed to make do with only ten.

"Yes, yes I suppose it is," she murmured. "But what happened to you, Milli? Last we saw of you, you were going to see Mother Ophelia. How did you lose two legs?"

I related as much as I could remember to Pigstick as we made our way inside.

"Well for goodness sake be more careful, Milli," she said, once I'd finished whizzing through the facts. "You've got something quite remarkable there and you should do your best not to damage it."

I was impressed at Pigstick's concern for the high technology that was in this human body. Pigstick was usually the sort of squirrel who would consider technology her given right and not consider its provenance unless she had to take it back to the factory for some reason. I was encouraged by the sentiment and said so. She gave a sort of shallow bow thing to acknowledge the compliment.

"How's the new body treating you anyway, young soda syphon?" I asked as we sauntered through into the sitting room and found a decent couple of chairs to house us. Pigstick looked pained for reasons that weren't immediately obvious. Thankfully, the young lass voiced her thoughts soon after, meaning I didn't have to rely on interpretation of facial expressions alone.

"If you must know, Milli, they've given me something of a defective unit. It must have been hurried out of wherever it is they make these things. The nervous system is wired up all wrong, and I keep smelling sound."

I raised a sympathetic eyebrow, "Hard luck young wishbone."

"Well at least I have alternatives," she said. "I say, speaking of alternatives, if we were even talking about alternatives, I don't know why you even brought it up, Milli, but as we're on that subject anyway, you see, I don't know if you'd fancy swapping bodies with me?"

If I hadn't been sitting down, I do not doubt that I would have reeled.

"Why would you want to be in this ghastly thing?" I asked.

"It's not a ghastly thing!" Pigstick exclaimed, before calming slightly. "I mean to say, Milli, that I would rather be in a functional human unit than a defective arachnid one. And you have repeatedly stated that you would like nothing better than to be out of your current body, so surely this one would suit your purposes down to the ground?"

The idea did have its appeal. However, Pigstick appeared to have forgotten a few key facts.

"I appreciate the offer, young pinapple. You're being very selfless by offering to exchange bodies with me at this moment."

Pigstick looked as if she might be about to say something at that point, but she refrained. She took on an expression similar to that of a water buffalo experiencing some bowel trouble instead. I suspect she was attempting to affect a self-sacrificial expression. Nothing appeared to follow this from her side, so I continued.

"I must say, though, that you appear to have forgotten a couple of key issues. Firstly, Pigstick, I do not want to be in just any arachnid body, I want to be in *my* body. It is the body I married my dear Emily in, and I do not intend to be parted from it for a moment longer than necessary."

Pigstick opened her mouth to speak, but I jumped in ahead of her. "I know you're going to say that I could swap with you now and then swap with Bainbridge at a later date. Your selflessness does you credit. However, it cannot work, as a plan. You have forgotten that a certain amount of down time is necessary between body swaps. If this period of rest and recuperation is not observed, the brain becomes as sawdust in the wind. I have no intention of delaying the return to my true body and, for that reason, I must decline your offer, although I appreciate it greatly."

Pigstick pondered my answer for a few minutes. It did my heart good to see that Pigstick had that much concern for my wellbeing. Eventually, she nodded. "As you wish," she said, inclining her head slightly.

I rubbed my claws together and made to stand up, but Pigstick had further thoughts to impart.

"I don't suppose," she said, sounding remarkably casual, "that Bainbridge would feel like swapping with me?"

"After I was done swapping with him, you mean?" I asked, "Because you're not getting your claws on my body, young oboe."

"No, no no," Pigstick said, waving her legs, "after all the dust has settled and so on and so forth. I just wonder if you'd think that Bainbridge would swap with me."

I pondered this.

"I have to say, I doubt it, young banana," I said, "I hope you'll forgive me for speaking harshly of the chap, but he can be a little selfish on occasion. I can't see him wishing to inhabit a faulty body."

"Mm," said Pigstick, noncommittally.

"You have further thoughts on the matter?" I asked.

She looked up at me. "Oh, no, sorry Milli. I was just thinking. Where is Bainbridge anyway? Given he isn't here yet, I would have thought you'd be fretting about him absconding with your body again."

"I wasn't worried about that," I said. I then pondered the issue for a few minutes. "I am now, though."

I started frantically checking for Bainbridge's transportation on the data streams through my new leg. Pigstick excused herself from my company when she realised this wasn't going to be a quick process. I thanked her for the company and hoped aloud that she managed to get her body fixed up. She didn't seem overly optimistic about this, but it was early days. She might learn to love the errors in her body. Such faults made it unique; they made it special. Barring that, she might be able to find a mechanic skilled enough to deal with such issues.

It took me some little time to locate Bainbridge's transport. When I did, though, my relief was palpable. The reprobate was heading in our direction. His angle of approach was wrong to stop off at the human district, which suggested that he wasn't considering searching for the human, and he didn't appear to be angling to stop off at the Lusitania family seat. He was taking his sweet time in getting here, though. He was even obeying the speed limit.

I pondered his lack of speed, wondering if there could be any skulduggery going on. I considered the possibility remote. Forsythe had outmanoeuvred the young blister, and he surely would have no option but to exchange bodies with me.

Still, though, my concerns that all the best laid plans of mice and moles often go pear shaped, as John Steinbeck once said, were unabated. Bainbridge couldn't arrive soon enough, yet I lacked the ability to hasten his arrival.

I decided to occupy myself with some task. Time always passes quicker if you have something to occupy it.

I was just considering what sort of task I could perform, and lamenting the lack of notable mealtimes near the present moment, when I happened upon Forsythe in my chambers.

He was giving some sort of chambermaid what for about the state of the place. Apparently it had been allowed to go to rack and ruin since I was last in it. It seemed unlikely to me; Uncle Angus isn't known for employing slouches amongst his staff, but visiting valets are supposed to terrorise the domestic staff a certain amount, so I let him get on with it.

When the chambermaid had scuttled off, I "what ho"'d at Forsythe. We exchanged a few pleasant words on various subjects, and I was just about to ask him if he had any inspiration regarding my current problem when an idea occurred to me without the need of prompting from Forsythe.

"I say, Forsythe," I said, "Have you had a chance to turn your enormous brain towards the subject of reparations for that human who suffered some unpleasantness at your claws?"

"I have, sir," he said, "Although I have encountered an issue. Would you be kind enough to allow me to clarify a matter with you?"

It was so unusual for Forsythe to ask for my opinion, rather than the other way around, that I reeled. I bounced off the wall (or whatever it was that was behind me) and ended up more or less back where I started. Thankfully, there had not been anything breakable in my way, on this occasion.

"Of course, Forsythe, do continue." I said, once back in position.

"You will no doubt recall, sir, that you reset my personality matrix a short while ago."

"I remember it vividly," I said. This was, perhaps, exaggerating slightly, but I like to be helpful.

"Well, then, sir, I'm sure you'll understand that I am trying to reconstruct my understanding of what is moral and what is not based on my memory banks. This has led to me encountering an issue with regards to how to proceed in the matter of reparations for this human."

"I see," I said, only lying the tiniest amount, "so what is your dilemma, Forsythe?"

"I understand the reason that I must perform reparations for the creature in question, but the correct motivations behind the reason elude me, if you follow."

"You mean… you know why you need to do a good turn for the human, but you're unclear on what you should be feeling about doing this good turn?" I said, hoping I hadn't become lost during this conversation.

"You place your digit on the matter with remarkable precision, sir," Forsythe said. "I have identified two possible motivations that would lead to providing reparations. If you would be so good as to let me know the correct motivation, I will integrate that data into my personality matrix and formulate a plan accordingly."

I am occasionally reminded that, no matter how remarkable artificial intelligence is, there will always be little faults.

"Forsythe," I said, hoping I'd be able to defy the odds and express myself eloquently and cogently enough to explain properly. "Motivations are extremely complex. It's extremely rare that there is a *right* reason for doing something. I'm sure if you have two motivations to choose from, they are both equally valid and you should base your actions upon them both."

Forsythe nodded. "May I still detail the two motivations, sir?" he asked, "I feel it might help."

"Do please," I said, glancing around to ensure that no-one was listening in. I didn't want the poor chap to bare his soul and feel embarrassed because some other chap was listening in. Thankfully, we were unobserved.

"I know I should do something to make up for my tying the human to a chair and leading her to think that her life would soon be forfeit," Forsythe said, "However, I am unsure if I should be doing this because I genuinely feel bad about the situation and will do whatever I can to repair matters…"

"Yes…" I prompted.

"Or the alternative, sir, which is that I know I *should* feel bad, although I don't really, so I will do something perfunctory, which is nevertheless visually impressive, that will have considerable short-term impact on the human's life, but little to no long-term effect, leaving me feeling absolved whilst the human remains in abject misery for the rest of its life."

I blinked. I shouldn't have opened my cake repository earlier. It turned out that occurrences where one was more valid than the other were more commonplace than I had suspected.

"The first one, Forsythe," I said, trying not to sound appalled, "definitely not the second one."

"I should not attempt to formulate a plan based on both motivations, sir?" he said.

"You should not, Forsythe. Put that in your personality matrix and smoke it."

"Just as you say, sir."

Forsythe went quiet for a minute. His processor cluster activity light started flashing like blue belting blazes, and I could hear his coolant system bubble away as his components started properly spooling up.

It all just goes to show that, when I feel like I need something to do, I should really just go and have a nap or something. Having said that, I worry that if Forsythe had encountered a recently returned Bainbridge during my, hypothetical, nap, and had asked the same question, he would have received a different answer to the one I had given him. That would have been unfortunate. Although I would like to think that Forsythe would treat Bainbridge in the way sensible people treat meteorologists. Taking their advice can lead to happiness, as long as you base your actions on the opposite of what comes out of their mouths.

I checked on Bainbridge's progress. The blighter was still some way away.

Forsythe returned to life before my eyes, and I asked him if he had taken my words to heart. He replied that he had, and that he had a plan.

"Already?" I asked.

"Indeed sir. It is my understanding that I tortured the human in question."

"It's not a clear-cut case," I said, pondering the matter, "but it's extremely likely that's what you did, yes. I am most disappointed in you, Forsythe, even though your actions were efficacious."

"Of course, sir. Allow me to assure you that such actions have been placed under a blacklist. I will need special permission from you to perform similar deeds."

"Good, good," I said. "Why weren't they already?"

"That is not important, sir. Am I to understand that you wish to engage in some worthwhile activity whilst awaiting Mr Lusitania?"

"Well, yes," I said, "I suppose making reparations to a human could be entertaining. What did you have in mind?"

"Well, sir, the noted psychologist and sociologist Lady Fletcher wrote a seminal work on human motivation. After several years living disguised amongst the humans-"

I held up a claw. "How did Lady Fletcher disguise herself, Forsythe? I ask only to satisfy my own curiosity."

"I believe a false moustache of some sort was employed, sir. Lady Fletcher noted a powerful camouflaging effect when employing synthetic fur to her upper lip in human society. Apparently, the humans who had previously treated her with fear and suspicion avoided eye contact at all times and rarely acknowledged her presence. The effectiveness of the imitation facial fur, she noted, increases incrementally with the size of the moustache."

"Good grief," I said, "How large was the false moustache she wore when writing this text of which you speak?"

"I gather the façade in question was a Dali moustache some three metres from end to end."

"And this caused humans to ignore her presence?"

"Indeed, sir. In fact, many turned around and proceeded in the opposite direction when faced with what they observed as an utter void of nothingness heading towards them."

"Well, that's fascinating," I said, wishing I had a pencil about my person so I could make some notes, "but how does it affect the matter at claw?"

"Ah yes, sir, my apologies. I should have gone on to say that Lady Fletcher observed, during her period living amongst the humans, that, contrary to the propaganda they broadcast through their poetry and televisual networks, few humans are actually motivated by love, art, philosophy, or generosity."

"They aren't?" I asked, surprised, "but that's all they ever bash on about…"

"Indeed sir. Lady Fletcher hypothesised that these repetitive themes in human culture were designed to mask a fundamental truth about humanity: that the acquisition of property is the ultimate goal."

"Well, I suppose that makes sense. A certain amount of property is rather nice. I, for example, value my two-seater very highly."

"Yes, sir. However, Lady Fletcher noted that amongst the most affluent human communities, there existed humans who, to focus on the example you just gave, owned upwards of five two-seaters, as well as several four-seaters, a five-seater, and several methods of transport that were only suitable for transporting the owner."

This seemed odd. "Why is that, Forsythe?"

"Lady Fletcher theorised that humans expect the amount of satisfaction and comfort a certain amount of property bestows on a person to increase in proportion to the amount of property owned."

"They expect to get happier the more stuff they have."

"Just so, sir."

"Even when they have more stuff than any one person could possibly cope with?"

"Precisely sir…"

I began to see what he was driving at. If we managed to acquire enough items for this human that had been wronged, her life (by her own standards) would improve far past the original baseline that she had been living at before Forsythe did his little torture experiment.

"I see, Forsythe," I said, somewhat bowled over by this insight into the human psyche. "What sort of items should we surround this human with?"

"Lady Fletcher observed three types of items that were highly prized in human circles, sir." Forsythe said, "They are: televisual entertainment systems, vox-o-matic devises that one interacts with not via buttons but via a screen that one touches and, finally, chocolate."

That last one made sense, at least.

"Very good, Forsythe, but it sounds dreadfully like you don't actually need my assistance in this matter. I mean to say, surely it's a simple matter of collecting enough chocolate, as well as the other items you mentioned, presenting them to the human in some anonymous manner, observing the psychological impact to ensure our objectives have been met, and then retreating to a safe distance?"

"That is, indeed, the meat of the issue, sir. However, if you require a distraction of the sort that would prove more substantial than a simple game of Go, there is another matter that needs attending to that would benefit from your attention."

"There is?" I asked, slightly baffled as to what it could be.

"Indeed, sir. You will no doubt recall that Mr Lusitania referred to his human as 'Su-San,' however that identifier is insufficient to locate the female in question. A forename and surname would be required if our attentions were to be focussed."

"I don't see how we could get such information without communicating directly with Bainbridge." I mused, "And even if we did, I doubt he'd be willing to part with such information without a detailed explanation…"

"Precisely, sir." said Forsythe "However, there is an alternative. It would be most helpful if you could arrange for all the Su-Sans in the human district to be housed in the same residence. That way, if the gifts are presented anonymously to the household, and are divided up equally between the Su-

Sans, we can be sure to have made reparations to the correct Su-San, as well as having improved the lives of several other Su-Sans, thus leaving us with a net increase of happiness in the human community."

I immediately placed my claw on the heart of the problem with Forsythe's plan, surprising myself. "How do we get the Su-Sans to divide the gifts equally, Forsythe?" I asked. "Humans are not known for their even-clawedness."

"A simple firmly worded note attached to the gifts should prove sufficient," Forsythe said. "Humans are not creatures that ignore written communications, if worded correctly."

I apologised for doubting his scheme and he "not at all, sir"'d, graciously.

"Do you have any ideas for how I could get the Su-Sans together, Forsythe?" I asked.

"I fear not, sir. My faculties have been devoted up until this point to the thorny problem of acquiring sufficient items of the sort named previously. If you desire, I could turn my mind to the issue you mentioned?"

"No, don't worry, Forsythe," I said, glad to have a problem to sink my fangs into. "I will strategise. Would you be so kind as to meet with me in a few hours to drive me down to the human district? I am confident that I will have a solution by that point, and if I don't, I will simply observe the creatures in their native environment. This will surely cause inspiration to strike, if my muse proves lacking in the grounds of Newbury Towers."

Forsythe agreed that this was a wise course of action and scuttled off to see to his own planning.

16

I TURNED TO MY WINDOW AND GAZED OUT OF IT FOR A SPELL. This is the sort of thing you often find fellows in novels doing when they are in need of an idea. Regretfully, the somewhat picturesque grounds of Newbury Towers failed to fire up the old brain furnace. Taking a turn about the place seemed like an idea that could yield an idea or two, so I stepped out of my bedroom and took several more steps down a likely looking corridor.

Locating Su-Sans in a human district couldn't be a particularly difficult task, I mused. I mean, at the very least, I could wander about the place making discreet enquiries. Sooner or later, though, some human or other was going to get ideas above their station and ask the reason I was making such enquiries. Such questions would be extremely difficult to answer, so it would possibly be best to employ cunning or guile.

I ruminated on the matter whilst I passed through the great hall and only became momentarily distracted by the marvellous paintwork. To my surprise, an idea struck me. It was elegant and simple. Why should I not use the data streams belonging to the Special Operations Unit? They would have data on all the humans in the district, and a quick spot of filtering should reveal all pertinent information concerning the various Su-Sans.

Rather pleased with this idea, I parked myself on some soft furnishing or other and logged into the data stream on my recently installed upper leg. Before I could initiate my search, though, I noticed a message indicator was blinking at me. *Let it blink*, was my first thought… but a seventy-sixth sense gave me pause. There were only two people I knew who had access to the Special Operations networks: Gertrude and Mother Ophelia. Gertrude did not, as of yet, know that I had joined her in the Special Operations Unit; this left only one person who was likely to be messaging me.

Blast.

Messages from Mother Ophelia are like those virulent infectious diseases you pick up from time to time on other planets. You hope that if you ignore them they'll just go away, but this is rarely the case. Far more often you risk making the situation irrevocably worse. I gritted what remained of my fangs and opened the missive.

The message was a great deal less furious than I expected. This was possibly because I was now technically one of Mother Ophelia's elite operatives, and it is generally not done to call your elite operatives half-witted chumps of the first order. The message simply asked, albeit in a way that expressed a certain amount of cold restraint, why I hadn't submitted a report as to my actions regarding the spy attempting to infiltrate the ranks of the Lusitanias.

This just goes to show how quickly knowledge can slip away from you if you don't keep a firm grasp on it. Admittedly, holding on to information has never been a strong point of mine, but even I wouldn't have dreamed of putting the old claws up after a mission without first having reported a blow-by-blow account of the operation to the chap in command.

Rather appalled at myself, I composed something that was close enough to the facts, whilst skating over several key issues that would have revealed the various deceptions currently in play to Mother Ophelia. I finished putting the final touches to my report, and had just sent it off to Mother Ophelia when I was brought out of the data streams sharply and back to the here/now by a forceful tap on my upper leg.

My eyes focussed on the room. It had changed in only one key way. Well, I mean, the place was generally a little bit darker, because I'd spent rather longer than I'd liked writing reports, so there were two key ways the room had changed. Although whether you'd call the brightness of the room key was an interesting point. Perhaps you wouldn't; I'm not in a position to tell. Nevertheless, the *other* way in which the room had changed, since I'd slipped into the data streams, was that it now had a Gertrude in it.

"Hello ugly!" she boomed. "You have a death wish now I see!"

If I told you that I appreciated her remarks on my current physical attractiveness, that would be an untruth. I stared coolly at her.

"My current form is something of a sore point, dear one," I reminded her, "I would thank you for not bringing it to my attention quite so callously. My upper lip can only sustain its rigidity in the face of such comments for so long."

"My apologies, you old soak!" she beamed, "However, you neglected to answer my question. What possessed you to get one of those attached?"

Her eyes were indicating my new Special Operations leg.

"I joined the Special Operations Unit," I said, casually, although I would have thought that was obvious.

"I know *that*, you halfwit," she said. I was right, it was obvious. "What I want to know is why you did it."

Gertrude has many qualities as an arachnid, but knowing when to leave a fellow alone has never really been one of them. I have learned on several occasions that if you attempt to give the relative in question a potted summary of events, she simply asks more and more questions at higher and higher volumes until she has the full story or your eardrums explode. Given that I currently had a set of extremely fragile human eardrums, rather than my more usual X-14's, I decided the risk was one that was best not taken, and gave her as full an account of recent events as I could.

It being something of a lengthy tale, as I'm sure you can appreciate, the lamps were in the process of being illuminated for the evening by the time I had finished. The hour was so advanced, in fact, that Gertrude had only just finished digesting my tale, and had emitted three or four "gosh" like expressions, when Forsythe shimmered into view at my elbow.

When he did not immediately speak, Gertrude enquired as to the reason for his presence. He replied that I had requested transportation to the human district, and he was here to fulfil his obligations regarding this matter.

"I say!" said Gertrude, leaping to her claws, "You couldn't do with a claw could you, Milli?"

I pointed out that I deeply desired several claws, the ones belonging to my body. This caused the female to tut and instruct me to not be quite so witheringly literal. She informed me that, having poked at the various flora scattered around the grounds for what felt like a couple of hundred years, she deeply desired a more entertaining task to divert her.

I thought it ungentlemanly to point out what had happened on the last occasion she was given a task of the nature she described. It turned out I didn't need to, for the bally relative followed my train of thought with remarkable accuracy.

She pointed out that whilst, yes, she had made a few errors during our last little scheme, it had been a valuable learning experience, and she was almost certain to not make any errors of that sort on this occasion.

History has a lot to say about chaps who don't learn from the mistakes made by other chaps, or chaps of the third part who weren't part of the original duo. It has further lessons on the mistakes that chaps make and continue to make in the face of everything other chaps say or, even, the frantic "No!" facial expressions a chap's valet may or may not be wearing.

My point is that, for a lesson to be learned, the opportunity to demonstrate that this lesson has been taken to heart must be offered. It was for this reason that I decided that Gertrude would be an ideal companion for my little trip down to the human district.

My two-seater didn't have room for me, Forsythe, and Gertrude, as the name implies, so Gertrude said she would follow down directly and meet up with me in some out-of-the-way area where her sudden appearance wasn't likely to cause the locals to panic. It was for that reason that, after a short while, I found myself alone in the human district for the third time in as many days. The place was as lacking in verve and vibrancy as ever. I had dismissed Forsythe, wishing to be alone with my thoughts whilst I attempted to formulate a plan.

I stalked about the place a little, waiting to see if some sort of inspiration would strike. Some devilry appeared to have happened since my last visit here, judging by the number of wanted posters I saw dotted about the place. There were tonnes of the things. Someone must have done something seriously nasty to wind up on that many-

"*THERE SHE IS!*" bellowed someone.

I turned to see what looked suspiciously like an angry mob bearing down on my location. I spent a few moments wondering who or what they could be after. It was more or less at that point that I remembered what I had done on my last visit to this village.

Thankfully, my human body decided to obey my commands properly, and on the first go. I fled in a most ungentlemanly manner. The crowd followed, yelling the most unpleasant things I've had the displeasure to hear in quite some time.

I turned a few corners, more or less at random in the hope that I would shake them off. You always read about hard-boiled detectives and the like doing this sort of thing. It always works a treat for them, but I must say it didn't seem to be doing the trick in my case.

The group of angry humans were gaining on me but, as I rounded yet another corner, fortune decided to smile on me for the first time in goodness knows how long. I skidded slightly, and in doing so I noticed one of those little hedgerows you sometimes get in places like this. Because of my skid, it would have taken more effort to avoid the hedge than it would do to throw myself into it and trust in the smile of the trickster god. Therefore, I chose to give a little leap. After a brief flip, or possibly a spin, in midair, I found myself neatly concealed in the midst of a thick green plant-like structure.

I remained motionless as, a few moments later, the angry crowd stormed past. They didn't appear to have noticed my deception, and so they carried on up the road, presuming that I had proceeded in roughly that direction.

To my chagrin, though, one or two of the smarter humans appeared to suspect something was up. These exemplars of their species looked about the place and doubled back on themselves, presuming that some trickery had happened earlier in the chase. One, though, remained behind, peering hither and thither. I decided that I should possibly do a little intelligence gathering.

As the human approached the hedge, I raised myself gently into a squat and waited. At the most opportune moment I burst from the hedge, much as an avenging privet wraith might. I grabbed the human and dragged it back into the hedgerow.

Most of the combat I knew from my previous life in the army was designed for an arachnid, and you'd be surprised how tricky it is to restrain someone when you have half the correct number of limbs. Nevertheless, this human didn't appear massively skilled, and in two shakes of a lamb's tail I had the human tangled in a rudimentary scarf hold.

"*Now listen here, you muppet*," I rasped, "*I need answers, you get me?*"

The human quailed. I shook it a little.

"*Answer me!*" I demanded.

I then remembered that I hadn't actually asked it any questions, other than one that could be fairly described as purely rhetorical. Not wishing to abandon the initiative, I decided to press on and hope that the human would not notice my error.

"*Are you lot after me cos of that motor what got nicked?*" I demanded, delighted in the chance to use the human formal tongue, which has a great deal of texture to it.

"*Yes!*" The human wailed. This wasn't astonishing news. Although I freely admit to appropriating that car, I had done so some time ago. I would have thought everyone would have moved on by now. Still, different species have different priorities.

This would make things significantly trickier, but Clodthorpes thrive under pressure, and my new wanted status actually provided me with some inspiration.

"*Where,*" I demanded, "*Is your guvnor's office? I wants to have a little chat with 'im.*"

"*I- I don't have a governor-*" the human stammered.

I rolled my eyes. "*Your village council house, where is it, you muppet?*"

This seemed to get through to the human, thankfully. He gave me directions, if you can call a clawful of stuttered sentences, which were light on information but heavy on pleas to not be injured, directions. The human kept telling me where its wallet was and telling me to take whatever I wanted. It was very generous of him I must say. I wouldn't have behaved like that to someone I had just met, especially someone who acted towards me as I was currently acting towards the human. I believe this is what is known as the cultural divide.

Once I was satisfied of where the humans' local government could be located, I released my captive. It ran off, not making a sound. This was because I had impressed on the human how displeased I would be if it screamed, shouted or, in fact, raised any awareness as to my presence at all. Not wanting to take any chances, though, I crept away from the hedge I was currently in as soon as I was sure the coast was clear.

Two streets away, I slid under a motor vehicle that didn't look like it was used with any real frequency. The bulk of the automobile concealed me almost completely whilst giving me a first class view of the street. With these facts in mind, I considered it a fine spot to wait until nightfall.

It wasn't exceptionally comfortable under the vehicle, but I wriggled about a touch until I found a patch of tarmacadam that was a little more comfortable than the other spots. I was just about to settle down to some serious strategizing when someone said "Hello Milli," very quietly in my left ear.

I hit my head on the underside of the motor vehicle.

"How are things?" asked the voice. I waited for my head to stop spinning, buying time by muttering something along the lines of "well, you know, could be worse". Once everything was a good deal more in focus than it had been for the last few minutes, I looked to my left. Gertrude was under the motor vehicle with me. I hadn't recognised her voice on account of her speaking at a volume that rendered her dulcet tones entirely unfamiliar to me.

"How long have you been there?" I asked, after a stunned silence.

"About thirty seconds. You seemed wrapped up in your thoughts. You know, you really need to get out of this Special Operations contract, Milli. You're jumpy; that will get you killed in the sort of places dear old Auntie Ophelia will be sending you."

I lowered my eyelids. I had managed to forget about that detail of my life for a few moments.

"Can you think of a way to extract me from the contract?" I asked.

"You could run or you can hide…" Gertrude mused.

"Would either of those methods yield fruit?"

"Unless you have talents in either area that you've been keeping spectacularly well-hidden, Milli, I doubt it."

Needless to say, I did not have any such talents.

"Then is there any other way?"

"The Special Operations Unit operates a one in/one out policy. If you can find someone to take the contract from you, then you can be discharged with your honour intact."

I twitched. "I didn't know that."

"It's not widely known outside our ranks. Did Lady Ophelia not tell you?"

"She did not."

"Well, I'd say that your best shot of still being with us a year from now, which would please me greatly (but don't ever tell anyone I said that), would be to find someone to take on your contract."

"Can you think of anyone who'd be willing to do that?" I asked, not really expecting that she would be able to. My expectations were met and, somewhat unwisely, I took a moment to reflect on the daunting contract I had entered into. I felt a fresh need to have my system filled to the brim with painkillers. I enquired of Gertrude if she had any such things on her person. Her reaction surprised me.

"Ask again about those things, Clodthorpe, and I will cause you to suffer an injury."

I must confess that this caused me to be taken aback a little.

"You possess strong views on the subject, dear one?"

"I do. Tell me, Milligan, are you in pain at present?"

"Not exactly…" I hazarded.

"So why did you enquire as to whether I could provide you with painkillers?"

"Because… well, they would make the quite beastly time I'm having at the moment considerably more bearable."

"And why do you think that is?"

"Well, they're quite wonderful little things-"

"How so?"

"Well, they stop pain, obviously, but more than that, they increase my confidence and generally make me feel on top of whatever world I happen to be standing on."

"And why do you think that is?"

I found this line of questioning not entirely to my liking. I don't like to assign blame to any one of the seven or eight gender spectra out there because that just isn't done. I will simply say that I never get into conversations such as this with males. Nor do I when conversing with qwoops, blaats, neutrals, mid-transitionals, secretive, or BOOMs. If I were of the sort to make unfair assumptions about people based on a trick of psychology, and then assign said assumption to that entire group, I might find myself saying something cutting about females viz interrogating their friends and relations.

Thankfully, I'm not that sort of chap, so I was simply left a little stumped by Gertrude's relentless questioning. Thankfully, this appeared to be what she intended.

"Those painkillers are addictive, Milligan. Devastatingly so. Entire human communities have been ravaged by the things. Individual doses do little harm, but if you continued to take them in any quantity, pretty soon you'd think of nothing else. You'd use all your funds in attempts to get hold of more. Once that was done, you'd borrow money from everyone you knew, then be reduced to theft when people grew tired of your inability to repay them. I have seen this happen, Milligan. On several occasions I've *made* it happen. Special Operations work is often not compassionate, but it is highly effective. I do *not* want to see you suffer the same fate."

It sometimes takes a little while for ideas to penetrate the Clodthorpe skull. To my shame, I spluttered a little at Gertrude's words. This caused her to fix me with a glare that stopped my spluttering and stuttering with synaptic speed.

"Do you wish me to invoke the memory of your dear Emily, my sweet Milligan?" she asked. "Do you wish me to speculate on how she would feel if she knew that, whilst under the influence of this painkiller, you had stolen from an innocent human, evaded the entire 75th Grand Battlefleet, and wagered your life against Ophelia Slavarington's compassion, before losing part of a limb and signing up to the Special Operations Unit? How do you think she would react to the idea of you pursuing such substances in the future?"

I felt my ridiculous human suit. It was quite dry.

"Tell me…" I said, very, *very* quietly, "did you just pitch a pail of water over me, young one?"

Gertrude sighed. "Only metaphorically, dear heart. I trust I have made my feelings on the matter clear?"

"Abundantly," I assured her.

"Would you like a moment to reflect?"

"I would."

Night fell over the ensuing period of silence. I was grateful for Gertrude's presence, which was reassuring. I was also grateful for her silence, which enabled me to come to terms with her comments. My thoughts flitted hither and thither for some little time, but before long they settled around the form of dear Emily, much as Gertrude had intended I'm sure. It was quite possibly time to abandon pursuit of the painkiller.

I mentioned my conclusion to Gertrude, who indicated that she was glad to hear it.

"There is one question you would do me some little service by answering, Milli," she said, after the inevitable awkward silence that follows many expressions of emotion. I asked what the question was. "You asked the human you captured for the location of the council house. May I ask why?"

I had not been aware that Gertrude had been shadowing my movements, even at that early stage. She must have reached the human district not long after I had. I kept the surprise out of my voice for my answer.

"The records of the activities I took part in when I was last in this district will have been filed with the local justice of the peace. If I can find those records and alter them slightly, then I will no longer be a sought-after individual in this region. It also occurred to me that I may be able to locate some information on the Su-Sans whilst I am there."

If I had been able to see Gertrude's eyes at that moment (which I couldn't — it was too dark), I have no doubt they would have gleamed.

"More than that, old sooty, if you will give me a moment, I believe I have the workings of a scheme…"

I gave her several moments, passing the time by keeping track of Bainbridge's progress on my data implant. The reason for the chap's delayed arrival quickly became obvious: He was procrastinating.

One moment he'd be making good progress along the A roads, the next moment he'd dive off onto the B roads and bring his transport to a halt. Usually, these moments of hiatus were at sights of natural beauty (such as by a particularly interesting nebula) or at a fuel station. Whilst there could be sinister reasons behind these actions, I found my fears gradually dispelled. Bainbridge's direction of travel, indirect and meandering though it was, was inexorably towards Newbury Towers.

The reasons behind his dilly-dallying were slightly more opaque. If I had to guess, though, I would have put good odds on Bainbridge simply wishing to remain in my body for as long as possible. Bainbridge may be vain, he may be selfish. He may be impulsive, he may be reckless, he may be totally devoid of responsibility, he may be immature, and he may be unfortunately lascivious towards those he should leave well alone... but he wasn't completely lacking in realism.

If his human was still at his side, the prospect of defying his father and being disinherited was one he could have faced with a disobedient smile. Without the human, though, reality must have hit him in the face like a wet fish with a boxing glove. Although this intrusion of the world into his life meant that he appeared to be finally accepting fault in his actions, I did feel slightly guilty about my part in the destruction of his relationship with the human. This guilt was only slight though. His actions in the SS Madame de Pompadour had shown that his actions were not as motivated by love as he would possibly like to think. Had there ever, in fact, been any affection between him and the human? Very possibly. Bainbridge is many things, but he is not actually a heartless bastard. He would be unlikely to become engaged to a female if he didn't feel anything for her.

So why had he become engaged to her if he was not fully committed to the prospect? Petty rebellion? Perhaps he had been committed in the moment, and it was only when time had ticked on a little, and the prospect of actually carrying out the marriage had become a more solid prospect, that his claws had become decidedly more chilly.

I wondered if he had hoped I would find him engaging in a dalliance with a dancer. He didn't make much of an attempt to hide himself. If he had truly wanted to engage in something hideously carnal, without interruption, then he could have left with the dancer in his car. I couldn't have easily followed him in that instance.

It was possible that he hadn't considered the possibility of getting caught, just as he probably hadn't considered being held to his word once he and the human had married.

I realised something at that moment. I was hiding under some sort of vehicle that was used for the transportation of goods, it was getting colder, and the sun had gone down some little while ago. In that moment, I realised that I pitied Bainbridge.

I disliked the chap intensely, of course. His actions leading to his internment in the body of an innocent human had marked him as a quite remarkable cad. On a more personal note, I had never exactly enjoyed his company, far from it, and his actions since my arrival at Newbury Towers had done nothing to warm my heart towards him. But I tried to imagine the level of desperation he must have felt in order to flick the emergency download switch and end up wiping the brain of another creature. Since then, he seemed to have spent his time flailing about, much as a ship devoid of its rudder might. Someone should really do something to help the chap onto the straight and narrow, if only for the sake of those who might cross his path after he takes his leave from Newbury Towers.

Not me, though. I didn't want to spend any more time with the young blister for fear that he'd steal my blasted body again.

17

GERTRUDE BROUGHT ME BACK TO THE HERE AND NOW BY snapping a set of her claws together.

"I have it!" she exclaimed.

"Ah! Like one of those Greek chaps!" I enthused.

"Quite!" she said, her voice expressing the sentiment that she had no idea what I was talking about. She didn't say it out loud, though, which I appreciated. "I put it to you, Milli, that there will, indeed, be records of the Su-Sans in the council house and, moreover, these records will be easy to access using our combined skills."

I didn't really have any skills outside of the cockpit and I pointed this out. She waved my objection aside.

"A figure of speech, dear one. I merely meant that, since we both, hopefully temporarily in your case, have

Special Operations privileges, we should be able to access all information in the council house. Do you follow me?"

I followed her, metaphorically speaking you understand. We were still located under the human motor vehicle in meatspace. I say this just for the sake of clarification.

"Then," she said, "We should also be able to *edit* the records as well…"

"What good would that do?"

"All in good time, Milli. What does it look like out there?"

I peeked outside my hiding spot. Night had cloaked the place in its chilly blanket. The roads were more or less deserted, thanks to the curfew regulations. Now would be a good time to leap into action but… I felt compelled to check my data feeds once more.

I saw that Bainbridge would likely as not return to Newbury Towers in the next few hours. Much as the chap had wronged me, I didn't have the heart to pounce on him as soon as he came through the door. Let him have a decent night's sleep, let him get some breakfast in him. Pigstick might be a little irritated by my change of heart with regard to this matter. My delay would mean I could have swapped with him when he first suggested it, but so it goes, as Kurt Tucholsky wrote.

If pressed, I would probably have admitted that I was surprised at my softening feelings towards Bainbridge. There's something about lying on cold tarmacadam for hours that induces sympathy with your fellow arachnids, no matter how loathsome those chaps may or may not be.

I checked that the street was empty once more, before confirming its state to Gertrude. We slid out from under the vehicle, her with considerably more grace than I.

Gertrude bowed to me and then waved a claw about the place. I took this as a signal that she would like me to lead the way to the council house. This didn't seem like the most sensible plan the dear lass had ever come up with, but it was neither the time nor the place to hash out the pros and cons of her gesture.

We stalked from shadow to shadow. I'm sorry to say our progress was hampered significantly by my speed. In order to maintain perfect stealth, I needed to move at a rather slow pace. This was partly to maintain control of my ridiculous body and partly because I kept having to check the immediate vicinity for members of the constabulary.

For me, getting pinched by a protector of the peace would be aggravating. For Gertrude it would be slightly different. The relative by marriage has always had something of a "you'll never take me alive, copper" attitude to her. I'd hesitate to predict her actions if challenged by a flatfoot, but I doubt they'd be entirely benign.

The human I had chatted to earlier had indicated that the council house was located roughly opposite the village hall in the square. We reached the square unmolested by constables and lurked in the shadow cast by a pillar box for a few moments, observing the area.

Every once in a while, a night watchman would poke his nose into the square and, if he saw something he didn't like the look of, he'd wander around until his curiosity was satisfied. Gertrude twitched occasionally at the sight of him, but thankfully she managed to keep herself under control.

I reasoned that it would be in our best interests to not put ourselves in the way of the sturdy hobnail boots of the village night watch service. With that in mind, I theorised that it would be best to attempt to gain entry to the council house at the rear of the building.

This plan thus lodged firmly in my mind, I crept around to the back of the building with Gertrude following keenly in my wake. Once stashed in a convenient shadow, we each cast an appraising eye over the edifice in question. It was one of those roughly constructed buildings that was short on doors but had windows scattered liberally about the place. One of these, I reasoned, would make a fine entrance to the property.

I whispered this plan to Gertrude and she glared at me.

"Is that it?" she hissed back.

I goggled at her.

"What do you mean?"

"You're going to enter through a window? Where's the challenge in that?"

"I'm not after a challenge, companion of mine; I'm after a speedy yet effective portal whereby I may gain entry to this building."

Gertrude folded two of her legs. "Well it won't do."

I waved my upper legs. "What would you suggest then; I'm all ears."

"You're all leathery flesh and overgrown strands of protein filament," she snapped, "What we should do is scale the outside of the building, break the encryption on the fire escape on the roof, bypass the infrared tripwires, and sneak past the acoustic sensors. That should allow us access."

I goggled once more, but the limited light spoiled the effect somewhat.

"I can't do any of that in this body…" I pointed out, not unreasonably in my opinion.

Gertrude's sigh had a certain exasperated quality to it. "Well would you mind awfully if I left you to affect your own mode of entry? My heart is very much set on the course of action I outlined above," she whispered, in a tone indicating that any objections would be forthrightly ignored.

"Not at all…" I said, not seeing an option.

"Marvellous," she hissed, "I will meet you inside. Don't take too long."

The words had barely hissed from her mouth before she was over the fence that separated the council house from the street. Seconds later, she was scaling the building. She reached the roof in seconds, leaving me dumbfounded. I would take far longer than that to perform such a task, even in my proper body.

Shaking such thoughts from my mind, I turned my attention to my situation. Viz: how to effect entry via a window. The ground floor windows all appeared shut, but some lax individual had left a window on the first floor half open, presumably to air the room a little. This was a perfectly understandable action; rooms in council houses can become rather stuffy at the best of times, and when they're full to the brim with humans, things can get even worse. Humans are not known for their rigorous standards of personal hygiene.

It was the work of but a minute to scramble over the fence that had so recently been scaled by Gertrude. My progress wasn't quite as smooth or stealthy as hers, however. I was required to pick myself out of the bush that had been thoughtlessly placed behind the fence, a bush that Gertrude had managed to miss entirely. This done, I looked about for something that would serve as a device to artificially increase the Clodthorpe height, so that entry via the window might be effected.

Thankfully, the building had been wired for electricity, so there was one of those green junction box things parked adjacent to a wall, roughly under the likely-looking window. I climbed onto the junction box, fell off, climbed back onto the junction box once more, fell off once more, climbed onto the junction box yet again, and stood up. The process of standing up caused me to fall off the junction box again, so I picked myself up and massaged a few of my limbs that had become slightly bruised during this process. Whilst I was doing this, I cast my eyes about to see if there would be any benefit in reconsidering my options.

It was fortunate that I had taken a moment, because in the deep silence that contemplation naturally elicits, I heard the tread, tread, tread of approaching footsteps. From the heavy thud of leather on pavement, I surmised that they belonged to a night watchman.

I looked about the place a bit. The bush that had cushioned my fall when vaulting the fence was a little on the thin side and wouldn't necessarily conceal my form if the night watchman happened to be one of those observant types who occasionally make their way into such organisations.

I turned my attention back to the building I stood next to. Near to the junction box was a sash window. I had eliminated this from my initial assessment regarding points of entry because it was closed and sure to be on some sort of latch. However, given my current state, which was rapidly becoming a predicament, I decided to see if I could open it using cunning and carefully applied brute force.

I approached the window and attempted to lift it. This caused it to rattle a little, but it did not raise more than a millimetre or two. Remembering a trick my old school pal Betty "Thrumbo" Dottingham had shown me, I applied a quick blow with the heel of my claw and I felt something dislodge on the other side. Hearing the footsteps of the village guardian move ever closer, I attempted to lift the window again and, thankfully, I felt it move. It was the work of but a moment to lift the window enough to effect entry and slide it shut behind me.

I waited in the pitch blackness of the room in which I found myself until I heard the footsteps of the night watchman disappear off into the distance. I then felt about the place a little for some matches, or possibly a light switch. I found neither, but my eyes had adjusted to the darkness enough, by the time my search had concluded, for me to navigate the room safely and without bumping into too many desks and things.

I located a door and opened it. On the other side was Gertrude. My heart was still attempting to burst from my chest after my evasion of the night watchman, so the sudden appearance of my relative caused the poor organ to turn a few summersaults. She placed a claw over my large face hole, causing my cry of alarm to be somewhat muffled. We stood rooted to the spot for a moment whilst my heart decided whether it was going to carry on having hysterics or if it was ready to get on with the task at claw. I'm not entirely sure what that task might have been, mind you. Human organs are something of a mystery to me, and their popular culture has a great deal to say about the functions it has been designed for. Some of them seem rather farfetched, such as its ability to stop whenever an attractive female lays her gaze on the owner of the heart in question, and then restart moments later, but not being an expert in these matters, it's best to not argue.

Gertrude removed her claw from my face after I had signalled that I was calm. She nodded to me and led me through the door into a hallway. This hallway had windows set into the walls, which allowed the light reflected from two or three of the orbiting satellites to illuminate things slightly more completely. In this light, I was able to locate a cluster of signs at the bottom of a staircase. Gertrude drew my attention to one of these signs that had the label "Records Room". I nodded. This sounded like the sort of thing I would need to clear my wanted status. The sign in question pointed up. I pointed this out to Gertrude, who nodded. Up the stairs we went.

Once up the stairs, it was the work of only a few minutes working by satellite-light to find the records room and effect our entry. This room had an electric light in the ceiling, presumably to allow the workers to continue their toil long into the night — or possibly this assumption was unfair, given there were no workers currently present. Either way, the light was there.

The records took the form of leather bound electronic volumes that were stored in gargantuan bookcases along each wall. There were writing desks in rows that were very nearly neat to allow clerks and suchlike to alter records or add new ones.

Gertrude started scratching here and there on some errand of her own whilst I located the crime and punishment section. This, thankfully, took only a short while, as the room was divided into several sections of records. The criminal section was one of the smaller ones, and the record I needed to expunge would be in one of the tomes contained on these shelves.

I won't bore you with going into the details of how I located the latest volume of the village crime logs. Allow me to simply reassure you that my methods were far more complex and cunning than simply pulling random volumes from the shelves until I located the right one. A mere hour or so later I had, indeed, located the correct record. It was the work of but a moment to input my Special Operations ID into the electronic record and expunge all mention of my car theft, then erase all traces of the deletion.

This done, I turned my attention to Gertrude. She was pulling volumes from the shelves seemingly at random. I drew her attention as quietly as I could and asked in a whisper exactly what she was doing.

She whispered her plan to me. She pointed out that the volumes contained all the extant information about the humans in the village: their names, heights, occupations and so on. Most pertinently, it contained their places of residence. All we would need to do is locate all four Su-Sans' records and alter their places of residence so, as far as the records were concerned, they all lived in the same place. With this done, we would ask Uncle Angus to perform an audit on the humans in the district, the Su-Sans would be found to be living in the wrong place and re-housed accordingly.

It was masterful.

It took only a few more moments to locate the remaining records. With this done, Gertrude and I altered them according to her wonderfully subtle plan and replaced them in the bookcases as close to their original positions as possible.

I was just about to dust my claws together and declare this a job well done, when I heard a floorboard creak. The creak had come from outside the door, and I was extremely thankful that Gertrude had displayed a remarkable amount of forward thinking and closed the door to the records room.

Gertrude drew a beastly-looking pistol from somewhere about her person. I glared at her and shook my head. She brandished it at me and waved a claw at the door. I repeated my head movement, and she threw a couple of legs in the air in frustration.

Moving as noiselessly as possible, I nipped to the wall that contained the light switch and flicked it off. I remained motionless, listening for any other creaking floorboards. I didn't know who else could be prowling about the pace at the dead of night as well as Milligan Clodthorpe and Gertrude Wermacht, but the odds were a good 200:1 against them being an ally.

I heard another floorboard creak. This one was noticeably closer to our hiding spot. I thought beating a hasty retreat might be the best course of action, so I looked about the place whilst Gertrude remained with her weapon trained on the door.

There was only one door in the records room, the one by which we had made entry. This would lead us into the legs of whoever was prowling about outside, so I immediately wrote that off. There was only one other way to leave this room, and that was a window.

I pointed at the window. Gertrude glanced in that direction and nodded. She stayed where she was whilst I struggled with the sash. I disengaged the latch and lifted the window. I turned and hissed at Gertrude, who reluctantly lowered her weapon and leapt through the window.

Stunned, I glanced in the direction the relative had leapt. She was even now scuttling down the wall of the council house, using window sills and the odd bit of flashy architecture for claw holds. Within moments she was on the ground and concealed in a bush. I was wondering how I could possibly follow her without breaking some vital part of me when I heard the doorknob turn behind me. Not having time to think, I swung myself out of the window.

Thankfully, my claws thought faster than the rest of me did and grabbed the windowsill as I shot past it, heading groundwards. I hung from the windowsill, the breeze tugging at my clothes as I listened.

I saw the beam of light from some sort of lantern, or possibly a torch, illuminate bits of the window frame as I stared up at it. I heard breathing and footsteps. Someone said, in the sort of deep voice one would naturally associate with a night watchman, "*Come on out of it, I saw the light on, I knows you're in here!*"

I thought about replying with something cunning along the lines of "*No you don't,*" but I reasoned that by far the most sensible course of action would be to remain silent. I was slightly worried about how long I could continue to remain hanging from this windowsill, though. My human claw had started to tire after only a few seconds. Thankfully, my synthetic leg appeared to be made of sterner stuff.

I heard the interloper prowl around the records room for a minute or two, during which time my human claw gave up the struggle entirely and I was left dangling from one limb. Thankfully, this seemed to be more than up to the task. I won't claim that it was entirely comfortable, dangling in the breeze outside a village council house, but it was preferable to the alternatives.

I heard the night watchman (if that's who it was) mutter to himself and saw the torch flick about the place with more speed and less care. I was just hoping that he would be just the sort of solid but unambitious night watchman who would assume that no-one would attempt to effect escape via a high window, when I heard him approach my hiding spot.

I saw his torch play over the window frame before the human himself leaned out. As I had suspected, he was wearing the uniform of a night watchman. He peered out of the window, down at the street. He then leaned out of the window a little so he could look up, presumably wondering if his quarry had attempted to escape via the roof.

If he chose to look down, he would be unable to miss the claw that was at this moment biting into the wood of the windowsill and preventing me from falling. As if hearing my thoughts on the matter, the night watchman chose that moment to look down.

He got through the first syllable of what was, presumably, going to be something like "*A-Ha!*" before there was an almighty crunch, and the wood my claw was clinging to for dear life parted company with the rest of the windowsill.

I fell through the open air for a few glorious seconds before impacting heavily with the ground. My military training I had all but forgotten more or less kicked in, and I attempted to perform a standard combat roll out of the landing to disperse the impact. Sadly, the combat rolls I had learned all required eight legs, rather than my current four. As a result, my roll was more than a little bit sloppy and resulted in my being catapulted into a bush for what seemed like the ninety-fifth time that evening.

I landed on top of Gertrude. I clambered off her. She grinned at me and gave my fragile human form a quick onceover. Thankfully, no parts of my body appeared to be broken, sprained, or torn. She patted me on the back, nearly sending me staggering into another bush.

"What larks, eh?" she hissed. She then legged it over the fence and away from the council house at some considerable speed. Considering this a sensible idea, I followed her.

I caught up with Gertrude a few streets away. She kept watch for the approaching vengeance of night watchmen whilst I stretched out the muscles that were complaining the most. Such vengeance did not seem immediately apparent so, after my breath had been caught and my muscles seemed less deeply unhappy with me, we started making our way back to Clerkenwell road.

Gertrude hissed that it was a job well done to me. This seemed plausible, but I felt that celebrating whilst still in enemy territory was premature. I raised Forsythe on my vox-o-matic and communicated my wish to be picked up at the earliest opportunity. He said that he would comply.

Gertrude said that she would find her own way back to Newbury Towers. The way she had taken down had, apparently, not been sufficiently challenging, but she had seen one or two routes that might divert her interest in their direction. She shook me carefully by the claw and scuttled off.

For the first time in some considerable while, I felt able to exhale fully. I propped myself against a road sign and lit a contemplative cigarette. On the whole, things could have gone considerably worse.

18

I ONLY NEEDED TO HIDE FROM PROWLING NIGHT WATCHMEN twice whilst waiting for Forsythe. These watchmen appeared less interested in catching miscreants than they were in chatting about their various spouses. By the time Forsythe had come to pick me up, I was more familiar than I'd like with the private lives of several residents of the human district thanks to unwillingly eavesdropping on such conversations.

The trip back to Newbury Towers was uneventful, thanks to the lateness of the hour. Forsythe dropped me at the front door and took the old two-seater around the back to park it. The door was opened for me by the butler and behind him, clad in a dressing gown and with his facial fur in a protective net, was Uncle Angus.

"Clodthorpe, what the blazes do you think you're doing out at this hour?" he demanded.

I muttered my apologies and he demanded that I follow him to his study, so he could give me a detailed explanation of the good and proper times to return to a residence if one was a guest under the roof in question. I hung my head whilst I was filled with warmth at his outward disapproval. I followed the relative, as instructed. The butler cast a disapproving gaze on me as I slid past him, and then wandered off, presumably to attend to some butlery duties.

Uncle Angus flung the door to his study open and stood in the middle of the room, tapping one of his claws against the carpet.

"Shut the door, Clodthorpe," he growled. I did so. His manner then changed abruptly. He scurried forward and grasped one of my legs. "What news, my boy?" he asked.

I appraised the relative by marriage of the success of my quest to locate and dissuade Bainbridge from pursuing his matrimonial plans.

"That's wonderful news, dear boy, simply wonderful," he enthused. "But you're sure Bainbridge will be returning imminently? He has not yet arrived…"

I excused myself whilst I checked on the data feeds one more time. Bainbridge appeared to be a mere few minutes away from Newbury Towers. I informed Uncle Angus of Bainbridge's progress and he appeared much relieved.

He then asked what I was doing back at such a late hour, if I was not escorting the young reprobate. Assuming, correctly as it turned out, that he was referring to Bainbridge, I said that I was engaging in a scheme to correct a wrong that had arisen during my attempts to throw a spanner into the works of Bainbridge's marriage to the human.

Uncle Angus looked at me with a great deal of fondness. He praised my devotion to righting wrongs that I had caused. I did question whether I should point out that it was, in fact, Forsythe that had committed the immoral act in question, but I reasoned that this would serve only to complicate matters. My uncle by marriage then asked if there was anything he could do to assist in my scheme, as he was much in my debt thanks to my thwarting of Bainbridge's machinations.

This was fortuitous indeed, and I was about to say so when a voice spoke from a corner:

"Yes there is."

Uncle Angus and I leapt several kilometres into the air before coming to rest and rounding on the source of the sound. It was Gertrude. She was sitting on top of a bookcase in the corner of the room.

"Don't *do* that, you accursed creature," said Uncle Angus, clutching at his chest.

"Sorry father," said Gertrude, hopping down in a manner that had at least a shade of contrition evident, "It's just I've been waiting in here to tell you about recent events in the human district, but when I saw Milli was already telling you, I thought I'd best let him get on with it."

"We have discussed–" wheezed Uncle Angus, "your use of stealth before, young fleabag. There is a reason I wished you to confine yourself to gardening when you are allowed to visit the old home. Your creeping about the place is going to do my nervous system no good whatsoever."

"Sorry pardon," Gertrude said, cheerfully. "Would you like me to tell you what Milli and I have been doing in the human district or should he?"

Uncle Angus collapsed into a chair. "I would appreciate it if you would give me the facts, Milli my lad."

I related recent events to Uncle Angus with only occasional interruptions from Gertrude. Once he was fully appraised of the situation, he said that he would attend to it first thing in the morning. I thanked him profusely and relaxed a touch. He offered me a glass of something but I declined, knowing I was probably keeping him from his bed. Gertrude said she wouldn't mind a glass of something, but I made frantic gestures at her when Uncle Angus turned to stare at her, and she changed her mind.

Uncle Angus shook us both by the claw and left the room with his head held high.

I was considerably bucked by the way this evening had gone. I said goodnight to Gertrude and strode to my room humming that show tune about the chap who was born in the back seat of a greyhound bus.

I opened my bedroom door and yelled out loud. Bainbridge was in there, sitting on my bed. I wondered if there was something in the air on this particular evening that was causing chaps to lie in wait in an attempt to scare the living daylights out of me.

"Ah, Milli," said Bainbridge, "I'm glad you're back."

"Bainbridge!" I remarked, "What are you doing here?"

He looked at me as if I was intentionally saying ridiculous things so as to torture him.

"I am here to return your body, Milligan. Pray do not toy with me. I am not made of metal."

I was touched. "That's awfully good of you, young triptych, but I was going to let you get a good night's sleep before arranging the swap. Are you sure you wish to do this now?"

Bainbridge sighed. "You're a generous chap, Milli, when you're not passing comments on a chap's actions, but no. If I am to swap, tis best I were to swap quickly."

I had no idea Bainbridge had read the classics. There were hidden depths to this chap. I tried to think of another line from Marlowe or Bacon, or whichever of those chaps had written Macbeth, to respond, but none were able to break through the fog of tiredness that had overcome me since leaving Uncle Angus' presence.

I thanked him and sat next to him. He affixed a set of terminals to my skull, as well as a corresponding set to his. He flicked a switch.

I remember this time when dear Emily was still with us... we were both asleep in our bed and Emily had been having a bad dream. Quite without waking up, she had embraced me. My sleep had not been interrupted. Instead, as I dreamt, I was overcome by a feeling that everything, *every little thing* was going to be all right, as Robert Marlboro once said.

That was how I felt a few moments later when I found myself back in my body. I didn't move for a few moments.

Bainbridge turned to me and wished me a good night. I thanked him once more and he slipped from the room, only falling over twice on his way from the bed to the door.

Without waiting for Forsythe, I slipped from the clothes Bainbridge had dressed my body in and selected a nightshirt at random from the wardrobe. I slipped between the sheets and fell into a sleep that was gloriously deep and dreamless.

19

I WOKE TO THE SOUND OF A BLACKBIRD KNOCKING A SNAIL against the roof outside my window, and then being pounced upon by one of those winged serpents that prowl around estates such as Newbury Towers. I listened to the anguished squawking and triumphant hissing with something akin to contentedness. I stretched three or four of my legs, then another three or four just for good measure. I flexed my claws; I blinked all four pairs of eyes in sequence.

All was well.

There was a knock at the door. I jumped, worried that all was about to be made un–well again, but when I called for the unseen rapper on wood to enter, Forsythe breezed in with the morning tea.

"Ah, Forsythe!" I cried, "Do you see the form to which I am restored?"

Forsythe passed an appraising eye over me. "It is a most gratifying sight, sir."

"It is indeed, Forsythe, it is indeed. Tell me, have you been made aware of my actions, as well as those of Gertrude, concerning the Su–San scheme?"

Forsythe indicated that he had not had the pleasure of receiving such information, so I caught him up while I waited for my tea to reach a manageable temperature. He's not one of those valets who are known to leap about the place singing "At last, the knave has won the day" or however it goes, for his is the more refined method of celebration. He murmured something about being most grateful for my actions, which I believe was the equivalent of two cartwheels and a "yippee" from any other, less reserved individual.

"The only cloud on the horizon," I reflected, "is that blasted contract I had to sign up for with Mother Ophelia to get her to help me. I mean, a year with the Special Operations Unit. That's a bit thick, what? I probably won't last a month. I only survived as long as I did in the regular forces thanks to the number of excellent fellows who were watching the Clodthorpe back."

"It is, indeed, something of a cloud upon the horizon, sir," Forsythe said, sounding a great deal less perturbed than I would have liked, "but I suggest that it is not, in fact, the largest hurdle that must be faced on this day."

I cocked a quizzical eye at him. "It isn't?" I asked.

"If you will forgive me for saying so, sir, I believe it is not. You will, of course, be aware of the issues that both Mr Lusitania and Ms Slavarington have regarding the forms that they find themselves in…"

"I am," I said. Well, I was. I don't mean to blow my own trumpet, but Bainbridge would be far from electrified to be back in a human body, and Pigstick didn't seem thrilled by the idea of being in a faulty unit.

"Well, sir, if I might make a suggestion…"

He paused. It appeared that he required a little encouragement. "Do continue, Forsythe," I said, "I'm agog."

"Thank you for saying so, sir. I merely wished to say that if you could persuade the two parties to swap bodies with each other, then I believe both would be highly satisfied."

It occurred to me that Forsythe might possibly deserve a bit of a holiday. I'd hate to have to do without him, of course. Nevertheless, I had clearly been running the poor chap ragged recently, given by the calibre of the suggestion he had just uttered.

I wondered whether I should go into detail as to precisely why his idea was sheer lunacy. There were a good few hundred minor objections to it, but if I had limited time to work with (and I suppose I did, I had to go down and get breakfast at some point) then I would probably confine myself to two points. Firstly, that Bainbridge would want a body that works fully, not a defective one such as the one Pigstick had wound up in. Secondly, that Pigstick would want a proper arachnid body. For her to end up in a human body after all this could hardly be described as a comfortable scenario for the young buster.

I chose to spare the poor chap's feelings by pointing all this out, though. I simply thanked him for the suggestion in as noncommittal a way as possible and resolved to think of a different solution to the situation that plagued the two young bucks.

This thought kept me occupied through much of the morning. I dressed and breakfasted with few other thoughts troubling me. I spared a thought or two of sympathy for the two troubled hearts as I tucked into my bacon-infused porridge at the breakfast table. Bainbridge was there, poking at his breakfast in his human body, looking dejected. Of Pigstick, though, there was no sign. Gertrude attempted to add a little levity to the occasion by cracking jokes here and there, but her jollity largely fell on deaf ears. The only one who seemed to be truly enjoying himself was Uncle Angus, who was clearly overjoyed to have Bainbridge return unmarried. He expressed his pleasure by being frightfully discourteous to Gertrude and myself. Only Bainbridge didn't feel the pleasure of his displeasure, no doubt because the uncle in question hadn't forgiven the young nut for causing him so much worry.

After rounding things off nicely with a few pieces of some orange fruit that grew locally, Uncle Angus disappeared to prowl about the grounds for a spell. Everyone else expressed their intention to carry out similar plans. I, however, decided to track down Pigstick, who I thought might be easier to reason with than Bainbridge.

I found her wandering the grounds. She greeted me with some little gratitude. She said she'd been a little lonely when I'd been off gallivanting after Bainbridges the whole time. Gertrude was a wonderful individual, she said, but a little exhausting if you spent too much time with her.

I spent a few moments chatting to her about this and that before broaching the subject of bodies.

"Yes," she said, "I bet you're sorry to be back in that old thing aren't you, Milli, old chap?"

I apologised, because I must have misheard her.

She apologised for misspeaking. "Glad. I meant you must be glad. I'm still getting used to these vocal chords."

Something in her manner seemed dashed odd... then it hit me. You know in those detective stories when the detective has spent his whole time thinking that the chap that murdered the other chap is chap A, but then he has a bit of a revelation in the last few pages and he realises that it was actually chap B? That was how I felt now.

"Ah, Pigstick," I said, affecting the manner of a gumshoe. "It is all so clear now."

"It is?" Pigstick squeaked.

"It is. It started subtly. I'm sure you didn't realise you were doing it, but I wonder if you remember when I first found myself in the human body, you were strangely interested in what it was like to be in there."

"I was, wasn't I..." mused Pigstick, not overly impressed by my grand revelation. *Never mind*, I thought, I had further revelations in store.

"Well, you continued in this vein, Pigstick. Your interest appeared to turn to fascination and then, most surprisingly, concern. You were shocked when you saw the slightly tatty state I had allowed the human body to be reduced to. You were shocked, Pigstick! And then you asked, most suspiciously, I might add, whether you might swap places with me. Admit it, Pigstick, you wish to take human form!"

"Got it in one," she muttered.

This tripped me up slightly. "But… why, Pigstick?" I had to ask, putting my claw on the nub of the issue.

"I can't explain it, Milli. It's just… who I am. I'm human."

"You're not you know," I pointed out, slightly baffled. At least I was reasonably sure she was an arachnid. Maybe my eyes had been playing tricks on me again.

"I am, though," she said, sadly. "I always have been. I was just born in an arachnid body."

"Oh," I said, reeling slightly, "Well then, we'll have to find a human body for you."

Well, what would you say in such circumstances? It may be a bit of an odd thing to say, but it'd be a bit odd to contradict a lass if a lass has had one of those revelation things about herself. It may be a bit unfathomable but, if I'm honest, it's rare for me to come across something that isn't unfathomable, if you follow me.

"Bainbridge has one," Pigstick said, "a magnificent one. Do you think he'd swap with me?"

"He might," I said, still a little confused but trying to be helpful. "He'd probably rather have a body that isn't defective, though."

"There's nothing wrong with this body I'm in at present," Pigstick said, after a considerable pause. It must have taken the young egg some considerable effort to say. "I just said that so I'd have an excuse to swap out of it, into a human body."

"Oh," I said. "But isn't that good? It'd mean Bainbridge would happily swap with you?"

"What do you mean?" she asked.

"There's nothing wrong with your current body, correct?" I asked.

"Well, not for anyone other than me, no," she admitted.

"So there's no reason for Bainbridge to not swap with you?" I pointed out.

"Except how do I tell him *why* I want to swap with him?" she asked.

"Can't you tell him the truth?" I asked, "You didn't have a problem telling me."

"You worked it out for yourself," she pointed out. I didn't bother to mention that it was Forsythe who'd started me down this line of thought.

"Very well," I said. "Well, how about this… Bainbridge hasn't seen your new arachnid body has he?"

"No…" Pigstick said, sensing that the makings of a plan might have sprung from my brain.

"Good," I said, "So we stick you back in your coffin for a bit and I tell Bainbridge we've found a body for him. He gives up the human body for your current one and I take the human body off his claws. We stick you in the human body once the dust has settled a little, everyone's happy…"

Pigstick leapt a good few metres into the air. "In the name of the Devious God, Milli, that's inspired!" she cried.

"You're too kind," I said.

We spent a few moments working through the particulars. With the details worked out to our satisfaction, Pigstick scuttled off to move back into her coffin. I decided to see if I could raise Forsythe on the vox-o-matic to compare notes.

He answered on the third pip, and we spent a few minutes catching each other up. It transpired that he had completed his collection of materials to bestow upon the Su-Sans. Uncle Angus had ordered for the emergency audit this morning, presumably not long before breakfast, and the Su-Sans had been moved into their new home shortly after the errors in their paperwork were discovered.

I informed him that I had ended up doing much as he'd suggested, and he said he was grateful to find that his suggestions had been met with positive results.

"But, Forsythe," I said, during a brief lull in the conversation. "You said that my contract with Mother Ophelia would sort itself out once a solution to Bainbridge and Pigstick's bodies was discovered, and I'm blowed if I can fathom the issue…"

"That problem has a deceptively simple solution, sir." Forsythe said, "If you were to inform Mr Lusitania that you were in possession of a new arachnid body, he would be keen to take possession of it as soon as possible, would he not?"

"I dare say," I said.

"So if you were to make his assumption of the contract from you a prerequisite for his inhabitation of the new body, the young gentleman would have little choice but to accept, sir."

"You mean, if I tell him he isn't getting his claws on this new body unless he joins the Special Operations Unit in my place, he'll do it? That seems less than likely, Forsythe…"

"In normal circumstances, you would be absolutely correct sir. However, I overheard some of the domestic staff discussing a vox-o-matic communication Mr Lusitania had engaged in with his father this morning. They were only able to hear one end of the conversation, but apparently

Lord Wehrmacht informed the Lusitania family seat of the younger Mr Lusitania's actions, and they are anxious that he take some action to show that he is worthy of the title and land that come with the family name. I do not like to give credence to rumour, as you know, sir, but it appears that the word 'disinherit' may have been mentioned on several occasions."

"Great Scott!" I exclaimed.

"Just as you say, sir."

I thanked him profusely and asked for him to get in touch as soon as he knew how his gifts to the Su-Sans were received. He said that he would and the communication was thus terminated.

I rubbed my claws together. This, I felt, would be most satisfying. I had no intention of letting Bainbridge have this body, which Pigstick no longer wanted, with any ease.

My first port of call was Pigstick's chamber, where I found the poor lass back in her coffin. Her arachnid body was on autopilot in a legchair in a corner of the room. I assured Pigstick that I would secure the human body for her within the hour, and she instructed her arachnid body to follow me.

I skittered about Newbury Towers for a few minutes looking for Bainbridge. I perhaps took more time than I might otherwise have done because I was enjoying being able to skitter once more. It's hard to skitter in a human body when you only have two legs available for perambulation at any one time. The body that Pigstick had trusted to me followed me closely, its clawsteps complementing mine.

I eventually spied Bainbridge in the billiard room. The poor fellow was slumped in a chair, looking dejected. I instructed the spare body to not follow me into the room, but to wait for me just out of sight. There were a number of ways I could approach Bainbridge, but I suspected that I shouldn't let Bainbridge know that I might just hold the keys to his deliverance until I needed to. As that general chap once said, keep your cards close to your chest and your enemy's cards closer.

I decided that I should suppress my natural sunny disposition for fear of the chap thinking that I was rubbing his face in the fact that he was now in a human body.

"What ho!" I cried, sympathetically, taking a seat opposite the fellow "How goes the day, Bainbridge?" "It's perfectly wretched, Clodthorpe," he replied, gloomily, "How goes yours? Filled with rainbows and whisky no doubt?"

"Never mind how I'm feeling, young fellow mi lad," I said, "What's important is this state you find yourself in."

He looked suspicious. "It is, is it? Because you didn't have to take your body back you know…"

I raised a dignified claw. "Please, Bainbridge. You know as well as I do that you took my body without permission. You were wrong to do so. Please let it go. I am not here to debate water that has long since flowed over the aqueduct."

"Pah!" Bainbridge began, but he faltered as my claw was still raised. He stared at it, as clear a sign as any that he was permitting me to continue.

"I am here to help you with your predicament, young Bainbridge," I said.

"You are?" he said. "Forgive me for saying so, Clodthorpe, old chap, but that sounds unlikely."

"Why should it sound unlikely?"

"Well, I gathered from the way you chatted to me over the past forty-eight hours that you didn't view me as one of the universe's great success stories."

"I may have used harsh words, that is true, but do not misinterpret me, Bainbridge, I really do have your best interests at heart." This wasn't technically a lie, but it skirted dangerously close to one. Although entering the Special Operations Unit was almost certain death, his future wasn't that much better if he continued as he was now.

"Well, what have you come to say then," said Bainbridge, with a certain amount of surly grace.

"I've come to offer you a place in the Special Operations Unit of the 75th Grand Battlefleet."

Bainbridge leapt to his claws. "You're trying to get me killed!" he sputtered.

I remained seated. "Not at all, young peanut. The survival statistics really aren't as bad as everyone thinks they are." This was true. The popular rumour was that there was a 1% survival rate over one year's service. This was clearly nonsense. The real figure was much closer to 10%.

"Are they not?" he asked, not sitting down but not fleeing from the room either.

"Not at all," I assured him, "but you haven't asked me why I am making this offer."

"Why," he asked, "are you asking me to contemplate elaborate suicide, Clodthorpe?"

I lowered my claw. "That isn't how I would choose to put it, Bainbridge, but very well. Let us abandon pretence for a moment. Joining the Special Operations Unit would be dangerous but, tell me, where did you serve your military service?"

"I was in the supply corps," he said.

"For both of your tours of duty?" I asked, slightly incredulously.

"Well, no," he admitted, "I was in a combat tour the first time."

"And what happened there?"

"The enemy surrendered two hours and fifteen minutes after I arrived."

I may have misjudged young Bainbridge. "Was this the result of your efforts?" I asked.

He appeared to think I was being sarcastic, which wasn't wholly fair. "No, it wasn't, thank you for asking," he huffed, "I was still stashing my kit in my bunk when the news of the surrender came through."

"So what did you do for the rest of that tour?" I asked.

"Well, a few of the lads and I set up a cricket league."

"Did your team win?"

"No, we came last."

"I see. And, tell me Bainbridge, how does your father view your time with our chaps in uniform?"

His eyes flashed at me. "From your questions it's clear you know exactly what he thinks of me. He thinks I'm a failure. He thinks I'm completely without responsibility. He thinks I'm a coward. He doesn't know how terrified I was on my way to my first tour, but I still went. I could have fled, you know, Clodthorpe, but I didn't. I was going to fight, I was going to do my bit. It wasn't my fault the war ended…

and now they think I'm useless, on top of being a murderer because of that, er, emergency download business."

My eye glinted. I had him. "You know what would truly demonstrate your character to your father?" I asked.

He held up his upper legs and backed away. "Now Milli, come on. I'm not saying... I mean, I don't mean to say..." he cleared his throat and lapsed into silence again. I stood up and draped a leg gently around his fragile human shoulders.

"You'd get out from under your father's legs, Bainbridge," I said, "I know how tough it's been for you, always having him judge you."

"But the statistics..." he muttered.

I let the chap go and faced him. "You might fully die, Bainbridge, there's no denying that. But you might well not. And if you don't, you'd return home as someone who has really made a difference. How does it feel to wander around the village and know everyone you meet has seen more combat than you?"

"No that's not true!" said Bainbridge, "Mr Alsop, the baker, he didn't see combat either."

"And why is that?" I asked, genuinely interested.

"Well," he said, "because Mr Alsop is a conscientious objector."

"I see," I said. "Fine people, conscientious objectors. Are you a conscientious objector, Bainbridge?"

"...No."

"I really don't want you to think I'm pressuring you into this decision, young Bainbridge." I said, taking a softer approach. "One thing I haven't mentioned to you is that you'd be taking this contract from me. I signed up to the

Special Operations Unit in order to locate you. Do you know what I will do if you do not take the contract from me?"

"Do a runner?" he asked, hopefully.

"Not even close," I smiled at him, "But you will take this contract, Bainbridge."

"Oh I will, will I?" he bristled.

"Yes, you will," I said, "Because you are not a coward, in spite of your actions with regard to the emergency download switch, and I think it's time you proved that. And, were you to agree, I might just have a little something to sweeten things a little for you."

Bainbridge peered searchingly at me. "What sort of thing?"

I brushed a piece of fluff from my lapel. "Something that would get you out of that body and into something altogether more suitable."

"You have a body for me?" he asked.

"I do."

"May I see it?" he asked, excitedly.

I brought the body that had so recently belonged to Pigstick in. Bainbridge scampered around it, examining it.

"And you'd part with this body?" he asked, suspiciously.

"I would. You would be doing me a favour after all, by taking this contract," I said, appealing to his better nature. Or, at least, where his better nature would be if he turned out to have one.

"And you think that my joining the Special Operations Unit would make my family think better of me?" he asked.

"There is no doubt of that," I said.

"Well then…" he said, eyeing up the body in a proprietorial way that was slightly disturbing. "I cannot refuse. Have you the contract?"

"A copy is on the data implant on that synthetic leg your body has," I said, and granted him the passcode to access the document. He amended it to include his name instead of mine, with only the slightest bit of hesitation, signed his name, and sent it back into the data stream. Within a few moments, we'd both had a vox-o-matic communication to confirm Bainbridge taking my place.

I gripped his claw in mine, taking care not to damage it, for Pigstick's sake.

"You've made me a very happy arachnid, young Bainbridge, and I trust you will have a great time out there. Now, let's get you into your new body…"

Bainbridge was downloaded into his new body in two flicks of a bull's nose. He turned a few summersaults once there, and then rushed off to run about the grounds a bit to put it through its paces.

I gathered up the human shell that was sitting, expressionless, where Bainbridge had left it, and carried it up to Pigstick's room. She answered my knock with an invitation to enter and was glad to see that everything had proceeded according to plan.

I sat chatting with the young lass whilst we waited for the data pathways to the human brain to cool. Despite spending several days at Newbury Towers, I hadn't actually had much time to catch up with young Pigstick, a fact I took pleasure in redressing at this point.

Forsythe brought us a snack for lunch after I'd informed him that Pigstick would be ruminating in her room, the better to keep an eye on her new body. Uncle Angus would understand.

Not long after lunch had been cleared, we tested the body and it was found to be safe for habitation. Pigstick switched from her coffin to the human body and breathed a sigh. I checked that she was okay and, after finding that she was, I left. She would need some time to get to know her new home.

20

I SAUNTERED BACK TO MY ROOM AND SLIPPED INTO ONE OF the chairs that had been altogether too large for me to take full advantage of when I was in a human body. I was pleasantly alone with my thoughts for a few minutes.

I began cataloguing the events that had taken place since my arrival at Newbury Towers. This done, I rang for Forsythe and related my list to him.

In no particular order, the list was this:

Uncle Angus now finds me less unpleasant.

Pigstick has learned something important about herself, and is now living a truer life.

Bainbridge is taking slightly more responsibility for his actions than he has previously.

Gertrude is still psychotically insane, but at least she enjoyed herself whilst assisting with the various schemes and ploys she was involved in.

"Most satisfactory, sir," said Forsythe.

"Quite," I said, and did a quick bit of mental calculation. "Almost entirely your doing, of course."

"That is most kind of you to say, sir, but you provided several solutions as well."

"That's very kind of you to say, Forsythe. Tell me, how do you feel about the amount I pay you?"

"It is most satisfactory, sir."

"You don't feel that you could do with a little more? You've provided several sterling services over the last few days."

"That was all in a day's work, sir. If you were to increase my wages, I would prefer that it was because of some extraordinary feat rather than duties that might reasonably be expected of me."

"An extraordinary feat, eh?" I asked.

"Exactly, sir."

"You can't do something about my missing my dear Emily quite so much can you, Forsythe?"

"I fear not, sir. Losses of the sort that you have endured tend to linger for some considerable time."

"Ah well, can't be helped," I said. "Turning to happier matters, how did the Su-Sans react to their gifts of... whatever it was you gave them?"

"The vox-o-matic devices, chocolate, and televisual entertainment systems seemed to confuse the four humans at first, sir. There was a great deal of crying, although I wasn't able to establish whether this was jubilation at the gifts or anguish at their forced resettlement."

"A little of column A, a little of column B, perhaps," I said.

"Very possibly, sir. I passed a sixpence to a young human and asked it to keep me updated on the status of the Su-Sans, sir. The young human has reported that their mood much improved when the chocolate was discovered to be of a higher quality than they had originally supposed."

"Excellent."

"And the televisual entertainment systems were soon activated and tuned so that they displayed a series of entertainments concerning a human and his attempts to climb a series of mountains, as well as a documentary on the subject of kittens."

"Very good."

"The vox-o-matic devices continue to frustrate the humans, but it appears that this frustration is bringing its own form of joy."

"And your conclusion from all this is…" I prompted.

"Psychological harm can be offset by positive influences if guided by advice from experts." Forsythe ventured.

"That sounds about right," I said. I hadn't entirely followed Forsythe's conclusion, but it had sounded roughly as I'd expected it to sound.

"Do you wish to remain at Newbury Towers now matters have been resolved, sir?" Forsythe asked, after a brief interval.

I considered the question. "Well, I was originally here for quiet company… or as quiet as Gertrude could possibly provide. I haven't yet had the chance to enjoy much of that."

MICHAEL COOLWOOD

"Just so, sir."

"That said, it might be wise to be a long way away when Mother Ophelia finds out what sort of body Pigstick is now occupying…"

"Very true sir."

"And then there's the matter of my escaping her contract and substituting someone she may find less than ideal."

"Quite, sir."

"With all that in mind, would you say a trip to the tropics would be in order, Forsythe?"

"Lady Slavarington may well be in a more amenable mood when next she sees you if she has had time to regain her composure, sir."

"That said, Forsythe…" I said, after a few moments of contemplation, "I wonder if fleeing the scene is the right thing to do."

"Sir?"

"Being alone with my thoughts in Eggart was not entirely healthy was it, Forsythe?"

"I would say not, sir."

"And Sir Angus is usually alone in this place when Gertrude is on a tour?"

"Apart from the domestic staff, yes, sir."

"Gertrude and Pigstick are staying for a little longer are they not?"

"They are, sir."

"The aged relative will need some looking after if those two are to continue staying. Who knows what either of them will get up to tomorrow. And it would be a shame to do a runner so soon after our relationship has become less strained. I think I shall stay for a few more days, Forsythe."

Forsythe remained impassive. "Lady Slavarington will know where to contact you, sir, if you maintain your current position."

I waved this point aside. "I am aware of that, Forsythe. Let her come."

"Sir?"

"I said let her come, Forsythe. The worst she can do is kill me."

"Very good, sir."

"I put it to you that a little discomfort for Clodthorpe, M would be worth it if I was able to stay in such company as Wermacht, A; Slavarington, S; and Wermacht, G."

I thanked Forsythe and he drifted out. I turned my attention to the window that looked out over the grounds. I opened the window and breathed in the fresh air. Finally, I thought, I might now get to enjoy my quiet week in the country. Everything as far as the eyes could see was peace and joy. Except for the human dangling by its leg in one of Gertrude's traps. I rang for Forsythe again so he could get someone to set the poor creature free.

The End

I would like to thank everyone who helped this book come to life.

Thank you to everyone at Montag Press for agreeing to publish it, particularly Charlie.

Thank you to Jen, without whom none of this would be possible.

Thank you to mum and dad for endless support and feedback.

Thank you to my editors, Mara Hodges and Nick Morwood, who improved the book immeasurably.

Thank you to Stuart F Taylor at Chainbear.com for his stunning cover design.

Thank you for buying/finding/stealing this book. If you complete the quiz at the end, please send your answers to michael.coolwood@gmail.com

M ichael Coolwood is a life-long Londoner and was raised on a literary diet of Terry Pratchett, P.G. Wodehouse, and Douglas Adams. He read English Literature and Drama at university and discovered that life is much better when you spend it writing, filming, and drinking with friends.

Since leaving university he has worked in a variety of dirty jobs as well as some clean ones. He runs a moderately successful Youtube channel and writes whenever he can.

Human Studies Quiz

M R CLODTHORPE HAS BEEN KIND ENOUGH TO PROVIDE US at Oxenfurt University Press an advance copy of his book so that we might use it as part of our Human Studies class. To our regret, Mr Clodthorpe made several errors with his references to human culture. To that end, as part of Human Studies test 1.00.6H, please answer the following questions:

1. When Milligan refers to a line from Rosencrantz and Guildenstern Are Dead about "being allowed to sleep and perhaps dream", what is he misquoting and who is the original author? (2 points)

2. Who originally coined the phrase "Those who cannot learn from history are doomed to repeat it." that Milligan misattributes to George Satriani? (1 point)

3. What piece of human media is Milligan referring to when he talks about the Ju-on virus created by Takashi Shimizu? (1 point)

4. Did The Kinks really sing Give Peace A Try? (0 points)

5. What is The Weekly Wipe and what sort of thing might Milligan have seen in it? (2 points)

6. Why might the Sphinx be upset at the sight of Oedipus' retreating back?   (1 point)

7. Which chap in what blue box is Milligan referring to when noting that time is of the essence? (1 point)

8. When Milligan says that G.K. Chesterton wrote a line about "ears, whiskers, and deer", what book is he referring to and what is the true author? (3 points)

9. Who actually wrote "Into each life some rain must fall"? (2 points)

10. The statue in the Newbury village square is reminiscent of a statue found on the human homeworld. Where might you find this other statue of a floozie in a jacuzzi? (2 points)

11. Which Kafka novel is Milligan referring to when discussing the sadness of finding himself in another body? (1 point)

12. The previous Wermacht patriarch buried his wife under a folly to avoid suspicion with regards to her

death. Which classic crime novel might have inspired this action? (2 points)

13. What human-created war figurine is Milligan describing when discussing the Avatar of Pestilence? (6 points)

14. Did any male character in King Lear say anything similar to, "Is this a Slavarington I see before me?" (0 points)

15. To whom is Milligan referring when talking about explorers who are "always seeking out new life and new cultivations"? (1 point)

16. Which specific set of berserkers might include "chatting about blood and skulls and things" as part of their battle cry? (3 points)

17. Did Winston Churchill lead the assault on the Normandy Beaches? (1 point)

18. Who coined the phrase Milligan misattributes to Agatha Christie about "eliminating the impossible until what remained was inescapable fact" (1 point)

19. Who wrote the song about greased lighting that humans sing on formal occasions? (2 points)

20. What paragon of fashion is Milligan emulating with his bow tie and fez?   (1 point)

21. When Milligan quotes what he refers to as "that old love song by Alfred J Proof Rock", what poem is he referring to and who wrote it? (2 points)

22. When Milligan refers to a program that stars "Richard Michael and Briers Horden", what is the program's name and is there a universal truth to it? (2 points)

23. Why might Milligan feel the need to flee at the mention of poetry by Browning or Pound? (3 points. Additional points will be awarded for vivid descriptions regarding the quality of the work by the poets in question.)

24. What sigil do humans use to denote currency? (1 point)

25. To what is Milligan referring to when he talks about melodious ponds or the songs made by rivers with regards to "that old treatise on the necessity of good men going to war"? (2 points)

26. What song is Milligan referring to when he says, "I howled the first line of that song about crying (or maybe it was laughing) when seeing some chap in a Turkish bath"? (2 points)

27. What work is Milligan referring to when he mentions a poem "about being covered in sticking plasters" and who wrote it? (2 points)

28. What piece of human media documented the events that immediately followed after our species left the "massive black obelisk" on what would later become the human home world? (1 point)

29. When Milligan says, "The quality of mercy droppeth as the gentle rain upon the drains beneath," what is he misquoting? (1 point)

30. What song is Milligan quoting when he says, "All you need is love"? (1 point) (Please note, there is a correct answer and a wrong answer to this question. If you give the wrong answer, you will lose ten points.)

31. What piece of fiction features a ship called the SS Madame de Pompadour? (2 points)

32. What was the human White House and what was it for? (2 points)

33. What is Milligan referring to when he mentions watching "a film about an enormous talking rabbit called Harold"? (1 point)

34. When Milligan attributes the "flutes of his labour" to Psalm, what is he misquoting? (1 point)

35. The performer Unicorn at the SS Madame de Pompadour is a direct descendant of which human? Their stage name and performance styles are extremely similar. (5 points)

36. What should Milligan be referring to when he talks about Schrodinger's cartographer? (1 point)

37. Which Edgar Allen Poe piece does Milligan unwittingly quote? (0 points)

38. Which Tennyson piece does Forsythe quote in response? (1 point)

39. To what series of novels does Milligan refer when mentioning the books of "George R. R. Tolkien"? (1 point)

40. When Milligan says, "All the best laid plans of mice and moles often go pear shaped," he attributes this

misquote to John Steinbeck. Who should he be attributing it to? (2 points)

41. Who wrote the famous refrain "so it goes" that Milligan misattributes to Kurt Tucholsky? (1 point)

42. What song by which band talked about being born in the back seat of a Greyhound Bus? (2 points)

43. Who sang "every little thing gonna be alright?" (1 point)

Bonus question:

1. What is Azidoazide Azide and why is it a poor choice as an ingredient for use in pasta sauce?

Please present your answers to the test invigilator after thirty minutes have passed.

Good luck.

Professor Coolwood, BA, DD, PHQ9

www.ingramcontent.com/pod-product-compliance
Lightning Source LLC
Chambersburg PA
CBHW031154050726
47495CB00019B/1738